HER EX-GI P.I.

(Former Title: *Go Home and Die*)

Peg Herring

Her Ex-GI P.I. © Peg Herring, 2017
Former Title: *Go Home and Die*

Her Ex-GI P.I. is a work of fiction. The names, characters, and incidents are entirely the work of the author's imagination. Any resemblance to actual persons, living or dead, or events, is entirely coincidental.

ISBN: 9781944502423

Carrie stood at the third-floor window, squinting as she watched Peter Callender in the parking lot below. The day was cool but bright, and the dumpy little man whose motives she knew so well moved busily in and out of her range of vision, disappearing several times down the alley and returning with a can of garbage each time. The overfilled receptacles were a lot for a man with spaghetti arms to carry, and she heard an occasional scrape as the can's metal bottom brushed the concrete. Determination provided strength for the task, and Peter dumped the contents of each can beside the last, forming a disgusting, noxious wall of garbage around the sides and rear of a cream-colored Cadillac parked in his designated parking space.

The Caddy belonged to Peter's brother and business partner, Jim Callender. Jim had usurped Peter's space so an attractive female client could leave her new, 1968 Mustang convertible in Jim's space. The car sat two spaces down, its chrome wheels sparkling in the October sunlight. Carrie could admire its sleek lines without losing track of Peter's progress.

Jim and the lady in question had gone off together for a "consultation," a term that caused Peter and the other partner, a cousin named Brad Callender, to roll their eyes each time Jim used it. Bluntly speaking, they had gone to a nearby hotel for a quickie, leaving both cars at the office for the sake of appearances. That left no parking space for Peter when he returned from lunch. While his Thunderbird sat in a One Hour Parking Only space on the street, Peter took his revenge, one gooey pile of trash at a time.

As she turned away from the window, Carrie sighed. Her work was almost finished for the day, but she wouldn't be leaving soon. When Peter had finished his juvenile prank and gone home, she'd trek down to the Caddy and un-barricade it before Jim returned. It was sure to be a nasty job, but office peace would be maintained—at least for a while.

Carrie had worked for the law firm of Callender, Callender, and Callender for almost two years, longer than any other secretary had tolerated the antics of the three adult delinquents. Decent lawyers, successful men, and responsible citizens in many ways, they hated each other passionately and aired their feelings at peak volume when the mood struck one, two, and sometimes all three of them.

Past secretaries had quit in tears, in anger, and in disgust, but Carrie stayed on, braving the shouting and the lunacy. Maybe she'd become used to their ways, or, as her mother said over and over, maybe she had no common sense. Mostly she couldn't face the prospect of looking for another job, since she didn't exactly inspire confidence in prospective employers. The Callenders liked her, though they didn't like each other. The coping mechanism Carrie had developed over time was to foresee and forestall trouble whenever possible.

Brad, the cheap one, had billed his own uncle at a ridiculous rate for preparing his will. ("Why not? The old geezer's rolling in money.") Carrie treated it as if it were her own clerical error and got Peter to fix it. When Peter dithered with useless detail until papers were late getting filed, she suggested a revolving system for proofing documents and left Peter out of the rotation when a deadline was close. She even managed sometimes to keep Jim's escapades with female clients a secret from the other two, though what they did know was scandalous enough.

Difficult as it was, Carrie made the office work, and for that the Callenders were grateful in their way. Still, it was awful when they went at each other, screaming, swearing, and shouting for hours on end, followed by a day, sometimes two or three, where Carrie was the only one any of them would speak to. Peter and Jim were the worst, but Brad egged them on, siding with Jim sometimes and Peter others. Occasionally the brothers united against him too. She never knew how it would play out.

That was why today she'd remove the trash from around Jim's car and hope neither man mentioned it in the morning. Peter would think Jim too proud to say anything, and Jim would never know he'd been the target of Peter's vendetta.

As Carrie started down the hallway to the stairs, broom in hand, she heard feet shuffling on the landing above and a voice called, "Where you goin', Miss Walsh?" She turned to see Bea, the building's cleaning lady, coming down the stairs. Bea, twice Carrie's size and age and suffering from bad feet, still did the work of three men. A static-y transistor radio broadcast Motown music from her belt, since Bea claimed she cleaned better with accompaniment. She was especially fond of the Temptations, but now she dialed down the volume to barely audible.

When Carrie shrugged, Bea answered her own question. "You're gonna clean up his mess, ain't you?"

No doubt all the tenants were snickering about Jim's stunt by now. Carrie shrugged a second time. "It won't take long, and tomorrow will be a lot easier."

"It ain't your job." Bea set the mop down with a thump, and folds of skin under her chin wobbled as she shook her head. "That copper-colored hair of yours don't give them the right to treat you like a red-headed step-child."

"They don't do it to me. They do it to each other," Carrie reasoned. "It makes things easier when I fix the things that are fixable."

"Like when you cleaned the spaghetti off the wall after Peter missed Jim with it, or when you bought a new lamp with your own money so Brad wouldn't know Jim busted his?" Bea shook her mop and the smell of pine wafted toward Carrie. "It ain't right, you babying them men. Lotsa better lawyers would hire a secretary good as you."

Carrie's laugh was mirthless. "I don't know any. They all want girls with an associate degree." She added somewhat wistfully, "And girls with—I don't know—class." Bea opened her mouth to say something, but Carrie pointed to herself. "I know what kind of impression I make with my frizzy hair and Twiggy body. I'm terrible with clothes. I blush when a stranger looks at me." She touched the black frames that hid much of her face. "And what lawyer wants a girl with Coke-bottle glasses and a squint to be the first one clients see?"

Bea put up a finger as if to argue, but Carrie went on in a burst of self-deprecation. "I'm lucky the Callenders are so hard to work for. It meant they had to give me a chance." She shoved her glasses into place with a quick jab, a habit of necessity since the heavy lenses caused them to slide down her nose constantly. "I'm stuck with this job, so I'll clean up Jim's little prank and go on."

Bea sighed as if to say she disagreed but wouldn't argue. Instead, she set her mop in a corner and pulled yellow cotton gloves from her left back pocket. "It ain't my mess either, but the two of us will get done twice as fast."

They went to work, Bea shoveling the trash back into the metal cans with a large dustpan and Carrie dragging them into the alley from whence they came. Bea insisted on taking the dirtier job, since she was dressed for it, though Carrie's brown skirt and sweater wouldn't have shown the dirt much.

It was five-twenty when Carrie, hauling the last empty can within Bea's reach, looked at her watch, "I have to call the courthouse before five-thirty. Let's go back inside, and I'll finish this later."

"This should be the last one," Bea said, surveying their work. "I'll fill it, and you can haul it into the alley on your way to the bus stop." She checked her watch. "It's Tuesday, so the boss-man will be stopping by to see if he can catch me goofing off." With a grin she added, "He always show up when the TNT Bar down the street has two-for-one-drinks."

"You're an angel." Giving the older woman a quick hug, Carrie headed upstairs.

She left work fifteen minutes later, having made her call and finished the office chores. The early autumn darkness had descended, and everyone else in the building was gone. Jim's car and the Mustang were still there, so it appeared the "matinee" was turning into an evening performance. At least he'd never know about Peter's nasty trick.

Hitching her purse strap higher on her shoulder, Carrie picked up the last trash can by its handles, feeling the cold metal through her gloves. The can smelled of mimeograph ink and something fruity, maybe peaches. It was full, and she concentrated on keeping it upright so as not to spill the contents as she entered the alley. Along the wall were the six cans she'd lugged back earlier, and she headed for the end of the line, waddling clumsily under the weight she carried.

Movement to her right caught her eye, and Carrie peered toward the opposite end of the alley. Two men stood over a third figure, all silhouetted against a lighter building across the street. Though Carrie saw only shapes, one man appeared to be searching the fallen one's clothing while the other stood back, separating himself from the action. Surprise caused Carrie to tip the can she carried, and its lid dropped to the pavement with a clatter. The two standing men looked toward her, startled. An instant later they reacted, disappearing around the building.

Carrie stood for a moment in shock, struggling to take in what she'd seen. When she recovered her wits, she hurried to where the fallen man lay flat on his back, very still. "Are you all right?" He moaned softly in response. After checking the street to be sure his attackers were gone, she knelt beside him on the cold bricks.

He was about her age, with even features that were pinched with pain. In the shadowy light Carrie saw his corduroy jacket and tight-ribbed sweater were stained with blood that bubbled from a wound in his chest. Instinctively she put her hand over it, trying to stop the flow. Could he live through the loss of so much blood?

The man seemed aware of her presence. His mouth moved, and he tried to form words. She leaned close, still applying pressure to the wound. "Lie still. I'll get help, and we'll get you to a hospital."

Surprisingly strong fingers gripped her hand, and the man tried again to speak, a whisper coming with each ragged breath.

9

Carrie listened intently. Whatever he had to say was important to him.

"Tell Jack—Namwise, Kali—Shurenz. Please—Jack."

Feeling the fingers begin to lose their grip, Carrie looked into the dying man's eyes and said, "I'll tell Jack exactly what you said. Now lie still." A strangled sigh told her no doctor could save the man. Instead, she stayed with him, holding his hand until the grip relaxed. Then, with tears in her own eyes, she closed his sightless ones and went to find a different kind of help.

CHAPTER TWO

Sergeant Bill Stevenson stood outside the small room where Carrie Walsh sat looking at mug books. As he waited, Bill looked out the second-story window at the street below. At the Genesee County Courthouse people moved in and out, either searching for justice or hoping to avoid it. Farther down the street, the Flint Cinema advertised Bullitt, Steve McQueen's new movie.

Too bad real life wasn't like the movies. Stevenson had a murder to solve, but no expectation it would happen. The girl in the next room had paged through books for an hour, ignoring the station's terrible coffee after a single sip, though she thanked him politely for it.

There wasn't much chance of success, but she was anxious to help, and she was a nice girl. From the thick glasses she wore, Stevenson figured Carrie Walsh wasn't a great witness. She'd seen only shapes in the alley, two men, one slight the other of better than average size.

Stevenson had already concluded it was one of the senseless deaths that made his job so frustrating. The victim was an average guy with no enemies, at least according to his business partner, Jack Porter. He hadn't been robbed, and it didn't seem like any kind of a sex thing. Two unknown men had dragged him into an alley, knocked him around a bit, and then stabbed him. Todd Sachs had died as a result.

It was even possible the two men Carrie had seen were just opportunists who happened along as Sachs lay dying. They'd been searching him, she said, but what they'd been looking for other than a few bucks, no one could say. Sachs hadn't even had a real job, though he and Porter had been working on it.

Private detectives—the thought made Stevenson snort softly in disgust. Just what Flint needed, two amateurs trying to sort out the mess that was Michigan's murder capital. At least these guys had the background for it: army training and combat experience. Not a bad idea if you were going to open an office on Dort Highway.

A chair scraped against the tile floor, and the sergeant turned his attention again to Carrie Walsh. She'd finished the last book, and she removed her glasses and leaned back to rub her eyes. Without the clunky black frames, the lenses that distorted her eyes, and the squint that appeared when she focused on something, she wasn't bad looking. Her long, reddish-brown hair had a lot of curl to it, even if the ends kind of frizzed out. Her green eyes were nice. Her pale, freckled complexion, which he bet she hated, was smooth, like fine china. Her clothes were about as attractive as his Aunt Mildred's, but she had long legs, a nice build, and—Stevenson stopped, reminding himself to be the businesslike, married cop he was.

"Anything?"

"No. I'm sorry."

He smiled, a quick bend of his lips. "I doubt the men you saw are in those books."

She gave him the already-familiar squint. "Really? I hoped we'd catch them."

Noting the *we*, Stevenson smiled to himself, though he kept his expression serious. He rose, moved to her side, took the book she'd closed, and slid it atop the others with a soft clunk. "This crime was probably random, someone looking for cash. They didn't get it because you showed up and stopped them." She nodded, accepting that at least she'd interrupted the criminals' plans somewhat. "They could be drifters who came in on a train and left town the same way. Lots of times criminals can avoid arrest just by staying on the move."

Miss Walsh nodded, putting her ugly glasses back on. "I've never seen anyone die before, and to die only because you were on a certain street at a certain moment—that's awful." He could have told her it happened all the time, but something in her innocent face made him want to shield her from the knowledge. She frowned at the mug books then turned to him. "Did Mr. Sachs have family?"

"No," Stevenson answered. "His parents are dead, he'd never married, and he had only one sibling, a brother killed in Vietnam a few years ago. His partner, Jack Porter, will be taking care of—matters."

"That's the Jack I was supposed to give the message to?"

"Probably, but the message means nothing to Porter."

"It meant something to Mr. Sachs. He insisted I had to tell Jack."

Stevenson shifted his weight. His knees hurt, which wasn't unusual. "People close to death sometimes seem to have something very important to say. They struggle to get it out, and others agonize over what it is. In the end it might turn out to be something like, 'The sky is blue.' It's death they feel coming over them, and all they want is to communicate with the living one more time."

Miss Walsh frowned. "Maybe I didn't get it right."

"It was probably nothing," he repeated. "You shouldn't worry about it."

"I'm sure you're right." The girl's smile was pretty, but if they'd passed on the street, he'd have looked right past her. What made her so—what was the word—frumpy?

Stevenson sincerely thanked Miss Walsh for being a concerned citizen. People had been known to ignore the dead and the dying on American streets, like a recent incident when a young woman had screamed repeatedly for help as she was chased, stabbed, and eventually murdered. That woman had died alone, but Carrie Walsh would have waded in, with her poor eyesight and her one-hundred-twenty pounds, and made a difference. Maybe not in the crime itself, but in the perceptions that cops like Stevenson had of the citizenry of the nation.

***

Carrie missed work Wednesday because of the police investigation into the death of Todd Sachs, but on Thursday she returned to the office, pale but composed. All morning the Callenders were quiet as she caught up on the most pressing items. With only the sound of her typewriter and the occasional phone call, the office functioned as an office should. By lunchtime, the Callenders were bursting with curiosity, and they began picking at Carrie to get her to tell the details of the murder she'd witnessed.

She told the story, neglecting to mention why she'd been in the building's alley so late. Sadly, their reaction didn't surprise Carrie at all.

"Drug dealers," Peter proclaimed. "It's just as well when they kill each other off."

"But the police don't think Mr. Sachs was dealing in drugs," she objected.

"Of course he was." For once Jim agreed with his brother. "Those guys come back from Vietnam addicts, most of 'em, anyway. The only way they can feed their habit is to sell the stuff."

"It's too bad you had to see it, Miss Walsh," Brad consoled, "but that's how the world is these days. We need to stay out of the affairs of little countries no one's ever heard of. Those people over there don't value human life, and our guys come back infected with their ideas."

The refrain was familiar, but she wasn't in the mood for it today. Carrie busied herself with work, and the Callenders moved back to their insular mini worlds.

Later in the day, her employers' interest turned to local affairs, at least to Jim's. Brad began it with an apparently innocent question.

"Jim, did you have time to talk with Mrs. Meyers about her divorce?"

"I've decided to handle her case," Jim replied, which set Peter off.

"That's what we call it now—handling her case?"

Brad tittered, and Carrie sighed at his phrasing. Jim thought if he simply refused to admit what he did, no one could censure him for it.

"I cannot believe you—" Peter began, and they were screaming at each other in no time. Brad took Peter's side this time. Even dumpier and more mealy-mouthed than Peter, he couldn't resist commenting on the length of Jim's "conference" with Mrs. Meyers and the lady's "assets." Jim, the only one of the three with any outward charm, had none within. His handsome face turned red and tightened to an ugly glare. Caught in his own lies and misdemeanors, Jim's usual response was, "None of your business." That was what he said—shouted—in this instance too.

14

Peter, usually the most composed of the three, lost both control and dignity when a battle began in earnest. He threw things, stomped around the office, and repeated himself to the point of idiocy. Today it was, "I can't accept this. I just can't."

The Callender fights were legendary and eerily similar in structure. When something happened that made one of the three unhappy, he commented on it persistently until he got a rise out of one of the other two. It sometimes took an hour or so for open war to break out. There were days when one or another even tried to avoid it, but eventually one of them would take a louder tone and a more aggressive style. Escalation was then quick and terrible.

"Can't accept what?" Jim sneered at his brother.

"Your behavior is a reflection on the firm and on the family. Dalliance with clients is unconscionable, and I won't have it anymore."

It had been said a dozen times, but Jim reacted as if stunned. "You won't have it? Who are you to tell me what to do with my life, Mr. Perfect? If we all operated the way you do, we'd have no clients at all."

Peter rose from his desk. "I work on business principles: fair profit for fair work."

Brad, whom Carrie's father would have called "Pencil-neck," stepped in. "We can't have your relationships with women dictating our practices, Jim. Why, last week you didn't even charge Miss Chaplain for preparing her will."

"Sometimes we give up something to get something," Jim retorted. "Miss Chaplain will return with her million-dollar holdings when she needs further legal help."

Peter snorted derisively. "And we'll lose the rest of the family if they learn how you carried on with a girl twenty years your junior."

"Fifteen," Jim amended huffily. "And age has nothing to do with physical attraction. Miss Chaplain is a legal adult."

"Chronologically," Brad corrected. "I'd put her mental age at fifteen."

"Shut up! You're so jealous your teeth are green." Jim's shout signaled the end of what might possibly be called discussion.

"Don't tell him to shut up," Peter growled. "It's your fly that should be shut up."

"I do not have to be insulted in my own office!"

"—Taking advantage of a woman in crisis."

"—How to run my life, especially not zeros like you."

"—Could affect our profits disastrously."

"—The best lawyer in this room! You need me, not the other way around!"

While Peter screamed at Jim and Jim swore at Brad for starting it, Carrie finished typing a letter required for the next day. Waiting until all three men paused, each trying to think of something scathing to shout at the other two, she said,"I'm going home."

All three Callenders turned to her in shock.

"Why?" Brad asked.

"Are you sick?" Peter added.

"Upset?" That was Jim, who considered himself sensitive to women's needs.

"I need time to think things over."

"What things?" Peter asked, but Brad elbowed him. Finally realizing her departure might have to do with their behavior, he mumbled, "Whatever you need, Miss Walsh. We'll manage."

Jim held her coat, and Brad picked up her hounds-tooth purse and black gloves and handed them to her. Peter walked her to the door, promised to close up the office, and patted her arm, awkwardly but with concern. She knew what they were thinking. Would she quit, as all the others had?

They stood watching her, three spoiled children with law degrees. Carrie caught a whiff of Jim's overbearing after shave and noticed Brad's moist forehead. Why did she put up with them? Words rose to her lips, threats that they'd better behave or she would quit, but she didn't have the heart. Promising to come early tomorrow and catch up, Carrie left.

On the stairs she met Bea, ascending with a bucket of cleaning supplies and Smoky Robinson on the transistor. The scent of Lestoil wafted around her. "Miss Walsh," she said earnestly, "I feel terrible about your scare the other night. I shoulda took that last can myself. We'd both been long gone when that poor man got killed."

"Bea," Carrie said tiredly, "Neither of us could have known it would happen."

Voices raised behind them caught Bea's attention. "They at it again?"

"Most days I can take it, but today..." She shook her head in frustration.

"You shouldn't have to take what the three stooges in there dish out. I can't imagine what those boys' mother is like."

Carrie grinned. "I've met Mrs. Callender. She's a dignified, serene lady."

Bea rolled her eyes dramatically. "Then their daddy musta been somethin' else."

"Peter Callender, Senior was a Michigan supreme court justice," Carrie informed her with a chuckle. "Makes you wonder if evolution doesn't sometimes go backward."

"I don't believe that evolution stuff anyway," Bea scoffed. "I ain't related to no monkey; I don't care what anybody says." Looking upward as a loud crash punctuated someone's viewpoint in the ongoing argument, she smiled grimly. "Monkeys would object to being related to them."

"Probably."

Bea patted Carrie's arm. "You go home and rest up. And think about whether you wouldn't be happier working where there's some sane people."

"I will." As she continued down the stairs Carrie thought, I'll think, and I'll wish, but in the end, I'll stay where I am. I'm the kind of person who keeps doing what she's been doing, even if it's dumb.

CHAPTER THREE

On the street Carrie stopped, unsure of what she'd had in mind when she left the office. Did she want to go back to her apartment and stare at four walls? Glancing upward, she saw three anxious faces at the window. The Callenders were worried, but what did they fear more: that she'd have a nervous breakdown or that she'd quit? A breakdown wasn't imminent, and she thought she'd handled violent death and police procedures well. It was the ridiculous fighting of her bosses that rankled today.

Bea's advice echoed in her head. Would she be happier somewhere else? Another question followed that one. Was she happy where she was? The answer was easy: no.

Todd Sachs's life had ended far too early. Had he had dreams, things he planned to accomplish that were impossible now? She turned the question around. What were her dreams? Would she ever reach for them? Did she even know what her dreams were?

Carrie hated working for the Callenders. Even when they were nice to her, they weren't nice people. They needed a babysitter, not a secretary. But her dreams?

Flint didn't offer a lot of opportunities outside the auto plants, and Carrie had been determined to avoid the grinding life there. A company town, Flint had no pretensions to charm and few touches of beauty. Many residents considered their stay temporary, even though it lasted twenty or thirty years. Factories offered stable employment at good pay, so people from all over the Midwest came to put in their time then go "home" upon retirement, whether to northern Michigan or to Kentucky, Missouri, or Tennessee. In the time between, they tried not to notice the grayness of the city, the despair of those around them, and the years that stretched ahead.

Carrie had felt lucky to get on at the law firm, having had only two clerical classes as preparation. The pay was all right, the hours regular, and the work well within her abilities. Only the Callenders themselves made the job difficult. Although she'd considered looking for a new job, she hadn't, mostly due to

Onalee Walsh, her mother.

Onalee made everything Carrie did seem odd and a bit distasteful. A beauty whose makeup was always perfect, whose nails were never without polish, and who moved about in a cloud of Chanel #5 had found it unbelievable that she'd produced a gangly, tomboyish daughter. Carrie felt clumsy and plain next to her mother, who could show displeasure with just a raised brow and a flare of her nostrils.

Though Carrie had never felt she and her mother were close, Onalee objected when her daughter moved out of their home in Flushing, a town outside Flint. "The downtown is taken over these days with hippies and freaks," she'd claimed. Mom hadn't approved of Carrie working for lawyers either. "You'll be dealing with criminals every single day!" Most of all she'd objected to her daughter's renting the upper story of a house owned by a local college professor. As soon as she met the man, she declared him "a bohemian and worse!"

Allan Fournier had been Carrie's instructor in Business English, and he'd taken a liking to her. When the Callenders called the college looking for a secretary he'd recommended her, unaware at the time of their office histrionics. Carrie learned later he'd worked on the Callenders, cajoling them into giving her a chance.

Once she got the job, Fournier offered the apartment in his home on Kensington, a stately street of brick homes, well-kept and separate from the seedier areas of downtown. It was a short bus ride to her new place of employment, and it was far enough away from Flushing to make visiting inconvenient for Onalee, who didn't like city driving. Carrie accepted Fournier's offer before she told her mother any of it.

For once Carrie had faced her mother's anger, assuring her Doctor Fournier was both protective and a perfect gentleman. He was those things and more: kind-hearted, intelligent, and flamboyantly gay. That she didn't discuss with Onalee.

Standing up to her mother back then had been hard. It would

be worse now to admit she hated her job and wanted out. Carrie imagined her mother insisting she return home and abandon plans for a career. "I've been patient with this idea of a career, Caroline, but you've had your fun," she'd say. "It's time to settle down before you're too old to find someone."

Back in Flushing, Carrie would suffer arranged meetings with sons of her mother's friends, men who would take her to a movie and paw clumsily at her chest in the darkness. That was what a girl was supposed to do: find a man and get married.

Only Doctor Fournier (and Bea the janitor, she amended) encouraged Carrie to think of work as a career and not a way to keep busy while she waited for Mr. Right. "I've been waiting for Mr. Right for forty years," Fournier joked. "I don't think he's coming."

That reminded Carrie her landlord had classes until eight today. She'd have no one to talk to if she went home.

A glance upward revealed three faces still peering down at her, so Carrie started off in the general direction of the bus stop. Wandering idly down several streets, letting her thoughts wander as well, she found herself outside a small deli she'd never noticed before. The plan must have been to serve lunches to busy workers, but the tables were deserted. Still, a cup of coffee sounded good. The afternoon wind had a bite to it.

The place smelled of cinnamon, coffee, and fresh bread, but the atmosphere was otherwise uninviting. A flat-faced, disinterested woman slouched behind the counter. A man with a very bad complexion leaned against an oilcloth covered table behind her. "What can I get for you?" The woman's tone was surly.

"I'll have a coffee to go, please," Carrie said. Then, feeling their disapproval at the tiny sale, she added, "and one of those sugar cookies."

The woman took a cookie from the tray with an irritated air. "She wants one cookie," she asked the man as if Carrie weren't there. "What should I charge her?"

The man looked at Carrie and apparently judged her too timid to argue. "A dime." Carrie glanced at the sign. Cookies were thirty-nine cents a dozen. Face burning, she gave the woman a quarter and received four cents change.

On the sidewalk again, her embarrassment turned to anger, No wonder they had no business: rude and cheaters to boot. Mostly she berated herself. She couldn't stand up to the Callenders or to her mother, couldn't find the nerve to say no to a ten-cent cookie. When would she grow up?

Her thoughts returned to the men in the alley. She'd faced them, at least a little. She hadn't run away from the danger, the blood, and the dying man. Suddenly Carrie wanted to talk to someone about Todd Sachs. The partner—Somebody Porter. Should she go see him? The building they'd rented was nearby, which was why Sachs had been in the area.

On impulse she turned and walked the other way, passing her office building again. Along Robert T. Longway Boulevard were the offices of doctors, lawyers, and other professionals, but at Dort Highway it was as if some invisible line had been crossed. Businesses had bars on their windows and metal grilles at the doors to prevent break-ins. The odor of automotive work permeated the air: oil, gas, diesel fumes, the smell of tires and ongoing welding. The area was the city's auto shop.

Where Longway angled into Dort, Carrie stopped. Half a block ahead sat a small building recently painted a crisp white. A hand-lettered board in the window said, *Eagle Private Detective Agency Opening Soon.*

Carrie peered in at the window, mustering her courage. The place looked like it had once been an auto-parts store. At the front was a counter and behind it a wall. A doorway led into the back of the building, which she assumed had once been for storage but would now presumably be offices. She tried the door hesitantly and found it unlocked. As she entered, a man in an office chair rolled past the open doorway. He never looked up, but at least someone was there. A radio announcer opined on Hubert

Humphrey's chances of winning the Presidential election. With Nixon's assault on the Democratic bungling of the Vietnam conflict and George Wallace acting as wild card, the analyst said HHH didn't have a chance in "H."

"Mr. Porter?" she said tentatively. After a moment a voice answered affirmatively. "May I speak with you for a minute?"

"We're closed." The voice was pitched low, but the tone wasn't friendly. Conquering her nervousness, Carrie stepped behind the counter and through the open doorway. As she'd guessed, the back was in the process of being converted to offices. There were two desks, neither in great shape, with a lamp and a telephone on each, a coat rack, some battered metal file cabinets, and nothing else. Nothing matched. The windows looked onto other buildings' blank walls and had no shades or curtains. The place smelled musty, as if the corners needed cleaning. Obviously, the renovation hadn't gotten very far.

From the terse earlier comment, Carrie vaguely expected a Scrooge-ish character, spare and tight-faced. Conversely, the man in the office chair was probably the most beautiful human being she'd ever seen. He had sun-bleached blond hair, curly and thick, and blue eyes so clear they appeared unreal. His shoulders were wide, his arms muscular. The only detracting factors were the glare of irritation with which he regarded her and his grooming, which was informal to say the least.

Jack Porter wore faded jeans and a sweatshirt slit open haphazardly at the neck, evidently for ease of movement. His hair was too long to be controllable, and he'd made no attempt to do so anyway. He needed a shave, and the skin around his fingernails looked positively raw. Not a look to inspire client confidence.

A few seconds later Carrie added another fault to slovenliness. Porter didn't rise to meet a lady but merely glared at her from his chair. *He needs lessons in manners and good business practices.* Carrie filled the silence by explaining her purpose.

"I'm Caroline Walsh: the one who found Mr. Sachs the other night...in the alley." Porter didn't comment and she wondered momentarily if he might be deaf. At least he could nod or something. "Mr. Sachs told me to give you a message. I know the police told you, but I wanted to say I'm sorry I couldn't make sense of it, and that he's...gone."

For a few moments she heard only the buzz of end-of-the-season flies beating frenetically at the window behind her. Porter's gaze remained on her, unmoving and unmoved. Carrie tried to imagine his grief at the loss of his friend, which might explain the rudeness. It was a lot to take in one day, though: the Callenders, the nasty pair at the deli, and now this.

She made herself wait for a response, to see what it would be. As she did, an irrelevant thought struck her: Porter hated his good looks and downplayed them with shaggy hair and careless clothes.

Finally he spoke, gruffly and with no response to Carrie's expression of sympathy. "Tell me what he said. Tell me everything."

Carrie reminded herself she'd come for this, but did he have to be so unfriendly? The look on Porter's face conveyed something close to hostility. His voice was a growl, the tone abrupt, as if she were an annoyance when she'd come to help. Best to deliver her message and go. She didn't have to be friendly either.

"As I told the sergeant, the only thing I understood clearly was, 'Tell Jack.' Then he said something like "namwise" or "nowise," and then "kali shurenz" or "keli shurnz." I didn't get any more than that."

"Think!" It was an order. "Did the last part sound like one syllable or two? Shurenz or shurnz?"

Carrie replayed the sound in her mind. "Two syllables. In fact, there was kind of a grunt between that and 'kali.' It could have been a three-syllable word, like assurance."

That interested him. "What else?"

"That's it. Namwise and kali something-shurenz."

"Nothing else?" His voice had become less angry, more human. It mattered to him.

"He repeated 'Jack.'" Carrie answered. "It was all he could do to get that much out." Porter looked disappointed, the first human emotion he'd shown, and she said again, "I'm sorry."

"Thank you." It was more a dismissal than a genuine sentiment. The chair creaked as Porter pulled himself closer and returned to sorting through the stack of books before him.

Carrie stood uncertainly for a moment then turned to go. Porter didn't look up again, though she glanced back once. It appeared he'd already forgotten her. He tossed a few books into a box haphazardly, almost angrily.

At the end of the first block, her head bent forward in the cold gust that came around the corner, a thought occurred to her. There was something else she should have told him. Carrie stood half-turned. Should she go back? Porter hadn't been the least bit welcoming, but he had seemed interested in anything she could remember. She wavered, literally, with indecision. The easiest thing would be to go home and forget Jack Porter and his dingy little office. Still, he'd been compelling in his insistence she tell everything. Did one more little thing help? Carrie turned back.

This time he saw her coming. Still behind the desk, he didn't stand or in any way welcome her. Someone should suggest a Dale Carnegie course: How to Win Friends and Influence People.

"Mr. Porter, you asked if I noticed anything else. It might not be anything, but it did strike me as odd. The men who killed—the men I saw standing over Mr. Sachs—I think they were talking to him while they searched his pockets."

She leaned forward and her purse bumped an unbalanced pile of 8-track tapes. The top one, the Rolling Stones, slid onto the desk noisily. She put it back in place and straightened the pile. Porter seemed not to notice but stared, waiting for her to finish.

"The police didn't pay much attention, but it seemed to me like they knew him. Their posture was angry, more than a mugger would feel for a stranger."

Porter reached a hand down and rubbed one knee thoughtfully for several seconds, taking his time with the idea. Carrie began to feel foolish for returning with such a little thing. With her thick glasses, he probably wondered if she'd seen anything at all.

"I get impressions of people from their posture," she told him. "I don't see well, so I kind of depend on what they call body language." She met his gaze. "They knew Todd Sachs, Mr. Porter."

"Jack," he corrected. Now they were on a first-name basis? "I believe you, not that it helps."

A long silence followed, and Carrie waited for an indication of where the conversation was going. Porter accepted her statement, which was gratifying, but he didn't seem willing to make any further contribution. Carrie felt an angry flush creep up her face. She'd been nice, and he hadn't even asked her to sit down. It was time to give up on Jack Porter. He might be sad, but people were supposed to be civil, supposed to respond to kindness.

Porter was obviously misanthropic, possibly misogynistic, and rude. Having never walked away from anyone in anger in her life, Carrie retreated into the cool politeness she used on difficult clients at the law firm.

"Mr. Porter, I've done as I promised Mr. Sachs. Is there anything more I can do before I go?"

The question was her way of ending an unpleasant conversation on a civilized note. Her brows rose in surprise when Porter said, "You could bring those boxes over here."

For a moment she almost refused. He was clearly no gentleman. Not once but twice he hadn't risen to greet a lady. He'd treated her with no courtesy, picking her brain as if the rest of her didn't matter at all. Now he wanted her to wait on him.

After two days of stress and unpleasantness, Carrie came as close to rebellion as she had in her whole life. Disgusted, she strode to the back of the room and picked up the empty boxes he'd indicated. Bringing them to the desk she set them beside it, perhaps with more force than necessary.

"There. Now I'll be going. I can't say it's been a pleasure, but I will make allowances for you, given the situation." She stopped, amazed she'd actually said what she was thinking. An apology formed on her lips, but she set her jaw stubbornly. This guy didn't deserve it.

Porter seemed to see her for the first time. His lips twitched, and his shoulders relaxed a little. "You're right." As Carrie stared in surprise, he leaned back and rubbed his fingers across his forehead then over his jaw and the shadow of light-colored beard. "I'm not fit company for anybody, but I'm sorry I took my bad mood out on you."

She responded at once to the apology. "You've been through a lot."

Porter's fingers beat a brief tattoo on the desktop. "I appreciate your visit, but you're right. It's best if you go." With that he dismissed her a second time, tossing items into the box she'd provided with clattering finality. Finally, Carrie got it. He was moving out, and he wasn't happy about it.

"You'll be closing the business?"

"Since it never opened, I can't close it," he contradicted, "but yes, I'm leaving. If I can get moved out of here by tomorrow, I'll get at least part of our deposit back."

She gestured at the cans of paint and a toolbox in the corner. "But you started the remodeling already."

"Todd was the handyman." She saw real sorrow on Porter's face.

"And your friend."

That was a mistake. Porter didn't want her sympathy—probably not anyone's. "He just came home from 'Nam two months ago. We had plans." He didn't explain further, and Carrie wisely made no reply.

CHAPTER FOUR

VIETNAM-1967

The Boeing 707 set down at Tan Son Nhut Airport on November 3, 1966. Out the window, PFC John "Jack" Porter saw a country of lush greenness and incredible beauty, except for craters that dotted the ground like unfinished spots on a landscape painting. Along with other confused, jet-lagged passengers, Jack made his way down the metal steps to the tarmac. Hustled into groups, they boarded buses headed to various destinations. His was the Bin Hue 90th Replacement Depot. There he was given a bunk and two weeks' in-country training on matters particular to prosecuting a non-war, an "armed conflict," in Vietnam.

PFC Porter's first duty consisted of emptying latrine drums. Fifty-gallon barrels cut in half and set under toilet seats made the soldiers' latrines, and every day those drums had to be dragged out with large hooks and new ones set in place. The contents of the old drums were then doused with diesel fuel and burned. Stirring was required to complete the process, and that task fell mostly to "cherries," new troops. No socially acceptable name for the duty existed, and no one assigned to it ever forgot the smell.

Todd Sachs arrived a few days after Jack did and ended up in the same unit. Looking up from a book, Jack had his first look at the man who would become his best—perhaps only—friend when Todd asked in a terrible attempt at an English accent, "Is this posh upper berth available for rent, old chap?" Todd was Jack's physical opposite: short and square with dark eyes, dark hair, and an ever-present, infectious grin. Though unalike, each man almost immediately sensed the other complemented his strengths and weaknesses.

Todd easily made friends with the men in the large tent that housed them, men to whom Jack had hardly spoken. He dragged his new friend into a poker game on his first night in camp and reacted with glee when Jack won easily. "A natural poker face," Todd crowed, clapping Jack on the back like a proud uncle. "He never gives away anything."

Long nights at the table with his dad's cronies had been Jack's training. By keeping track in his head of the cards played, he could figure out what might be left in the deck and judge the odds he'd fill a straight or get a third ace to bump his pair to a chance at winning. His analytical mind had stood him in good stead growing up in Chicago, where figuring things out might keep you from getting your ass kicked. Other than cards, his dad had taught him nothing, unless there were lessons to be learned in watching someone drink himself to death.

Todd had his own demons, different but no less haunting. His working-class parents had died five years earlier in a freak accident in Swartz Creek, Michigan, when their home exploded from a faulty gas line. Todd had lived with his older brother until Randy enlisted in the Marine Corps, planning to send Todd to college on his military pay. But Randy had died in a firefight after only three weeks in country. Todd had enlisted in the army two days after his brother's remains were buried with full military honors.

No one would discern Todd's tragic background from being around him, and even Jack didn't learn about it for months. Outgoing and friendly to all, Todd loved practical jokes and dramatic storytelling. About once a week he was threatened with disciplinary action by one officer or another, but not one ever followed through. The guy was just too likeable to put on report.

There was the time when Corporal Belarski, not beloved to the company, came strutting through the camp showing off his (in his own opinion) magnificent body. He did attract attention as he sashayed past nurses and villagers wearing only a towel and his usual smirk. The situation quickly changed when Todd sneaked up behind him, grabbed the towel, snapped his rear hard enough to raise a welt, and took off with it. Instead of heading for cover, Belarski had chased Todd all over the grounds, trying to retrieve the towel and exact revenge. The company commander spoke sternly to Todd afterward, and Todd expressed regret. Both recognized that neither meant it.

Jack was drawn to Todd, and to his surprise, Sachs liked him, despite his terse communication and stony expression. The two became inseparable, watching each other's backs, as Todd put it, once they arrived at Phu Bai and began the work of their tour. Assigned to the 101st Airborne as MP's, their duty to the U.S. military was to guard convoys from camp to camp, assure the good behavior of both GI's and Vietnamese citizens, and stay alive— probably in that order, they decided between themselves.

The two found commonality in things like a lack of mail from home, indecision about what they would do with their lives (if they still had them) when their tours were over, and a belief that courage and training didn't get a man through war experiences. It was mostly luck, they agreed. The account Todd finally got of his brother's death revealed no reason why he had died and not the men on either side of him. It was war, and war makes no sense.

"Signing up felt like something I should do," Todd told Jack as he uncapped another beer for each of them one night. "If you live through combat, you know what you're capable of. Most people never know, because they're never tested."

"True." Jack took a swallow of his lukewarm, earthy anesthetic. "But once you've seen this, you'll never be able to look at life the same way again."

Todd nodded. "Yeah, it's bad. Still, I like knowing what kind of person I really am."

***

They'd known themselves pretty well after Vietnam. Jack knew he was capable of killing but not murder, capable of rudeness—enough people had told him that—but not unkindness. Todd had come to understand he couldn't change the past, couldn't atone for the death of his brother or make sense of it. That knowledge gradually transformed him into a man who acted, despite his effervescent personality, logically and with some deliberation. That's why it wasn't fair. After ten months in combat, when Todd had just started to forgive himself for being alive when the rest of his family wasn't, his life had ended at twenty-two years of age.

Returning to the here and now, Jack examined the woman who stood before him. She was in many ways like Todd, a child of the middle class who believed everyone's motives were the same as her own. It wasn't her fault she'd come at a dark moment, when the loss of his friend, who was also the reason Jack himself was alive, was still only dimly grasped. His brain felt like it was being torn into shreds, but he admitted to himself this girl had come with the best of intentions.

"Look," he began, careful to keep his voice even. "I appreciate your coming here. Right now I've got a lot of cleaning up to do, because without Todd, I have to give up the office and the business." Jack wondered if he sounded as defeated as he felt, "It's the end of a lot of planning we did together, and I'm not happy about it." He reached over and turned off the radio, cutting Paul McCartney off in the middle of a line about something in the way she moves. "It's best if you leave me alone."

She was probably concluding he was a gloomy type, more Poe than Dickens, and she was correct. He wasn't the type to generate happy endings. Bending to pick up the purse she'd set down to fetch the box, she noticed his crutches in the corner behind the desk.

"You've hurt your leg!"

Jack felt his lips curl into a sneer. "My leg isn't hurt. It's gone."

The girl blushed. Now she'd leave as soon as possible, escaping the cripple and his problems.

Instead, she took a deep breath and said, "Mr. Sachs' death puts you at a disadvantage in more than the loss of his friendship."

Jack kept his face as blank as concrete. "You might say that."

She gestured at the stacks and piles around them. "I could help you clear the office. I have the afternoon off, and I know how to keep quiet."

Jack regarded the girl who'd disturbed his grief and anger, a girl with an earnest face and too-thin body. Her coat was plain. The white blouse beneath it had all the appeal of a blank sheet of paper, and the brown pleated skirt didn't add much interest. She wore no makeup in a time when most women her age wore layers of the stuff. Thick glasses made her eyes look distorted and goofy, and she had a primness about her he'd never found attractive in women. Still, her offer came from kindness, the innocent assumption one must be good and do good, and the world will repay. Though she was probably wrong, he couldn't hold that against her.

What the hell. It would get him out of here quicker if she toted things out to the pickup. He planned to take only a few things. The landlord could keep the furniture the Eagle Agency would never need. Her offer came from pity, but he need never see her again after today. He'd probably move back to Chicago.

Jack nodded. "Thanks. It's hard to carry boxes with the crutches."

"How long before they fit you with a prosthesis?"

He'd returned to filling boxes with office supplies, and he looked up in surprise. Most people avoided talking about his missing leg. This woman talked about it as a matter of fact, which it was. "I don't think that will happen, I walked out--" He smiled at the incorrect phrasing. "—I mean, I left the hospital with no intention of going back."

"I won't say I know how it feels to be in your situation," she said, "but I do hate hospitals. They give me the creeps, and they smell."

"Yeah. You're..." he stopped, unable to find the right words.

"Out of control," she suggested.

"Yeah. Doctors, nurses, even candy stripers, tell you what you can and can't do."

"I hated the 'we' part. They'd say to my dad, 'Now Mr. Walsh, we're going to drink this al-l-l-l down.' They didn't have to drink the awful stuff, but it was always we."

As she parodied a stereotypic nurse, her primness vanished, and Jack saw a different woman. He found himself adding to her comment. "They call you 'honey' or 'sweetie' like they care, but it's really because they don't remember your name." His voice turned bitter, "To them you're the amputee in Bed 6."

"My dad died in the hospital," she said. "Mom and I left to get something to eat, and when we got back it was over. The nurse said it's like they wait for their families to leave the room, but I felt awful." She added quickly, "So did my mom, of course."

Jack thought of how his father had died, coughing up blood but refusing to go to the "goddam hospital." His mother hadn't minded becoming a widow much. She'd had a new man within two weeks.

The girl apparently thought the tone had become too morbid. "Okay, point me to where this stuff goes." They worked diligently for half an hour, Jack filling boxes and the girl transporting them to the Ford F100 pickup parked behind the building. "The truck is Todd's," Jack told her. "He got an automatic so I could drive it, but I don't know what happens to it now. Maybe I can buy it from his estate."

She paused with a box of books. "What will you do now?" Hands full, she performed a face-scrunching gesture he would come to know well, using a cheek muscle to push her heavy glasses back into place.

"I don't know."

"What made you decide to become a private detective?"

Jack smiled for the first time. "Back in 'Nam Todd had the idea we'd become police officers. We were MPs, and we'd learned a lot about procedures and criminal justice and all that. When I got hurt, Todd just changed the idea around." Jack shrugged. "We couldn't be cops, but we could do private investigation, me doing the paper chasing and him the legwork. You couldn't rain on Todd's parade; any obstacle could be overcome."

Jack had been at times jealous of his friend—his enthusiasm, his determination, and most of all his loyalty. Todd could have become a cop without Jack, but he'd revised his dream to include him.

"What kind of investigating were you going to do?" the girl asked when she returned for the next box.

"We thought missing persons and stuff like that. We even had a prospective client."

"Really?"

"An old acquaintance of ours contacted Todd, Crate Somers."

"Crate?"

Jack wiped some matted cobwebs from a book with his shirttail. "Todd never called anyone by his real name. He called me Joker, a combination of jack like the playing card and a comment on my approach to life. He always said I'm too serious." The girl didn't say it, but he saw agreement in her eyes. "Crate was Todd's nickname for a guy we met in 'Nam named Packard Augustus Somers. A Packard is an old crate, so Packard became Crate, and the name stuck. Even Somers liked it better than Packard."

"Todd sounds like a real character."

"Never a dull moment." Jack felt a stab of pain, recalling he'd never see his grin again, but he went on with the story. "Crate wanted to find an old army buddy or something, and he contacted Todd a few days ago. He'd been looking through army records on Tuesday. That's how he ended up..."

"I'm sorry," she said in the softest voice possible.

He shook off the sentiment. "Wrong place at the wrong time, the cop said."

She pushed her glasses into place again. "He told me it happens all too often."

"It's not fair, Todd was..." But that was too much emotion for Jack. He let the rest of his thought hang in the air.

CHAPTER FIVE

"Joker, can you handle organizing stuff without me this afternoon?" Todd asked on the last morning of his life.

"Sure," Jack remembered saying, hardly looking up from the stacks before him. They'd collected a ton of reference works to aid them in locating addresses, zeroing in on streets and sites, and finding agencies that could provide needed information. Jack intended to create a system that allowed easy access to all of them, but the mixture of telephone books, maps, typed lists, and pamphlets made organizing difficult.

"I'm going to do a record search at the courthouse. Remember Crate Somers?"

"Who could forget old Wrong-Way?"

"He called last night. He's back home and pretty much fully recovered—got a job and a house and everything."

"That's good." The name brought to mind Crate's Vietnamese wife, and Jack hardly listened as Todd relayed Somers' concerns. Instead, his mind was eighteen thousand miles away. He and Crate Somers were alike in one way. They'd both left Vietnam different men. In Jack's mind the difference made him a lesser man.

***

"Maybe you should let this Crate know you can't help him out," the girl was saying. Jack forced his mind onto the less emotional track her words evoked. He was more distraught than he let on, but he was unwilling to show it in front of a stranger. Apparently unaware, she went on, "It was on the news, but he should hear from you."

"I'll see if Todd left a number." Jack scooted the chair from his desk to the other one, where he sorted through Todd's papers. When he came out from behind the desk for the first time, he saw her glance down. The amputation was at the knee, and he'd cut the left leg of his jeans off below it and sewn it shut. Did she think his wife had done that for him? He caught himself short, rolling his eyes. Why would she be thinking about his wife, or thinking about him at all? She was helping out the crippled vet. That was all.

Finding a legal pad with notes on it, he located the number and dialed the phone. The girl picked up a box of phone books from various areas of the country and took it out to the truck. Jack felt the draft when she opened the door. The October afternoon had turned much colder, and predictions said it might snow. It wouldn't stay this early, but he wasn't ready for the cold and the ice that was sure to plague a one-legged man.

When the girl returned, shivering, he was sitting behind Todd's desk, the phone in one hand and one finger holding down the cutoff button.

"What's the matter, Mr. Porter?"

"Somers' mother answered the phone. Crate had an accident, and he's dead."

"Dead?" She repeated the word in shock.

"He fell off the roof of his house. Broke his neck."

"I'm sorry, Jack."

"Yeah."

She leaned toward him anxiously. "Listen, I'm going to go somewhere and get us some coffee. Are you okay for a while?"

He nodded numbly, still staring at the phone. When he looked up, the girl was gone.

***

Carrie knew instinctively that Jack Porter needed time to get himself together after yet another heavy blow. Still, leaving him alone for too long might push him into the pit of despair she guessed had been widening since his injury. It sounded like Todd Sachs had kept him from descending in it, but Todd was gone. Would the anger she'd seen earlier return, or would something worse be the result? Carrie walked a little faster. She had to get back and offer Mr. Porter support.

At the same deli where she'd felt insulted earlier, Carrie bought coffee and a couple of doughnuts. The two behind the counter were as surly as before, but they were only a minor annoyance this time. Returning to the Eagle, she found Porter calmly sorting through papers again, putting some in a box and most in a wastebasket.

Carrie set a steaming, aromatic cup of coffee in front of him. Jack looked at the coffee then regarded her closely, his jaw jutting slightly. Knowing he assumed her actions stemmed from pity, Carrie was direct.

"At six years old I started wearing these glasses, so I know what it's like to be stared at. I hate them, but I can't go without them." She touched the heavy black frames. "Even with my bad vision I see that first glance people take before they look away, embarrassed for me." She waved away her embarrassment and indicated the crutches. "It's much worse for you, since you didn't grow up with those."

"You're saying you're a cripple too?"

"I'm saying I know what it's like to depend on something you need but hate."

He smiled grimly. "I do hate those things."

"Anyway, I'm not feeling sorry for Jack Porter the cripple. I think you've done well. You decided not to sit back and live on disability pay. You get around by yourself, and you were going to clear this office alone. That shows determination. I'm sorry you lost your best friend and another friend within forty-eight hours. You deserve a little sympathy, and I'm the only one here right now. So have a cup of coffee on me, will you?"

After a pause, Jack chuckled, and she heard genuine humor in it. "Only if you'll tell me your name again. After you left, I thought, 'I don't know who this woman is.' I need to thank you for your help—really thank you."

She felt herself blush. "Caroline—Carrie to my friends. My last name's Walsh."

Jack nodded, "Well, Miss Walsh, thanks for being here, for the help, and for the coffee. Now do I smell doughnuts too?"

Carrie couldn't believe what she heard herself propose a few minutes later. Sitting in the uncomfortable chair across from Jack, she'd handed him a cruller and taken a bite of her own. As she sipped the coffee, which was much better than the deli owners' manners, a thought that had circulated in her brain since she'd left the office came bubbling out. "What if you had someone to do your legwork, Jack?" She didn't know when he'd become Jack in her mind, but the name slipped out naturally.

He didn't even wince at her poor choice of term. "What do you mean?"

"You're qualified as a private detective? With a license and all that?"

"Yes, but—"

"It's difficult for you to get around right now, but someday you'll be able to. Why throw away what you've started here? If you had someone to do research and interview people...and I can type and file, too," she finished lamely.

Porter's face showed disbelief. "You want to be my partner?"

"Of course not!" She felt the blush in her cheeks again. "I'm no detective. But I have two years' experience in a law office. I deal with people well, even difficult people. Until you're able, I can do the stuff that requires getting around. You can do the detecting."

Jack's expression was unreadable: distress? amusement? horror? "But you have a job," he finally said.

"Which I hate." The words almost exploded from her. "My bosses are idiots with law degrees." Quoting Bea she added, "It's like I work for the Three Stooges."

"Carrie." His voice was soft, almost gentle. "You can't quit a solid job on the hope this little agency is going to take off. I have my pension to fall back on, but what will you do if it folds in six months?"

Suddenly more confident than she'd been in months, she replied, "There are other jobs. I heard this morning unemployment is at its lowest in fifteen years, and earlier, before I even met you, I asked myself, 'When are you going to do something you want to do?'" She sighed. "I want to be part of a business, not just a secretary but really part of it. You need me," she hoped she hadn't gone too far. "I need to change my life."

Porter sipped his heavily sugared coffee, looking thoughtful. His hair was even more disheveled than it had been earlier, as if he'd run his hands through it over and over. It took a long time, and Carrie sat very still, aghast at her own boldness. What was going through

37

his head?

After a few moments he leaned forward and stuck out his hand, which Carrie realized meant they'd shake to seal the deal. "I know you're willing, and I think you're able. Let's do it."

She shook hands, though she'd never done that as a business gesture. Thoughts flew through her head: she would no longer be the secretary everyone ignored, but an investigative assistant. She'd take classes at Flint JC and see where it went. Out of nowhere came a question. "Why the Eagle Agency?"

"We were 101st Airborne," Jack explained.

Carrie frowned, recalling the little she knew of the army. "Paratroopers?"

"All crazy enough to jump out of perfectly good airplanes." Draining the coffee cup, Porter rubbed his thigh in an almost enthusiastic gesture. "Our first job is to undo all the sorting and loading of the last few hours. If we're going to open this agency, I'll need all this stuff back in place, so finish that doughnut and let's get to work, Miss Walsh.

CHAPTER SIX

The next morning Carrie spent an hour debating with the Callenders, who were for once united in disbelief she would take such a rash step.

"Miss Walsh," Peter argued. "Think of what you're doing, leaving a job where you have security to take up a fly-by-night possibility. If he were here to advise you, your father would not approve."

Jim Callender made it personal. Putting an avuncular arm around Carrie's shoulders and squeezing briefly, he regarded her with eyes aslant. "Carrie, is it fair for you to leave us in the lurch like this?"

Brad mentioned a possible raise, making Peter sniff in alarm. Steering away from money and back to guilt Peter asked, "What does your mother say about this?"

"I haven't told her yet." That sounded defensive. The worst part would be telling Onalee what she'd done, but if she'd already given notice, her case was stronger.

"Carrie." Now Peter's powers of argument were focused. "A young woman doesn't always do wrong because she's willful. It's usually because she doesn't consider the consequences of her actions." He paced as if he were in front of a jury. "What every parent wants for a daughter is a husband and a family. Now these are things you might have and still work here at the Callender firm. We're more than willing to have you take time off for your wedding, for having babies, and we'd welcome you back. But at a one-man agency, and a private detective at that, will you have those options? The hours will be uneven, the pay sporadic, and you have no guarantee of this man's character. Porter might be some sort of cad."

He's probably worth half a dozen Jims. Carrie bit her response back. No sense leaving with hard feelings, in case she had to come back for a reference.

Peter retreated and Brad stepped in, rubbing his soft hands together as if applying lotion. "Why don't you speak to an uncle, your pastor, or maybe Judge Clayton? The advice of a mature man interested in your welfare might help."

"For the sake of your good name," Jim put in. "Even if this Porter is honest, what will it look like to a boyfriend when he finds out you work all day alone in an office with this man? How can he avoid thinking there's hanky-panky going on?"

Carrie's lips tightened. "It would be none of his business."

"I didn't say you'd ever do that, Carrie. I'm simply saying how it will look to men you might meet and want to date."

It went on like that, with Carrie not bothering to answer most of the arguments they thought were so clever. Not for the first time in her life, she resented the assumption she couldn't think for herself. If this move turned out to be a mistake, she'd admit it when the time came, but everyone she knew seemed to believe a single girl's decisions required an okay from a simple majority of her adult male relatives.

In the end, her bosses suggested she take the day off to "think this idea over very carefully." Since it was Friday, she'd have three days, at which time they hoped she'd be over this insanity. She informed them Monday would be the first day of her final two weeks and left the office echoing with the silence of their reproach.

Descending the stairs, Carrie heard Jim, always the loudest of the three, comment to his partners. "I hope that little lady doesn't regret her action. You know what they say: 'A man doesn't buy a cow when he can have milk for free.'"

"Guttersnipe!" Carrie murmured a word she'd always liked but had never said out loud before. Far from intimidating her, the Callenders' pompous advice had made her determined to disprove their dismissal of her as a fluffy-headed female. The Eagle Detective Agency would succeed if she had anything at all to say about it.

It took all of five minutes to walk from the law firm to Jack's office, but Carrie worried all the way he'd had a change of heart. They'd taken on a lot. Could she do as she'd promised and perform half the work? She knew how to drive, though she hadn't done it much, and knew the city pretty well, having grown up there.

She could set up a bookkeeping system and keep track of things, but Jack would have to be patient while she learned the basics of detective work. He badly wanted the agency to succeed, so maybe that would help.

When she arrived, Carrie saw with some relief that efforts had been exerted to make her feel welcome. Jack had rolled his chair to the outer office, where he was laying out paper, pens, a blotter, and other supplies in an attempt to make her space, the reception area, supplied with everything he could think of.

He was dressed in a sweatshirt and jeans again, but today his hair was combed. "I wondered if you'd done the sane thing and changed your mind." His manner was tentative.

"I went to give the Callenders two weeks' notice."

His face clouded. "I forgot you have to give them time to find someone else."

"It won't delay us too long," she hastened to assure him. "I'll come afternoons and finish the painting and get the building ready."

"I can paint." His tone was truculent.

"Good," she replied. "You can scoot that chair of yours along the bottom while I stand on a chair and do the top." She held up a zippered case. "Clothes for the job."

In a few minutes they began, Carrie in jeans and a bright blue sweatshirt. She pulled her hair up into a ponytail and tied it with a scarf to keep it out of her way while Jack stirred the paint and draped both chairs in old sheets. Carrie approved of Todd's color choice, an eggshell tone that brightened the almost windowless room.

They worked in silence until they'd established a rhythm, sharing paint while staying out of each other's way. After a while Jack asked, "Do you think they'll be able to find a replacement for you in two weeks?"

"It won't be easy, not because I'm so good, but because the Callenders are so bad. Their reputation precedes them all over town."

"Are they crooked?"

"No, difficult." Carrie didn't elaborate on her bosses' shortcomings. "I did have an idea on the way here though. I have a friend who'd love to get out of the Buick plant."

"Would she be a good secretary for a law firm?"

"I think so. In fact, she might be good for them."

"Meaning?"

"Meaning the first time the Callenders start screaming at each other when Marsha's around, things might get interesting."

"Marsha is the assertive type?"

Carrie grinned, "She's likely to give them more than they bargained for."

"She sounds perfect. Why don't you give her a call right now?"

She was pleased Jack seemed anxious to get her away from the Callenders. "I will this weekend. Her sleep schedule is a little weird."

Jack rolled his way to the tiny window at the back of the building, where he'd set two Cokes on the sill to keep them cool. Sticking one in each pocket of his jacket, he returned to the front. Popping the caps on an opener mounted beneath the counter, a leftover from the building's previous use, he handed one bottle to Carrie. "To Caroline Walsh and Jack Porter, total staff of the Eagle Detective Agency. And to Todd 'Squatty-Body' Sachs. Wish you were here, buddy."

Carrie's dad had had a reply for such occasions, and she raised her Coke and responded, "To absent friends."

Jack set the bottle on the counter. "If Todd were here, we'd be having warm beer."

"Warm?"

"Yeah, we couldn't get it cold in-country, so we got used to drinking it warm. When he got home, Todd couldn't tolerate cold beer, so he'd warm it a bit."

Unable to picture life without ice Carrie murmured, "Warm beer, yuck!"

"Rum and Coke is even worse." Jack's face relaxed as a memory arose. "Todd always said if he ever had a son, he'd name him Bud. A daughter would be Pabst, and twins would be Bacardi Light and Dark."

"That's terrible." She felt Jack's tenseness letting go. He was accepting Todd's death. He could remember his friend and tell stories that made him real to her. Suddenly she laughed. "Bud, Pabst, and the twins, Light and Dark. Too much!"

First Jack smiled at her amusement. Then he chuckled at the silliness of the joke. Carrie began laughing louder, unable to stop. Soon they were both laughing harder than the situation warranted. Stress letting go of them, she recognized, releasing the awful things they'd both faced over the last few days. Carrie set her Coke down as she laughed helplessly. Tears leaked from the corners of her eyes, steaming her glasses up. Still humming with humor she removed them. Without their correction she saw Jack's face only dimly, but she could tell his expression had grown serious.

"You look different without those." Silence crashed down around them. Carrie tried to hold her smile steady as she replaced the glasses, all her good feeling gone. Jack realized what he'd done.

"I'm sorry." He looked it. "I guess you could tell me I'd be more fun with two legs."

"It's okay." She tried to make her face match the words. "In school, I used to go without them to dances and things like that. I never knew who stood next to me or what the score was, but I felt— prettier, I suppose." She chuckled dryly. "Until I realized my squint ruined the effect I was going for." In a burst of honesty she added, "Mom used to call me her Ugly Duckling."

Jack frowned at her, shocked. "Your mother said that?"

"Actually, she called me Duckling, but I got the idea." Carrie defended her mother, as she had all her life. "She doesn't mean anything by it. It's just that Onalee was the all-American girl: Homecoming Queen, voted Best Looking in her class. She even won a beauty pageant, Miss Southeast Michigan or something." She moved away, testing the blinds for dust with a finger. "I'm used to the way I am. No point in fussing about it."

Jack's expression said he didn't agree, but he wasn't going to argue. "The police called. They're releasing Todd's body, so I arranged a service for Sunday afternoon."

She seemed grateful for the change of subject. "Would it be all right if I came?"

He grinned, "I was hoping you would, since I don't know any of his friends from around here." He handed her an index card with the date, time and address printed in bold strokes. "Now, show me how you like your desk set up, and I'll try to leave things where you put them for the next two weeks—until you really become the other half of the Eagle Detective Agency."

That evening Carrie roamed her apartment restlessly until eight o'clock then finally forced herself to pick up the phone. Dialing her mother's number, she pictured Onalee, still slim at forty-five, clipping down the stairs in her hard-soled little flats to the phone near the front door. A second phone hung on the wall in the kitchen, but her mother never went there if she could avoid it.

Onalee Walsh dressed every morning as if she were meeting Pat Nixon for brunch. Makeup carefully applied hid the passage of time on her face, and clothing painstakingly shopped for and purchased did the rest. A master of illusion and a genius at highlighting her attributes, Carrie's mom downplayed her few physical failings expertly. The irony of it was Onalee went nowhere important and saw no one special. Creating a perfect look had dominated her days for so long she knew no other way to behave.

The call connected, and Carrie heard a click as Onalee removed one earring as she brought the receiver to her ear. "Walsh residence."

"Hi, Mom, it's me."

"Caroline, you sound odd. Are you ill?"

"I'm fine. I have something to tell you."

"Will I like it?" Carrie's heart sank at the expectant tone. Mom was hoping the date she'd recently forced on Carrie, the son of a friend of a friend, had been successful—she'd finally "met someone" and had called to announce, if not her engagement, at least the acceptance of a promise ring. The truth was the men her mother dug up for her were pathetically unsuited for Carrie, and she for them.

Better to be blunt. "Probably not. The news is I've taken a new job."

"Did the Callenders decide to relocate?"

"No. I wanted to try something different."

"I knew you wouldn't like working there. People who need a lawyer are either criminals or next to it."

It wasn't going in the direction she'd hoped. "I found something more interesting."

"Interesting?" Her mother was off on her favorite topic. "I'll tell you what you need to do. Find a job where you meet good men: not criminals, not sleazy lawyers, but real, eligible men. Maybe you could still get in at Hurley." Onalee's dream was that Carrie would go to work at a hospital and meet an eligible doctor. Arguing that she had no interest in the work did no good.

"Mom, I'm going to work at a detective agency."

A long pause followed, "A what?"

"I met a man, Mr. Porter. I saw his partner get murdered this week. He needs help to keep the agency going, and I offered to work for him."

"Oh, my God. You saw a murder?"

That should have come out more gently. "I passed an alley and saw—the end of it."

"I told you about downtown! The place is a jungle."

"That's not the point, Mom. I'm going to work for Jack, uh, Mr. Porter. He needs me." A stretch, but she was desperate.

"I cannot believe you would throw away two years at a respectable law office to go to work for someone you just met who is obviously a low-life or his partner wouldn't have been killed in an alley." Suddenly the law firm was respectable?

Picturing Onalee wrapped in the phone cord as she paced the fake-marble inlaid in the foyer, Carrie tried for logic. "We don't know why he was killed. It might be completely unrelated to the agency."

"The agency," her mother mimicked. "Aren't you the professional shamus? Really, Caroline, come to your senses. The Callenders will take you back if I call them and explain we've reconsidered."

"No!" Carrie surprised herself with the vehemence of her protest. "I've given them notice, and in two weeks I will join the Eagle Detective Agency." Taking a breath she finished, "I called to tell you, not to ask your permission."

Onalee made a sound of disgust. "All right, Caroline, I'll tell you what. Go ahead and do what you want to do, but remember, when this falls apart, when this so-called business fails and you have to come begging for financial help, there will be strings attached. Serious strings."

Carrie didn't argue. At this point she'd learned to simply listen, since interrupting only delayed the end of the lecture.

"I've been patient with your wanting a career, but let's be honest. Good men don't marry so-called career women." Her tone was scornful. "They're tough and they're tired and they look fifteen years older than they really are. Men want to relax when they come home, Caroline. They want their wives there to keep the children quiet, to have supper ready, and to look nice for them. Those Women's Libbers say differently, but they're wrong. When you wake up and realize that, I hope it's not too late. I really do."

With that Onalee hung up the phone with a decisive clunk, leaving Carrie angry, frustrated, and hoping that on several salient points, it was her mother who was wrong.

CHAPTER SEVEN

A week later Carrie left the law office at five, locking the door behind her. Her bosses were still tight-lipped and reproachful about her decision to leave, so work was a little uncomfortable. Unable to comprehend how difficult they were to work for, the Callenders assumed Carrie's leaving was some sort of female whim. They showed their disapproval with all the pomposity three lawyers in agreement can exert.

The day wasn't bad for mid-October. The sky's shade brought to mind the phrase from a poem she'd had to memorize in grade school, "October's Bright Blue Weather." Cool but not cold, the air felt clean in her lungs. As she waited for the light to turn green before crossing to the bus stop, Carrie reveled in the sunshine, as Northerners must in the autumn. There'd be little enough of it for the next five months. The walk light came on and she started across the street, still thinking pleasant thoughts.

Suddenly a voice from behind her shouted, "Look out!" Carrie came out of her reverie to see a black car speeding directly at her. Reacting instinctively, she pushed hard with her back foot, propelling herself toward a parked car to her right. She landed hard, half over the hood of the car, but it was enough. The oncoming vehicle missed her, roaring past and disappearing down the street.

The kid who'd shouted the warning approached. About thirteen, he wore jeans and a flannel shirt and sported a buzz cut that said his dad still made the tonsorial decisions at his house. "Are you okay?"

Shaking, Carrie asked herself the same question. One of her penny loafers lay in the street, squashed by the car's tire. Her hands and one hip stung from the force with which she'd landed against the metal hood of the Pontiac she now leaned against for support. Her breath came in gasps, but she was alive. "Yes," she told the boy. "Thanks to you. I didn't see that car coming."

"You had the light," the kid said disgustedly. "I checked the traffic myself before starting across, but that guy came out of nowhere."

"I guess that's why pedestrians have to be so careful," Carrie said ruefully. "Can't assume just because we have the right-of-way, we should take it." She laughed nervously. "That car seemed really big coming at me."

He nodded. "LTD—sixty-three, I think. If you want, I'll help you file a police report."

If the police couldn't solve the murder of Todd Sachs, how much effort would they put into an almost hit-and-run with no injuries? Thanking the boy again, she declined his offer, dug out fifty cents so he could buy himself a sundae, unfolded the flattened shoe he handed her, and continued on her way.

***

On October 26, Carrie locked the office of the Callender firm for her last time and handed the keys to a frosty Peter Callender. After Todd's funeral, she'd called her friend Marsha who'd shown up "spiffy and aromatic," as she put it, for an interview. Though the Callenders had been skeptical, Marsha charmed them, as Carrie knew she could.

Marsha Kazubowski Wozniak was petite and blond, with blue eyes and a ready smile, on first impression a perfect Polish princess. Carrie knew, but did not share with the Callenders, that beneath her pert exterior lurked a strong personality. Though not college-educated, Marsha was smart, confident, and not easily cowed. All three partners had been willing to hire Marsha after the interview, and, giving up hours of precious sleep, she'd started working mornings with Carrie in order to learn the office procedures. Carrie herself had gone directly to the Eagle each day after work, where she and Jack set up their own office policies and procedures.

Jack seemed pleasantly surprised with her contributions. In addition to giving the place a thorough cleaning so it no longer smelled like dust, she set her mind to making the business viable. Jack and Todd hadn't considered things like advertising, assuming clients would accrue through word of mouth. While that was possible, it could also take a long time. Carrie suggested ways they could spread the news of their business discreetly but effectively. For example, though lawyers never advertised, the Callenders were aware the placement and size of a listing in the yellow pages could attract notice.

Other things Carrie suggested were designed to streamline procedure, make clients more comfortable, and assure quality record-keeping. Jack claimed the Callenders had lost a valuable resource, a fact they'd realize soon enough.

For her part, Carrie marveled at how much Jack changed when he was busy. Sometimes she looked up from painting or came in from outside to find him absorbed in a task, his blue eyes focused intently and his hair tousled. At those moments she would think: *This is a man.*

The day finally arrived when Carrie unlocked the Eagle's front door at 8:40 a.m., causing a small bell over the entry to ring cheerfully. For her first day as an associate she'd bought a business-like outfit in burgundy, adding a pink stretchy headband to hold her hair back from her face.

A few minutes later she placed an official-looking Open sign in the window. An equally official-looking sign hung over the sidewalk as well: Eagle Detective Agency/Discreet Private Investigations. In the outer office, Carrie sat behind the counter, newly enameled until it shone. Through the inner doorway was one desk where there had been two, but she'd found a second-hand couch to fill the other corner and make the room more inviting. She'd scrounged up some comfortable chairs at the Bargain Barn, and tasteful tan curtains of rough, open-weave burlap now covered the windows, hiding the fact there was no view. An inexpensive braided rug pulled the room together nicely. The office looked good, possibly even classy. Jack said he didn't get it, but he'd trusted her instincts and paid the bills.

That first morning was long, since not a soul entered the office. Both Carrie and Jack tried to pretend it didn't matter. For two weeks they'd worked, discussed, and planned. Now the business was a reality, but what if it flopped? Carrie feared Jack would sink into depression, and she guessed he feared she'd have to move back in with her mother.

***

Jack's stomach felt as if there was an anvil at its bottom. The business was going to fail, and Carrie, a girl he liked more than he had any right to, would be left high and dry, with no job and no ability to pay her rent. She'd only have one choice, and though she never criticized her mother, Jack knew moving home would be awful for her. Though he hadn't met the woman, Onalee Walsh sounded like a spoiled brat who manipulated her daughter, apparently just for something to do. It had evidently been quite a struggle for Carrie to move out in the first place, and going back would indicate failure in more ways than finance. She loved the little apartment that signified her independence.

Though he couldn't tell her how important the agency was to him, Jack knew it could save his sanity. Carrie's offer to help meant he could continue with his plans, despite the loss of Todd and his confident assurance. He felt a debt of gratitude to the skinny girl who'd found something in him to trust. He was sick thinking he might let her down, as he'd let down others before her.

Listening to the woodpecker-like sound of the typewriter as Carrie pretended to be busy, Jack reminded himself she'd wanted this. She'd wanted to find her place in the world, not as a copy of her mother, not as an under-appreciated employee. Busy earning a living, she was only dimly aware of the protest women staged at the Miss America Pageant in Atlantic City that September, earning them the mistaken but popular term "bra-burning feminists." While they'd painted the office furniture one day, she'd admitted feeling the call of women's liberation. "But I don't think a movement can change a person," she said. "It can only make you think about who you'd like to be."

Carrie had no idea how unusual it would be for a woman to be actively involved in criminal investigation, and Jack hoped she wasn't stretching herself too far. Would she panic when faced with a client who was crude or even violent? He raised an eyebrow at that thought: what client? Carrie might never be tested at all, in which case he hoped the Callenders would take her back. He wasn't up to feeling responsible for another person, not now, maybe not ever again.

Resolutely cheerful, Carrie appeared to be busy until noon. She'd even brought lunch: two sandwiches, a thermal bottle of coffee, and some cookies she shyly admitted to making herself. "Dad loved cookies, so I learned to make lots of different kinds. I figured chocolate chip was a safe choice."

Jack showed his approval by biting into one. "You and your dad were close?"

Carrie smiled at the memory, "Dad was the best, though after thirty years in the shops he was deaf as a post. Within months of his retirement, they found lung cancer."

"I'm sorry."

"Thanks. Mom and Dad..." She paused and rephrased. "She's beautiful, you know? He married her thinking she was someone she wasn't, and I guess she made a mistake too. They grew apart in a very short time, but by then I was there, his little shadow. He took me fishing while Mom did her nails."

There was no bitterness in her tone, only acceptance. Though she didn't say it, Jack deduced Onalee had found her husband as uninteresting as she found her own child.

Jack pictured Carrie as a kid, a little girl with strong glasses who'd felt ugly next to her beautiful but cold mother. That girl had discarded at a very young age any thought of growing up pretty. Mothers like Onalee should be banned, along with the Bomb.

***

After they finished lunch and Carrie had wiped away the crumbs with a napkin dampened in the bathroom sink, a feeling of flatness descended. Where would the customers come from? How long could they afford to wait? While Jack pretended to be busy in the back, Carrie made two calls. The first was to Sergeant Bill Stevenson. She asked him to keep the agency in mind for cases where the police couldn't put in the time they'd like to. Stevenson said he'd pass the word around, but it was obvious he thought she'd been insane to quit her job.

The second call went to the Callender office. She reached

Marsha, who reported things were going well. She asked to speak to Peter.

"Yes, Carrie?" His tone was formal.

"Mr. Callender, I believe I know of a way we can help you."

"What do you mean?" His tone was still slightly hostile, but she knew Peter well enough to know he liked things tied up neatly.

"You had a will to execute for Benjamin Allcore. We never found the beneficiary."

"That's correct. Mr. Allcore's grandson."

"Mr. Porter, my employer, specializes in missing persons."

"The firm already has an investigator."

The world's oldest living P.I.! What she said aloud was, "Mr. Chapman plans to retire and move to Florida this winter."

"Why hasn't he told us?"

"To tell the truth, he's afraid you'll throw a fit. But he told me."

A click told Carrie Peter had signaled someone else to listen in, probably Brad. She added, "Mr. Porter is willing to give you a reduced rate due to your kindness to me."

A pause followed, and she imagined the two of them mouthing things to each other. After a while Peter said, "I'll check with Chapman. If what you say is true, we'll consider it." Clearing his throat he asked, "What would the rate be?"

Chapman charged fifty dollars a day. "Forty dollars a day plus expenses."

"Done." Brad said before Peter could respond, but Peter stepped in quickly.

"I'll have Marsha call you back."

"Could I speak to her again, please?" she asked before he could hang up. When Marsha came on the line, she explained the situation. "If they have you call us, speak directly to Mr. Porter, and don't tell him about my call."

"Sure, honey," Marsha agreed. "I think I get it."

"And don't mention money. Give him the information on the case and tell him you'll work out the financial details with me."

Half an hour later the phone rang for the first time ever. Carrie was purposely up watering the small philodendron she'd bought as a sort of office-warming present. Jack answered, and despite his South Side Chicago background, spoke professionally to Marsha, jotting down notes as he agreed to look into the whereabouts of one Jason Allcore. The young man had disappeared into the drug culture of Detroit some months ago and was unaware of his grandfather's death and his subsequent inheritance.

Once he understood the facts, Jack passed the phone to Carrie. "I guess protocol is that bosses don't do the money part." When she finished the call, he gave her a speculative look. "Did you tell your former bosses we needed work?"

"I mentioned your specialty is missing persons," she said smoothly. "I guess they remembered it when the need arose."

It took Jack less than two hours to get a lead on young Allcore, and Carrie marveled at what he could do with only a telephone. She was also surprised to hear him humming as he searched the directory. He began by calling Flint Junior College, where Jason had attended classes, at least in theory, the year before. Claiming to be an army recruiter, he got Allcore's mailing address and phone number from the registrar then called the building manager and got the name of Jason's flat-mate, who still lived there.

The call to the roommate might have been a dead end, since he claimed he and Jason hadn't been close. As he told the other detective, the young man said, he had no idea where his former roommate had gone. Jack was patient, asking questions designed to jog the young man's memory. Who were Jason's friends? Was there anything left in the apartment that hinted at his favorite haunts?

It turned out a beer mug full of pencils sat next to the phone, inscribed with the logo of Malone's Bar. Jack thanked the young man, hung up, and called the bar. He reached a very chatty waitress named Ally who knew young Jason well, it turned out. Due to Ally's more-than-adequate volume, Carrie heard every word as the barmaid recounted shenanigans she found hilarious.

"Jason will eat a shot glass for a dollar—takes a great big bite out of it! You should see people's faces when he does that. Once he put a firecracker in his mouth and lit it." She giggled, adding, "The guy is really a cool head. He's just a little crazy!"

Jack indicated his estimate of Ally's I.Q. by rolling his eyes at Carrie. She smiled agreement, having heard the incessant crack of gum echoing through the phone line.

"Have you seen him lately?" Jack asked.

"No. I heard he took off with Melody." Her tone turned disgusted. "No accounting for taste, is there? She isn't even that pretty."

Jack betrayed no impatience with her side comments. "Does Melody have a last name?"

"Something like Prune, Pruitt, maybe. I know she lived in Flushing, because I had to stuff her into a cab one night after the bar closed. Why do people assume bartenders will see they get home? We don't even get paid overtime for that."

Ally's information led to calls to all the Pruitts and Pruetts listed in the Flushing phone book. It only took eight to find Melody's parents. They weren't pleased with their daughter's lifestyle, but they did have a phone number for her in Detroit. From there it was a matter of sweet-talking a smoky-voiced landlady into climbing the stairs to the apartment where Melody and her boyfriend were staying. Jack grinned at Carrie when the woman admitted the boyfriend's name was indeed Jason Allcore. He tilted the phone so Carrie could hear the rest of the conversation.

Listening to faraway strains of Iron Butterfly's "In-A-Gadda-Da-Vida," she eventually heard Jason stumble to the phone. He sounded stoned, but once he grasped the idea he'd inherited money, he tuned in. There was a problem, he told Jack. He had no way to get to Flint, and both he and Melody were broke. With a sigh of resignation, Jack told the kid he'd be down the next morning to transport him to the law office. "Make sure you bring some I.D.," he warned. Jason responded with a request not to make it too early. After ten was better.

Carrie expressed amazement that Jack accomplished so much so soon. "A lot of investigation is luck," he replied. "If any one of those people had been out, I'd have spent at least another day on it. Mostly you ask questions until something bubbles up from somebody's memory. Some people don't want to be found, but when money's involved... "Jack snapped his fingers to demonstrate the power of cash.

"So what's next?"

"Tomorrow you guard the fort while I fetch the black sheep of the Allcore family."

"My job is supposed to be doing the running," Carrie objected.

"I'll go," he answered confidently. "I've been to DEE-troit a few times, since that's where Todd and I got our P.I. credentials. I'll collect the dapper Mr. Allcore precisely at ten a.m. and bring him back to hear the good news from your buddies at the law firm." Grinning ruefully, he stuck the file into a drawer and slammed it shut. "I think I'll drop him at the door though. You can send the Callenders a bill."

"I'll be glad to." Carrie guessed Jack didn't want her to see the way guys like Jason Allcore lived, and she was flattered. She was also pleased his confidence had risen now that their first case moved toward completion. Would he have driven to Detroit two weeks ago? She thought not.

CHAPTER EIGHT

The agency's second day started differently, and Carrie was totally unprepared for it. Unlocking the door at 8:40, she entered and set her bag on the desk. As she moved into the back to hang up her coat, she jumped and let out a tiny squeak of surprise. A blanket-wrapped person was sleeping on their couch. As she stood there in shock the prone figure groaned and the blanket flipped back, revealing a beautiful Asian woman who sat up sleepily and looked at Carrie. "Where Jack?"

The woman knew Jack, and she obviously had a key, which he must have given her. "He had to go to Detroit this morning. Are you a friend of his?"

"His wife." Glossy-black hair fell straight to her waist as she sat up. It immediately took on a smooth look that Carrie, in constant need of a hairbrush, could only envy.

"I'm sorry?"

The woman seemed irritated. "Wife! I not say it right?"

Carrie's face took on the same blank look she used to mask her pain when Onalee said something particularly cruel. "You said it perfectly. I'm pleased to meet you, Mrs. Porter. I'm your husband's associate, Caroline Walsh."

"Call me Li." She glared at Carrie. "What he do in Detroit?"

"He's picking someone up." If she was really Jack's wife, shouldn't she know where her husband had gone and why? And where had she been for the last few weeks?

Guessing her thought, Li regarded Carrie with undisguised disdain, "I gone long time. Out of town."

"I see." Carrie didn't see at all, but the woman's arrogant manner left her unwilling to ask for explanations. "I'll get some coffee going." She retreated to the outer office, but Li Porter followed. In snug jeans, a yellow blouse, and black slippers, she looked fabulous despite just waking up. Her hair smelled of something exotic and expensive.

"Your eyes very bad, heh?" She indicated the glasses.

Carrie clenched her jaw. "I do all right."

"So when Jack hire you?" She was direct, with hard eyes unlike

Carrie's preconceived notions of Asian women. Stereotypes were wrong, she reminded herself.

"A couple of weeks ago, but we only opened yesterday, so this is my second official day." What if the wife wanted the secretary's job? Would Jack let her go? What then?

Again Li seemed to read her mind. "I never can do this. I not good with English, and I not good with be nice to people sometimes." She smiled archly, proud of the announcement that put Carrie in her place. An employee had to be nice.

Having no idea what to say in reply, Carrie began her daily tasks. First she made the coffee. At 9:00 she called the Callender office to let them know of Jason Allcore's arrival time. She also checked with their message service and learned there'd been a call from a Mrs. Packard Somers. It took her a moment to associate the name with Jack's friend Crate. As she wrote Jack a note and laid it on his desk, Li watched her closely. "Would you like some coffee, Mrs. Porter?"

"No." In a moment she added, "I no like this taste."

"I might have a teabag in my purse," Carrie offered.

"No." Her voice was commanding. "I wait for my husband." It sounded like *huzban*. "You do work." She plopped into a saucer chair in the corner and fixed her eyes on Carrie, waiting for her to obey.

Face burning with resentment, Carrie turned to her desk. Who did this woman think she was? The answer came quickly: Jack's wife, that's who. Carrie, who had thought to rescue Jack Porter from despair and help him climb out of his loneliness, had been wrong. Jack had a wife, beautiful and haughty, who had returned from some extended absence and turned Carrie's pitiful dream of being needed into dust.

Would she have changed her life so completely if she'd known Jack was married? Had she hoped subconsciously that he'd come to depend on her? Like her? Love her?

Stop! You took this job to change your life, not to catch a husband. Jack's marital status doesn't change the fact that he treats you like an equal, unlike the drippy Callenders. The wife just admitted she couldn't do the job, so he needs you. It should make no difference that Jack doesn't need female companionship in the bargain.

After her mental lecture, Carrie cast about for something to do that would prove to Li Porter that she earned her keep. She must have delayed too long, for Li stood up and approached with an eyebrow quirked, clearly indicating she was waiting to see something get done. Resentfully Carrie began typing up a bill for the Callenders. She'd fill in the transportation costs when Jack returned. Anything to appear useful to this...virago. She'd only read the word, but it applied. A petite bundle of force that didn't care what or who was in her way; that was Li Porter. Miserably she asked herself, *Why didn't Jack tell me he was married?*

An uneasy pall hung over the office all morning. Carrie tried to keep busy. Li sat either gazing into space or staring at Carrie with no attempt to disguise her curiosity. When the phone rang, she came instantly alert. Carrie answered, "Eagle Agency, Miss Walsh. May I help you?"

"So you really are working for this detective?" said her mother.

"Hi, Mom. Yes, I really am." She made her voice cheerful.

"How many murder cases has he solved?"

"Mom, we opened the office yesterday."

"So how do you know he's any good?"

"I guess we'll have to wait and see." An aggressive Asian and her mother both in one morning. Too much.

"Is he good looking, like Robert Mitchum?"

"Not like Mitchum, but okay." She glanced at Mrs. Porter, hoping she would miss most of this conversation. "Look, Mom, this is a business phone, so I can't chat. Was there something you wanted?"

"I am interested in my daughter's well-being." Onalee sounded miffed. "I won't call you at work again if you're going to be snippy."

"Why don't you stop in on Saturday if you're in town?" Onalee often shopped at the downtown stores on the weekend if the roads were clear.

"I can't make any promises, but Caroline, if you need to go shopping, please wait until I can go with you. Don't throw your money away like you did with that awful pantsuit with the three-inch belt."

"Okay. I'll hope to see you on Saturday."

As soon as she hung up, the phone rang again."Is this Jack Porter's office?" It was another Asian woman, but this one used precise English pronunciation.

"Mr. Porter isn't available at the moment. I'm his assistant, Miss Walsh. Can I help?"

"I would like to speak to Jack."

"May I take a message and have him call you?"

"I left a message last night."

"Yes, Mrs. Somers. Mr. Porter isn't in yet today, but I expect him soon. I'll relay your message and have him call you right away."

"I appreciate that."

"May I express my condolences for the loss of your husband?"

"Thank you." Dignity and pain sounded in her voice. "Jack knows?"

"I believe he learned the news from your husband's mother."

"Oh, yes. She stayed here to help after the funeral." At the stage of grief where one can't predict when emotion will overcome, her voice broke suddenly.

Carrie struggled for something comforting to say. "Mrs. Somers, Jack and I will do whatever we can to help." She caught a flicker of movement from Li. One eyebrow rose sardonically, but Carrie ignored her. "Jack will call you later today. I'll make sure of it."

"Thank you again. I'll be here all afternoon."

As she hung up, Li approached the counter. "Who calling?"

"Someone for Jack."

"You said Mrs. Somers. It was Su." So she knew Jack's friends.

"I don't know her first name."

"Su, I just tell you. She marry Crate Somers."

"Yes, Crate was her husband."

Li she caught the word was. "Crate dead?"

"Yes. He had an accident."

There was a flash of something in Li's eyes. "What kind accident?" she demanded.

"Mr. Porter can give you the details." Carrie busied herself with adding Su Somers' number to the Rolodex, wondering if Li knew of Todd Sachs' death.

Li's thoughts went in a different direction. "You mean Jack. You say Jack before."

There was no answer for that. Looking around for a change of subject, Carrie saw that it was after twelve.

"I'm going to lunch, Mrs. Porter. Can I get you anything?"

Li looked at Carrie as if she were a bug, but she must have been hungry. "Yes, you get me lunch. I will have hamburger with cheese an' pickle, French fry, an' Tab." Li counted the items off on her fingers then returned to her chair, making no offer to pay.

Carrie had a sudden urge to walk away and not return. How could Jack have forgotten to mention his snide, exquisite, Vietnamese wife? Not that she was attracted to him, she reminded herself, but they'd talked a lot in the two weeks they'd worked to get the office ready, and nice men weren't supposed to let their secretaries think they were single when they weren't. At some point, his being married should have come up.

Carrie left the office half hoping the interloper who called herself Li Porter was a crook who'd run off with the petty cash. At least then she wouldn't be there when Carrie returned, and she and Jack would be back to where she'd thought they were: two friends who had no secrets from each other—especially unexpected spouses.

CHAPTER NINE

VIETNAM, 1967

Lucy's Bar outside Phu Bai was a shack made of scrap tin with no bar at all, just a few tables scattered haphazardly. A phonograph blared in one corner, the music jumpy due to a bulge in the record that made the needle skip a bit on each revolution. Several GIs sat sipping "Tiger Piss," a warm liquid in long-necked brown bottles that passed for beer. Todd and Jack entered watchfully and were greeted with blank stares. Nobody much liked MPs, but nobody messed with them either.

The place was depressing. Towns like Phu Bai were off-limits to ordinary soldiers, so make-shift bars sprang up outside the compounds. Men went there to get away from officers, to get drunk, and to meet women. Most of the women weren't anybody's dream, but on this night, when the two M.P.s came in search of a private who was possibly AWOL or possibly just too drunk to tell time, they saw Li.

She sat on a stool in the corner, wearing a traditional dress of white and looking like a lost child. Obviously waiting for someone she looked up when they entered then quickly looked away. Todd and Jack glanced around the place, failed to find Private Santelli, and left.

"Kinda makes you want to use the old, 'What's a nice girl like you doing in a place like this?' line, doesn't she?" Todd commented.

They'd gone on to three more places. In the last one they learned Santelli had been found by some of his buddies and taken back to camp to sleep it off. That was best for all concerned, and his CO would deal with him in the morning. The two men returned up the dusty track that passed for a road, but as they came past Lucy's, a flash of white caused Todd to stop the jeep and shut off the engine. In the silence that followed, a woman's muffled cry and a man's curse came from behind the bar.

The two MPs moved silently and quickly, rounding the shack with professional caution. As Jack pressed his back to the corrugated tin and peered around the corner, he saw the girl in the white dress struggling with an ARVN, a soldier of the Army of the Republic of

Vietnam. He'd apparently waited for her to leave the bar and accosted her.

Todd hit them with his flashlight beam and shouted, "Hey!" The man released his hold and stood, swaying in confusion. The girl bolted away from her captor and straight into Jack's arms. A flood of Vietnamese followed which neither man understood, their command of the language being limited to polite phrases and requests for directions. Jack calmed the girl, who was half-scared and half-furious, while Todd demonstrated to the ARVN soldier the impropriety of his actions. He overcame the language barrier with physical punctuation and sent the man on his drunken way with a kick. That mollified the girl somewhat, and she called out something in Vietnamese that was unlikely to be a wish for a pleasant evening. Turning to Todd and Jack, she bowed gracefully and spoke more calmly, too fast and beyond their limited grasp of the language. Then she started off.

"Wait," Todd called. "We'll take you home."

The girl turned, standing imperially to her full four feet, ten inches, and pointed in the opposite direction. "No, You GI *didi mau* (go away)! I no girl for you." With that she disappeared into the night.

***

When Carrie returned to the office Jack was there, and tension crackled in the atmosphere like lightning. His jaw was tight, and he'd returned to the dark mood she saw the day they first met. She had prepared herself to appear perfectly unmoved by the appearance of Jack's previously unmentioned wife. When he saw her blank expression, his whole face seemed to sag, as if more weight had been added to an already unbearable load. Li watched from the couch, a smile playing on her lips.

"Miss Walsh, you've met Li?"

"Yes, Mr. Porter. Your wife and I introduced ourselves." Setting a bag before Li that smelled of hot grease, she turned to Jack. "Did you see the message from Mrs. Somers?"

"I'm about to call her."

"Everything went well with Jason Allcore?"

"Yeah, no problem, except I had to tolerate his opinion I'm a casualty of the imperialist machine in Washington. I should sue my congressman."

Carrie made no comment, nor could she force a smile. "Do you have an accounting of expenses? I can finish the bill and get it off to the Callenders today."

His gaze held hers for a second, pleading for understanding, but she remained impassive. Finally, he scribbled a note with time and mileage figures, and she returned without further comment to the outer office. Li's smile turned to a smirk.

The exterior door opened, and a woman came in off the street. Greeting her, Carrie learned she wanted to locate her deadbeat ex-husband in hopes of getting some of the two years' child support he owed. Carrie escorted her in to meet Jack, who threw off his bleak demeanor and listened carefully as the client gave the details of her case. A new case was good. Not only did they have their first unsolicited customer, but they had something to focus on besides the tension in the office as well.

When the woman left, Jack called Su Somers. After expressing his sorrow, Jack told her the circumstances of Todd's death. Carrie couldn't hear her response, but Jack said, "You had a lot on your mind, and Todd had no family to send condolences to anyway." He listened and then said, "And I'd have come to Crate's funeral if I'd known."

She guessed Su asked about the crime, because Jack told her, "They call it chance, but I find that hard to accept. Todd didn't look like an easy mark for muggers." After a few seconds he said, "Yes, he mentioned he'd talked to Cr—Packard a few days back."

At that point Jack motioned for Carrie to come close so she could listen in. She crouched beside his chair and heard Su Somers say, "What I have to say will sound odd, but you know me, Jack. You know what I have lived through, and I hope you believe I am not a hysterical woman."

"Su, you're the least hysterical person I know." Carrie caught

Jack's glance at Li, now napping on the couch. Her face was even more beautiful without the superior look she wore when awake.

"I don't think my husband fell by accident."

"What?" Li frowned at his raised voice then readjusted her shoulder on the cushion and continued her dream.

"I told you it would sound strange. Packard had cleaned the gutters the week before. He didn't like going onto the roof when there was frost because it became very slippery. Still, when I returned from grocery shopping, I found him dead at the bottom of the ladder." Her voice wavered on the last sentence, but she got through it.

"Su, maybe he changed his mind."

She wasn't finished. "A few days after Packard died, the little boy who lives next door told me it was lucky they both didn't fall off the roof. When I asked him what he meant, he said he saw a man up there earlier in the day."

"You told the police this?"

"Yes, but the child is only six. They think it's a story, since he said it was GI Joe."

"The toy?"

"He has a large collection of the soldier dolls, and his father says he makes up stories about them all the time."

"But you don't think that's the case?" A car backfired on Dort and Jack jumped, his elbow knocking against Carrie's chin. He smiled apologetically, and she guessed he had to resist an impulse to hit the floor at any unexpected noise.

Su went on, as Carrie tried to pretend the blow hadn't hurt. "Packard called Todd about something connected to your time in Vietnam. He told me Todd would know what to do about a man who called our home several times recently. My husband said this man was not in his right mind, because he claimed someone had caused his wife to die in a car accident."

"Was Crate afraid of the guy?" Jack picked up a lighter Carrie knew Todd had carried in Vietnam, the only souvenir he'd kept of his friend. He ran a finger over the lettering etched on the smooth metal surface.

"Not of him, but the man warned Packard he might be in danger."

"What did Todd say about that?"

"He intended to locate the man and talk to him."

"And did he?"

"I don't think so, but Packard intended to stay near the telephone in case Todd called. That's another reason he wouldn't have gone up on the roof that day."

Jack promised to look into the matter, repeated his sympathy for her loss, and hung up. Carrie waited for him to say something about what they'd heard, but he merely sat there. Finally he said softly, "Todd and Crate were thrown together by the war. Now they're both dead in the same week."

***

VIETNAM, 1967

Crate Somers was assigned to Transportation when Todd, Jack, and another MP were sent to guard a convoy of munitions on its way to a forward post near the A-shau Valley. The three MPs were in the rear jeep, doing "dust duty." Ten trucks roared along in front of them, and at the head of the convoy another MP jeep led the way. The day was no hotter than usual, but dust was everywhere—in their eyes, throats, noses, and ears. When they had to stop after a truck up ahead broke down, Packard Somers came back to share a couple of lukewarm Cokes he'd brought along.

Somers was a gangly kid with huge ears and blond hair that wouldn't lie down, even in the heat of Asia. He'd found out that Todd came from the Flint area, and since Crate himself hailed from Bay City, he figured that made them neighbors. Despite his wrestler's build, Todd had been well known in southeastern Michigan, an area noted for good basketball teams and players, for his excellent ball skills and long outside shots. He tolerated Crate's obvious hero-worship good-naturedly. Waiting at the tail of the convoy, the four men talked for fifteen minutes or so before the grind of engines ahead signaled movement.

Half an hour later the dust was so thick they could hardly see three feet before them. Jack drove with his foot hovering above the brake, fearing they'd rear-end Crate's truck if it stopped suddenly. After ten minutes or so, Todd shouted in Jack's ear, "The kid missed the turn! That's it to the right, but he went on."

Jack hit the brakes, and the three men squinted ahead at a lone truck going straight while the other vehicles moved east. Crate had missed it. Todd had been watching the map and had seen the turnoff ahead.

They sat for a few seconds wondering what to do. "We've got to get him back," Todd urged. "He's going straight into North Vietnam."

"He'll see he's alone and turn around," said Nolan, the gunner. "We could get into serious trouble in there."

"So can Crate," Todd answered. "We've got to catch him before he goes too far."

"Our orders are to guard the convoy, and it went that way," Nolan argued. "The guy screwed up. He's on his own."

Jack voted with his foot, gunning the jeep straight ahead. Traveling as quickly as the pitiful road allowed, the three MPs craned their necks for twenty nerve-wracking minutes before they spotted the truck ahead of them. Crate had stopped, finally aware he wasn't following anyone. He stood beside the vehicle, his cap in hand and a stark line between his shiny forehead and the dust-caked area below. His whole face lit when he saw the jeep approaching.

"Am I glad to see you guys! Didn't know who'd be coming up behind me."

"Find a place to turn that thing around, Crate," Todd said, keeping his voice calm. "We'll show you where the turnoff is then follow you to the firebase." There was no use letting the kid know how much danger they were in, and he happily obeyed. Jack's neck bristled all the way back, waiting for gunfire, attack, and captivity.

When they were safely back at the base and Crate learned the extent of the danger, his hero worship expanded to include Jack. "They came and got me right out of North Vietnam," he told anyone who'd listen. He didn't care that he painted himself as the hapless idiot of the event. Crate was just pleased to have two heroes to worship.

Later Crate had married Su, whom Todd and Jack never met. She came from a wealthy family, and when Jack wondered aloud what she saw in Crate, Todd put it succinctly: "a ticket State-side."

***

Su seemed genuinely grieved by Crate's death, Jack thought as he flipped Todd's lighter open and closed absently. Perhaps their marriage had been more than outsiders assumed. It certainly wasn't easy for a GI to marry a Vietnamese girl. The army and both governments made their disapproval of such unions clear with lots of red tape. Still, love blooms in war zones, and soldiers in love have brought home foreign wives since Biblical times. Of course, Jack thought glumly, love was not obligatory.

CHAPTER TEN

The Callenders called again three days later, this time on their own. Delighted with the speed of Jack's work in finding young Allcore, they offered another job. Carrie calmly informed them the introductory rate had expired, and they'd be charged forty-five dollars a day. It was still less than Chapman's rate, and Brad would have to settle for that, which he did after one whining comment about expecting more loyalty from Carrie.

Though a little less appetizing than the first, the new case presented a challenge. The Callenders had done work for a client named Jeffrey Tate, who'd skipped out on his bill, leaving them short over a thousand dollars. The address he'd given was false, and they feared the name was too. Carrie took down the information, pleased when Jack complimented her thorough notes.

"It helps that I met the man," she told him, sweeping dead flies from the windowsills with a soft brush into a dustpan as she spoke. Their relationship had settled into a working camaraderie, with both of them careful to speak only of business matters. "I have an idea where to start looking for him."

"That would be good."

"The guy was a chatty type, and one day they had to wait a while." A not-quite-dead prospect buzzed against the pane and Carrie opened the window and shooed it out.

"He broke down and told you he was a fake?" Jack asked facetiously.

"No, but people often let their guard down with secretaries. They tell little things they don't think are important, like he mentioned he always stopped at Maria's when he was downtown at lunchtime. Someone there might remember him."

"Then we'll have lunch at Maria's today," Jack declared. "A business lunch." He tried to make his tone light, but he watched Carrie's face as he said it.

"I'll drop you off," she answered. "I'd like to borrow the truck for an hour. I can pick you up at one."

Jack's eyelids drooped, hiding disappointment. "Sure." Pulling his chair close to the desk, he busied himself with work.

When Carrie picked him up Jack reported the bartender at Maria's didn't recognize Tate's name. "I wish we had a picture."

Carrie frowned. "He brought a woman once. He introduced her as his wife, but..."

"You didn't buy it?"

She shrugged. "She was pretty friendly for a wife, patting his arm and cuddling up close. He claimed they'd been married for fifteen years, but that didn't seem right to me."

"Did you say anything to the Callenders?"

"No. In the first place, Tate was Jim's client."

Jack grinned. "He's the expert on women, right?"

"Right. He wouldn't have listened to me."

"He sounds like a louse, but then, so does Tate."

"Maybe the woman could help us find him."

"Do you know her name?"

"Well, no, but—" Carrie grabbed the phone book, flipping through its thin pages with a businesslike rustle. "Like I said, people chat with the secretary, and she mentioned she gets her hair cut at the Genesee Valley Mall, by Jill, I think. She said I should ask for her." Carrie had taken the comment as a hint her hair needed attention, but she'd ignored it. "I'll bet they'd know her real name."

"That's how detectives work," Jack complimented. "Observe and remember." He tilted his head a little. "Why don't you call over there and schedule a haircut, on the agency? While you're there maybe you can find out who the fictitious Mrs. Tate really is."

"A haircut?"

Jack looked uncomfortable, "I'm not saying...you don't have to if you don't want to. I just thought it would be an easy way to get the staff there to talk."

As a child Carrie's haircuts had been done at home, sitting in the kitchen with a towel wrapped around her shoulders and her tight curls falling in a circle on the floor around her. She'd begun cutting her own hair in high school, taking off a couple of inches every few months to keep the ends from splitting. Onalee encouraged the economy. "Your hair's impossible," she'd say. "You might as well save your money."

She'd never thought about letting a professional work on her hair, though her mother went to the beauty shop every week and came out with a hairdo sprayed hard enough to last until next time. She recalled wanting to touch it as a child, to feel its sticky elasticity, but she'd never wanted her own hair to be like that.

Still, Jack would never darken the doorway of a woman's hair salon. Though some men were beginning to move to "Unisex" stylists, men like Jack went to barbers, period.

She touched her unruly mane. "It might be fun to see what a stylist does with all this."

"Great." Jack looked like he wanted to add something, but it never came out. Consulting the phone book again, she dialed the salon.

"Hi, I'd like an appointment for a haircut. A friend recommended one of your stylists, but I'm not sure I remember the name. Is there a Jill who works there?"

"No," the receptionist replied, "but we have Jillian. She's in tomorrow."

In thirty seconds, Carrie had an appointment for first thing the next morning. She spent the rest of the day half in dread and half pleased to take a step that should help the agency complete its latest case and might result in a more interesting Carrie as well.

Li Porter came in most days and sat for hours. She seldom spoke, and Jack said nothing to her that wasn't necessary. He was different when she showed up, cold and silent. When Li left, whether to go to Jack's apartment or somewhere else, Carrie never knew, his mood lightened. He moved more, smiled more, and talked more. Carrie kept her distance, making it clear to him—and to herself— theirs was a business relationship.

She gave up trying to decide if she'd ever hoped for more. After all, they'd just begun to know each other when Li's arrival changed things. What had she felt for Jack? Had she pitied him, defeated and hurt by so many things in his life? Why had she made the jump to this tiny business with an insecure future? Was it Jack or her own desire to do something interesting with her life? It had to be the latter. At least it did now that Li had shown up.

Carrie presented herself with outward but not inner calm at nine the next morning at the salon across from Fannie May Candies in the mall. She hadn't been to Genesee Valley many times, malls being places she had little interest in, but she did love the chocolates at Fannie May's, especially the mints. Bypassing the candy counter and crossing to the salon, she met with intriguing and slightly frightening odors: soft shampoo scents, sweet hair sprays, and the nose-wrinkling smell of permanent-wave lotion. A girl in a white smock approached. Her hair was parted in the center and cut below the chin line so that it hung in two perfect crescents, framing her pretty face. The style, though charming, would never do for Carrie's hair, which was curly to the point of irritation. Why, she asked herself for the thousandth time, did she have the natural curl her mother's friends found so desirable in an age when the style for people under Methuselah's age was very, very straight? In high school her friends had ironed their hair to get the curl out, but after burning her face once with the iron, Carrie dropped that idea. What sort of haircut should she ask for?

In the end, she let Jillian decide. As soon as she stuck her head around a partition and called, "Come on back, hon," Carrie liked her. Jillian was perhaps thirty-five, pencil thin and heavily made-up, but her genuine smile and take-charge manner inspired trust. "Been cutting your own hair, hon?" It wasn't an accusation, just a conversation starter.

"Yes, but now I'd like a haircut I can manage myself."

"Are you willing to lose most of it?" Jillian stood behind Carrie as they both looked at her hair in the wraparound mirror. She lifted the hair, feeling its weight and texture, "You'd look real cute with a shag."

"What's that?"

Jillian indicated a picture on the wall. The model's hair, cut short and combed forward, made a pixie-ish frame for her face. The hair in the back, left longer, fell in tousled curls down her neck. It looked modern and carefree, like the girls on Laugh-In.

"It's a good style for hair like yours, with a lot of curl to it," Jillian told her. "The short part makes it easy to keep, and the length in the back means you don't feel like a boy. You've got nice hair, but it's so heavy it hides your face. What do you say we make you look like Goldie Hawn?"

Carrie chuckled. "With these glasses? I doubt that, but do what you can." Once she was shampooed and upright in the chair again, she said casually, "A woman I met at work recommended you. I don't remember her name, but she's really gorgeous: long legs, dark hair. She reminds me of Jane Russell in those old westerns."

Jillian separated Carrie's hair into sections with deft movements and pinned them out of her way. Carrie felt the clips slide smoothly into place along her scalp, one after another. After a few moments the stylist smiled. "I bet you mean Miss Harris. She is really pretty; in fact, I think she's done some acting or modeling, something like that."

"Harris—that might be it, but I don't remember her first name."

"Me neither. I call her Miss Harris."

That avenue exhausted, Carrie watched as Jillian cut off an alarming amount of reddish-brown hair. As it piled up on the floor, doubt about the decision crept into her mind. In the first place, she could already hear Onalee wailing about her cutting "all that gorgeous hair," even though she'd always called it "hard to manage" before. In the second place, who was Carrie to think she could keep up a stylish hairdo? Would Jack think he'd wasted his money?

As Jillian worked, the style began to take shape. The hair on top, lay in soft curls that fluffed as they dried, framing her face. Longer tendrils in the back curled around her neck, making a feminine and, to Carrie, astonishing difference.

Jillian sprayed on something she called "setter" which added shine and smelled like lemons. Finally she proclaimed the job finished and handed Carrie a small hand mirror, turning the chair as they examined the hairstyle from all angles. It really did look good. The cut emphasized her high cheekbones and her not-bad hazel eyes.

Of course then she had to put on the glasses, which ruined a lot of the effect. Jillian must have been thinking the same thing. "There's an optometrist down the hall. Something lighter would go better with this hairdo."

Thanking Jillian wholeheartedly, Carrie stopped at the reception desk to pay her bill. The cut didn't cost as much as she'd feared, and seeing herself looking so different was worth it. Adding a generous tip, she told the receptionist, "Miss Harris was right. I'm very happy with the cut I got from Jillian."

"That's good to hear," she answered, "We like happy customers."

As Carrie struggled to come up with a way to ask Miss Harris' first name, the woman supplied it without being asked. "We should give Elaine a commission. That girl knows tons of people."

"Thanks." Carrie intended to head for the truck, but she found herself veering off toward the optometrist Jillian had mentioned.

The office intimidated her a little at first, all light and openness with hundreds of frames lining two long walls. Carrie had always gone to Doctor Guzman, an aged optometrist who said little and smelled of Sen-sen. When she was younger it had seemed the ancient machines in his office waited in the corners like sleeping monsters to test her and find her wanting yet again. Dr. Guzman had always clucked and shook his head over her poor vision, and they had always bought the cheapest frames. "No since paying a lot," her mother would say. "Kids just break glasses or lose them anyway." Carrie, who had never broken a single pair nor lost them, never argued.

Dad had objected once. "Can't you get her something nicer?" he'd asked, unaware she was nearby.

"Her eyesight is so bad that the glass has to be thick. She needs heavy frames to support the weight," his wife had replied. "And what difference does it make? She's skinny, she's plain, and she's got your side of the family's hair."

Carrie had concluded from Onalee's tone, and from Dad's lack of further argument, that she really was hopeless.

"Can I help you?" a young man asked as Carrie perused the frames displayed along two walls. She turned to him and said, "I'd like to talk to someone about new glasses."

Carrie left the shop with a lighter step. She'd be returning to the mall the next day to consult with an optometrist. The young man who'd approached her, an optician, claimed great strides had been made in the field. Glasses were becoming lighter through the use of plastics, and frames were smaller and less obtrusive. He seemed eager to help Carrie find glasses she'd like.

Probably considers me a challenge she thought as she parked the truck behind the agency. She didn't go inside, dreading Li's reaction to her new hairdo. It could wait until tomorrow, when she'd had time to get used to it herself.

When she arrived the next morning Li was already there. Her eyes narrowed to a glare when Carrie removed her scarf, and she turned away abruptly. Jack's eyes signaled approval, but he said only, "Good morning, Miss Walsh," before returning to his work. Telling herself no comment on the new look was best, she reported only that she'd gotten the name they sought.

"It's a pretty common name, Harris, so it might take a while to find her."

"True," Jack replied, "but you helped a lot. I'll see what I can do."

***

The optometrist appointment brought more surprises. The doctor finished his tests then looked critically at Carrie's glasses. "Are you satisfied with those?"

Carrie shrugged, "I guess I have to be."

"There's the prospect of contact lenses, if you're interested."

"They're dangerous," she replied. "They can scratch your eyeball and leave it scarred."

"Now who told you that?" His tone betrayed amusement.

"My mother read it somewhere."

"Well, she's mistaken, People have worn contact lenses for

74

years now, and they're quite safe if used properly. We could get some for you to try if you're willing."

"They're not bad for your eyes?"

"No." The man saw a chance to expound on a topic that fascinated him. "The possibility of lenses on the eye came to light during World War II when the material that airplane windshields were made of shattered and sprayed into some pilots' faces. Instead of shredding the eye, as people feared, they floated harmlessly on top."

"Wow." Carrie had never considered the possibility of freedom from glasses. Her head already felt lighter without her heavy mane of hair, and she felt a jolt of pleasure at the prospect of leaving glasses and the accompanying red marks on her nose behind. Then reality hit. "Contacts are expensive, I can't afford them just for vanity's sake."

The doctor frowned as she unconsciously parroted her mother's words. "It's not vanity. Contacts actually improve a person's vision. Let me give you some information and show you some prices." He picked up a nearby pamphlet, "I think you'll be pleasantly surprised. Learning to wear contacts takes persistence, but if you're willing, you can leave your glasses home within a month or so."

***

When Carrie returned from her appointment Jack was out, and Li stood talking with a middle-aged Asian man. They obviously hadn't expected her back so soon, and they looked uncomfortable at being found together. Li didn't offer introductions, but it appeared the man knew who Carrie was. He looked pointedly at her face, taking in the heavy glasses she'd have to wear a while longer. Touching Li's arm as if to say he'd handle this he said, "I am Lin Ghiavali. Mrs. Porter and I are old friends."

"I see," Carrie replied. Though she didn't know why, the man gave her the creeps. He appeared respectable, fashionably dressed, scrupulously neat, and perfectly groomed, but something in the way he looked at her was unsettling, as if he was measuring her for some unknown reason. "Do you live in the area, Mr. Ghiavali?"

Both he and Li smiled deprecatingly, apparently amused at the idea that he would choose a city like Flint for his residence. "Thailand, miss. I only pass through on my way to Chicago, and I must be going now." He bowed politely to Carrie then to Li and left, closing the door with a slight click. Li offered no further explanation of the visitor, and Carrie wouldn't ask.

CHAPTER ELEVEN

Whenever Li was in the office, Carrie called Marsha and met her for lunch. Their long-time friendship had begun when Marsha and Roy moved in next door to Carrie's family, and Carrie had babysat for them. Six years older than Carrie, Marsha had served as confidante to the insecure teen, and their friendship continued over the years. Marsha had been pleased when Carrie moved out on her own, away from her mother's constant belittlement. She wasn't shy about pointing out Onalee's manipulative ways, though Carrie always argued she was wrong. Moms were like that, she contended.

Now the stories they shared about work brought them closer. Marsha knew Carrie understood her situation—babysitting the Callenders—and in turn she was interested in Carrie's new job as a detective. When they met the day after the haircut at a little restaurant near the colleges, Marsha was ecstatic. "You look so good!" she cried, hugging her friend. "Your pretty face shows without all that hair."

"Silly." In response Marsha stuck out her chin, which was a sign she was trying to keep quiet. "Say what you're thinking. We've been friends too long for you to give me that face."

"I just keep thinking it isn't fair."

"Me? I'm unfair?"

"No, goon, not you. Your mom." Marsha watched Carrie's face carefully, judging how much she dared say. "Onalee's jealous of you. She tries to make you feel like you're hopelessly homely."

"That's crazy." Her mother had always been critical, but jealous?

"When you two go shopping, what does she tell you to buy?"

Carrie shrugged. "Stuff that will last a long time."

"Clothes she wouldn't wear in a million years."

That was true. Along with the information about contacts, the pleasant optician had offered frames that flattered her face, assuring that her prescription could be set into them. Even if Mom was afraid of contact lenses, why hadn't Carrie ever had a pair of cute glasses? Were her mother's negative comments calculated to destroy any confidence her daughter might develop?

She couldn't admit that, even to Marsha. "I'm sure you're wrong."

Having planted the seed, Marsha backed off. "I'm just saying Moms can be tough on their daughters. Speaking of shopping, do you want to see what Hudson's has on sale this weekend?"

"Who can afford Hudson's?" Carrie scoffed. "They do have nice stuff though."

"I always wanted to design clothes for them."

"Until you met Roy and started wanting to be Mrs. Wozniak." Carrie slurped the last of her malt then idly unwound the paper straw. "You do make really cute clothes though."

"I love to sew." Marsha stirred her lemon phosphate. "I could make you stuff."

"Why not sew for yourself?"

"I do that, but you're tall and thin, the kind of woman who can wear anything." Carrie was amazed. Did Marsha know how embarrassing it was to tower over most men? Not Jack, of course. He was several inches taller than she.

And that matters why?

Marsha had gone on. "When I design for myself, I have to think shrimp-size, but for you I could do some neat stuff. I'd like to open my own shop someday: Marsha's Fashion Mannequins or something like that. You could be my walking advertisement." Marsha made a model's moue and waggled her head in an attempt to look snobbish.

"Only if you let me pay for the materials." Carrie piled the remains of her meal neatly, covering the sticky ketchup with a napkin. "I don't guarantee anyone will ever consider me glamorous, but I would like some new clothes." Nothing brown, she promised herself.

"Good, I can't wait to get started."

So how are things with the Callenders?"

"They are strange little guys, but I think they're starting to realize who the boss is these days."

"And what has brought this revelation on?"

"Well." Marsha leaned against the booth. "Mr. Brad decided to strike some sparks and see if he could get Mr. Peter and Mr. Jim at each other's throats. He mentioned a certain Mr. Tate who paid his retainer with a bad check, asked for several documents to be drawn up, then disappeared, leaving the firm holding the bag."

"That's the guy they want Jack to find for them."

"Right. But Pinhead (my private name for Brad) told Uptight—"

"Peter," Carrie supplied.

"—that Rat Fink didn't check on the guy, being hot for the wife."

"Who turns out not to be the wife, but a Miss Elaine Harris." Carrie tapped a nail on the Formica table as she made her contribution. "Jack's trying to locate her right now."

"Interesting. Anyway, a discussion followed that became more and more like a U.N, debate starring Khrushchev. Rat Fink was outraged, Uptight was reproving, and Pinhead egged them both on."

"Sounds pretty typical."

"I don't know how you stood it. After fifteen minutes of swearing and threatening, I was about to go out of my tree."

"It's been known to last for hours."

Marsha smiled. "Not anymore."

"What did you do?" Carrie was half-admiring and half-aghast.

"The same thing I do when my kids fight. I sent them to their rooms, or in this case, their offices."

"You didn't!"

Marsha's smile was slightly sheepish. "I said to stay there until they could act like civilized human beings." She reached into her purse and pulled out a compact and lipstick. Clicking one and then the other open she repaired her makeup, peering into the tiny round mirror to see that her lip-line was correct.

"And they went?"

She raised her brows. "It was an hour before Jim came out, sweet as you please, and asked me to get you on the Tate case right away. The other two stayed put, and the office was peaceful for the rest of the day."

Carrie shook her head. "When I grow up I want to be just like you, Mrs. Wozniak."

Marsha closed her compact with a snap. "I think you're growing up fine as yourself, Miss Walsh. I see a definite trend toward independence."

As she walked back to work, Carrie considered Marsha's statement. Was she becoming more independent? Looking back, she thought she was. She'd begun at the law firm, taking matters into her hands that her bosses didn't handle well. Then she'd taken another step, joining the Eagle Agency, where Jack treated her as a partner rather than an employee. She supposed that was how independence came, in steps a person didn't notice in the daily process of living.

Back at work, Carrie found that Jack had located six Elaine or E. Harrises in the many local phone books. He called each one, saying he had a message from Mr. Tate. The first three didn't know Mr. Tate, but the fourth Harris did. Carrie bent to listen.

"What's the message?" she asked. Her voice was sultry and cautious.

"He might need your help again," Jack said. "There are new developments."

"Why didn't Jeff call?"

"He's out of town. He asked me to set it up."

"And you are...?"

"Jeff's brother."

"I don't think so." The line went dead with a clink.

Jack grimaced. "At least we know we've got the right Harris. Now how do we get her to talk about Jeffrey Tate?"

"She'll be suspicious of a strange man after that call." Carrie's eyes lit. "If I can catch my mom's friend Hilda at home, I might have an idea." Jack looked at her expectantly. "Miss Harris might be interested in a visit from the Avon lady."

"And that's Hilda?" Jack asked, still confused.

"Hilda is with Avon, but who's to say I can't join the ranks of the Avon ladies for one afternoon?"

"Okay. I'll watch the office. He'd tracked down the deadbeat ex-husband, and the client was coming in to get the information. He also planned to talk again with Su Somers.

"I don't know if she's delusional or not," he told Carrie, "but Crate was a buddy, so I have to help if I can."

Carrie understood that men who'd been in Vietnam felt a responsibility for each other. The nation wasn't sure how it felt about returning soldiers, but those who'd served knew how they felt about each other. The animosity vets saw in the faces of protesters made them keep each other close, as did the phrase engraved on the lighter Jack never used but always kept on his desk: For those who have fought for it, freedom is something the protected will never know. Carrie didn't know whether the war was right or wrong, but she knew guys like Jack hadn't been fighting for Shell Oil.

CHAPTER TWELVE

For her visit to Elaine Harris, Carrie bought a creamy white sweater from the sale rack at Penney's and found a green-and-blue necklace that added color. Then she experimented with makeup, figuring an Avon lady should wear at least some of the products she sold. She was hopeless with eyeliner and couldn't get foundation to look even, so she skipped those and stuck with powder, lipstick, blush, and a light application of eyeshadow. The Carrie who peered back at her from the mirror was unfamiliar, but she didn't think she looked fake or cheap.

She took the pickup that had become Jack's after the reading of Todd's will. For a happy-go-lucky guy, Todd had been precise in legal matters, and the truck and everything else he owned went to his partner. He'd paid cash for the vehicle with money saved during his tour, and he'd added an AM-FM stereo and 8-track tape player. Jack reported that when the dealer offered the choice of red or blue, Todd had said he didn't care as long as the vehicle wasn't olive drab green.

Carrie pulled into the small town of Bancroft a few minutes before eleven and, aware of her geographical shortcomings, asked for directions. She asked a woman, hoping for what she called landmark directions. Men said things like "turn east then go south." Women said, "Go past Mike's Market and turn at the green building."

Parking the truck a block away, since it didn't suggest Avon, she walked toward a little clapboard-sided house numbered 210. Elaine Harris had seen her coming, and the door opened as she came up the steps.

"Hi," Carrie began. "I'm Cathy, your new Avon lady."

"What happened to the old one?"

"I really don't know. They just gave me the territory." Jack had advised keeping the misinformation to a minimum. Less chance of slipping up that way.

"Come in." The door opened enough to allow entry.

Carrie hurried inside. The day was blustery and cold, and Elaine shut out the bitter wind with a slam and a "Whooh! Winter's anxious to get here, huh?" Most conversations in Michigan seemed to open with the weather, and Carrie wondered if other places were the same.

Elaine Harris was as knockout gorgeous as she remembered, and she led the way to her living room with an unconsciously sensual saunter. The house was decorated in Mediterranean style: lots of dark wood, red and black furniture covers with fake swords and wrought iron on the walls.

Lighting a cigarette with a table lighter that had a matching ashtray, Elaine invited Carrie to sit down. A dark-haired, dark-eyed beauty with lots of curves and long legs, every bit of her clothing and makeup had been chosen to highlight her looks. A green pantsuit of flowing fabric with a matching belt accentuated her full chest and tiny waist. Gold earrings hung almost to her shoulders, sparkling against her hair when she moved. Carrie wondered if she would ever get that dressed up to go out, much less to sit around an apparently empty house. But then, she reminded herself, her mother had done it every day for as long as she could remember.

Despite her beauty, there was something a bit wild, even childish, about Elaine that canceled the initial impression of beautiful in Carrie's mind and left only pretty. Chatting with Elaine as people do when they're getting acquainted, she realized her hostess was one of those girls men refer to as "fun-loving." meaning they didn't ask questions about a man's marital status if he bankrolled the entertainment. Elaine Harris wasn't a prostitute or a call girl, just what Onalee would have called "loose."

Elaine offered Vernors', and from the clink of glasses in the kitchen, Carrie guessed she laced her own portion with liquor. Returning, she sat in a chair opposite Carrie, setting the glass of ginger ale on the coffee table before her.

Carrie explained she had recently moved to Bancroft and hoped to earn extra money with her Avon business. As she'd hoped, Elaine was an enthusiastic customer of the makeup company. She expressed disappointment that the previous Avon lady made her rounds late in the day. "I'm working second-shift at Walli's," she told Carrie, "so I'm never home when she comes by." Thrilled to have a chance to shop at home, she paged through the catalog Carrie had borrowed from Hilda, chatting amiably.

Though the supper club was her income-producing job, Elaine's real love was acting." I get into local theater productions whenever possible, but this job has definitely got in the way of that." She looked at the wall over Carrie's shoulder as she added, "One reviewer said I reminded him of Julie Newmar."

Suddenly her brow wrinkled. "Have I seen you somewhere?"

Carrie licked her lips. "I used to waitress at Maria's downtown."

"Maybe that's it. I remember because of the—" She thought better of her comment and let it trail off, looking at Carrie's neck and not her eyes.

"I remember you now," Carrie lied. "You came in a couple of times with a guy who was really nice-looking."

She shrugged. "We don't see each other anymore."

Carrie confided in a gossipy tone, "I've seen him with other women."

Her hostess smiled. "Like I said, we weren't serious."

"Oh." Carrie feigned disbelief, hoping to goad Elaine into saying more, and it worked.

"I did him a couple of favors. Business stuff."

Elaine changed the subject, perusing the book and asking Carrie's opinion of cream versus powder blushers, lip liner pencil or brush, and several new fragrances. Carrie faked her way through, letting Elaine do most of the talking. Finally she steered the conversation back to men. "That's a popular one with guys if you're starting to think about Christmas gifts." She pointed out a bottle shaped like a horse's head.

Elaine gave her an arch look. "Honey, they're supposed to buy stuff for you, not the other way around."

"I only attract grocery clerks," Carrie said ruefully. "Where do you meet men like the guy I saw you with?"

Elaine lit another Benson & Hedges. "That one I met at a hockey game."

"Really? I love hockey! I wish Flint had a real team."

"They're working on it, but for now Port Huron is the closest one."

Carrie knew that, but she let Elaine elaborate. "I'm not such a big fan myself, but it's a great place to meet men. They're in a good mood at the rink, and lots of times the wives stay home."

"So you met that guy at Port Huron?"

"Yeah. It's not much of a drive, and the Flags have done okay the last few years."

"Maybe I should try it," Carrie said ingenuously. "I never thought of a hockey game as a place to get a date, but if that guy is any example, I wouldn't mind."

Elaine spoke as a more experienced woman. "We had some laughs, but men like Jeff go back to their wives, no matter how bad they tell you those wives are."

The phone shrilled in the hallway and, excusing herself, Elaine set her cigarette in the ashtray and went to answer it. Carrie sat idly on the couch for the first few minutes, trying to wave away the smoke that seemed to home in on her like a missile. As Elaine's conversation continued, with lots of laughter and purring on her end, she took a picture album from the octagonal end table and began paging through it. There were snapshots of Elaine beside a swimming pool, Elaine in front of a Christmas tree, Elaine wearing a fitted sheath dress...and Elaine with Jeffrey Tate.

Tate tried for the Engelbert Humperdinck look: long sideburns, longish hair, and Edwardian suits that only worked for Engelbert. In the photo she was sitting on his lap at what looked like a party. Why had Tate involved her in his scheme to cheat the Callenders? Why bring a fake wife to the office with him?

Carrie recalled the scene. The false Mrs. Tate had been dressed to kill, and Jim's tongue had practically hung out of his mouth.

Was that it? The presence of a sexy woman had made Jim less careful than he should have been, which meant he hadn't checked Tate out as well as he should have.

A shift in tone brought Carrie's focus back to the phone

conversation, which was ending. Without making a conscious decision, she took the photo from the album and put it into her purse. The album went back to the end table, and she was sitting calmly, if a little flushed, when Elaine returned to the room.

"Sorry about the wait. That was a guy I haven't heard from in a while, and you hate to rush them when they want to talk, you know?"

Carrie said she knew, though she could hardly speak for the guilt that had already begun tormenting her. Rising, she said she had another appointment. She'd bring the order next week and collect payment, she promised, stuttering so much she must have seemed an idiot. Leaving the house, she wondered if her biggest mistake was stealing the photograph or thinking she could ever be a real detective.

CHAPTER THIRTEEN

Jack didn't have to call Su Somers. As he escorted the deadbeat's ex-wife to the door (which Carrie had made him promise to do unless she was around to do it), Su sat in the outer office, clutching a packet of pictures and documents.

Jack's first thought was that Su had made a better transition than Li had. Though her build was square where Li was lithe, her face rounder and its features less defined, there was a pleasantness about Su that made her attractive. Where Li was sulky and petulant, resentful of things she didn't have, he guessed Su had settled into the life Crate provided and loved him for it.

Su had brought tea, which she shyly offered to share. "I didn't know if you had a way to make it, but I thought it would be nice on such a cold day." Su's command of the language was excellent, revealing her determination to fit into her new country. Jack tried not to compare her precise speech to Li's mangled English.

"That was kind of you," he said. "I'd love some tea."

She opened a shopping bag and took out a thermal bottle, two cups wrapped in a towel, and a small packet of sugar. With some ceremony she poured them each a cup of tea. The precise movements told Jack the process was meant to demonstrate friendship between them and honor to him.

"Packard worked so hard to give me things," she told Jack as they sipped their tea. "He worried I wouldn't have money if something happened to him."

"Did he have reason to think it might?"

Su smiled sadly. "He thought himself unlucky. You know, of course, about the time he strayed into North Vietnam. He often told me how you and Todd got him out." She sipped her tea before going on. "He also hurt himself many times in his life, sometimes seriously."

Knowing two examples of Crate's clumsiness, Jack chose to comment on the less serious one. "He told us once he fell out of his bunk during training and broke an arm."

"It's true." Su rubbed her own arm as if in sympathy for her husband. "We adopted two little girls last year, because of course we could not have children of our own."

***

VIETNAM, 1967

Todd came into the hooch and told Jack, "My little buddy over in Transport got hurt."

"Wrong Way Somers?"

"He shot himself climbing out of a Deuce-and-a-half. He's gonna live, but he can't make it with a woman anymore."

"Geez, what a rotten thing to happen."

Todd used his t-shirt to wipe the sweat from his neck. "I feel bad for the kid—I mean, he seems like a kid, even if he's our age. He can't do anything right, you know?"

Jack could think of only one consolation. "At least he has a ticket out of this place."

They'd gone to the hospital to see Crate and wish him well. Though he'd been pretty doped-up, Crate relayed surprising news. He was marrying a local girl who would follow him to the States soon. "I'll have a wife to take care of me," he said sleepily. "A friend is arranging everything."

Todd had been incredulous. "Crate, the brass doesn't let this kind of thing happen."

Crate had ignored that. "Su's a nice girl. She'll take care of me."

Though he was no bigot, Todd was concerned that Crate was making a mistake. "We like Crate, but he isn't exactly any woman's heart throb. He'll be crushed if she's just using him to get to the States. What if she disappears on him?"

There was no doubt Todd disliked the idea of Jack's marriage to Li just as much, but he'd been smart enough not to say so, then or ever. Like Crate, Jack wouldn't have listened, at least not the Jack Porter who existed at that moment in time.

***

Su Somers sat opposite Jack, grieving for the man they'd once thought she was taking advantage of. Crate had been the lucky one, despite his many accidents.

When their tea was finished and the bottle and cups removed,

Su placed the packet she'd brought on Jack's desk. "I brought pictures Packard had of people he knew. Maybe you have the same ones."

"I don't have any at all," Jack told her. Belatedly he attempted a smile to take some of the bitterness out of it. You're not mad at Su, he chided himself. Carrie often reminded him, in her gentle way, that the world requires politeness, tact, and grace. It wasn't a lesson Jack took to easily after years of surly silence, but he was trying. "This man who called Crate and said someone murdered his wife. You never learned who he was or why he thought she'd been killed?"

"It was something about insurance."

"Life insurance?"

"Maybe."

"Did Crate have life insurance?"

She nodded. "As I said, he worried about my future. Adopting the girls added to his worry, so he bought a policy from an ex-GI named Green."

"Green." Jack had picked up the lighter, and he ran his fingers over the engraving. "I don't remember him."

"I think he helped Crate get permission for us to be married. I remember him being there, but my English wasn't very good then. Mr. Green came to our house once a month to collect the premiums. Two days after Packard died, he called to say I would receive money. He brought it to me himself a few days later."

"May I ask how much the policy paid?"

"One thousand dollars."

Probably not enough to kill for. "What else can you tell me about him?" Jack took up a pencil. The insurance man might know something if he'd been in 'Nam with Crate.

"I think his first name is Sean. He's been very kind to me and the girls."

That reminded Jack he hadn't asked about her plans. "What will you do now, Su?"

"I have a friend who is building a Chinese restaurant on Miller

89

Road. He will hire me to work there." She smiled grimly. "He says Americans don't know Chinese from Vietnamese, so I will be safe."

Jack wondered what this tiny woman went through every day, facing loneliness, grief, and the bigotry of Flint's ample population of rednecks. Watching Su accept her lot with dignity and humor, he promised himself he'd be nicer to Li.

"Okay, I'll look through this stuff and see if anything rings a bell." Jack slid the packet toward him, peeked inside, then let out a sigh of frustration. "I wish I knew which direction Todd was going with this. He said he wanted to look at army records, but I never asked him why. He said he'd fill me in when he got back." Caught unaware, a wave of terrible grief washed over him. *We should have been doing this together. We were supposed to be a team, like in 'Nam.*

Su was silent for a moment then she rose briskly and collected her coat and gloves. "I should let you get back to work." As they walked to the door, Jack noticed she slowed her pace to allow him to keep up. It made him angry, but again, not at her. "It's odd, their dying within hours of each other. Is it possible Todd found out something and both he and Packard were killed for it?"

"It's possible," Jack answered, "but it could also be a coincidence." Su smiled politely, but her eyes said she did not believe her husband had died by chance.

***

VIETNAM, 1967

Jack was driving an army jeep through the village when he saw Li for the third time. Head raised proudly, firm body under strict control, she walked down the street ahead of him, a basket over her arm. He slowed the jeep to a crawl to watch her. She was beautiful to be sure, but there was something else that held his attention. Maybe it was the way she ignored everyone on the street, as if the crowds around her didn't matter. When she entered a store, Jack obeyed some demand from inside himself, parked the jeep, and followed.

A bell over the door sounded as he entered, and those beautiful eyes glanced up from some piles of fabric. He saw recognition in them, but she looked away quickly. Dust hung in the air of the shop, not the dust of outside, but particles from yards and yards of cloth shifted and sorted all day long. It created a kind of filter that blurred his view and softened it, like the ads for Breck shampoo in magazines back home. She appeared idealized, softer and lovelier than normal girls.

He moved toward her, trying to telegraph friendliness, but she turned away. She probably hated Americans, and he understood why she might. He believed the U.S. meant to help her country, but she probably saw only an army of invaders. So why was he chasing the poor girl around bolts of cloth?

In a moment the storeowner approached, offering the generous-sized, complimentary beer most businessmen gave out to insure GI goodwill. The locals considered it a worthwhile investment, since after visiting a few stores, the soldier's heightened alcohol content made it likely he'd buy something. Jack waved the beer away, aware he'd be in enough trouble if anyone knew he'd stopped. He had papers to deliver, and he'd best get to it. With a final glance at the girl, who had turned away, he left, feeling like a teenager with a foolish crush.

Two days later, a skinny Vietnamese man approached as Jack crossed the compound. "Sergeant Porter? You Sergeant Porter?"

"Yes."

"I talk to you, hey? I tell you something you like."

Jack had heard stories of guys with grenades concealed on their person getting close to a soldier in order to blow him up, but this guy didn't have any place to conceal one. He wore only a pair of shorts with holes that let skin show through. Besides, the suicidal types tried to get guys in a group rather than one at a time, making the sacrifice of their lives worth more.

He let the man lead him a short way off the path. Camp life flowed around them, men headed for showers that relieved the sweat and heat for all of five minutes, guys on duty moving listlessly at various necessary but tedious tasks, and the few favored Vietnamese allowed into the camp: washing women, ARVN officers and apparently, this one, who had no visible purpose. Jack got down to business, unwilling to spend a lot of time on a guy with breath like a Chicago sewer. "How do you know my name?"

"I very smart." The little man laughed. "I know lot of tings." Though he seemed old, it was hard for most Americans to guess age among the Vietnamese. This one had only a few teeth, and his hair seemed to have been cut with a machete. Still, he appeared to be harmless. "I know you like one girl name Li. This girl very nice family. She number one beautiful, like Audrey Hepburn."

Jack got it. "No, thanks, pal. I'm not looking for a woman." He turned to walk away.

"No, no, you not understand." The little man hurried along beside him. "She no whore, this Li. She good family. Her father big ARVN army man—general."

"So?"

The man put a claw-like hand on Jack's arm, and he recoiled instinctively. "She no whore, not for other GI. She go to U.S., be number one wife. You take her Chicago."

The guy knew Jack's name and his hometown, knew of his interest in Li, knew he was single. "Where does all this come from?"

"I very smart," the man repeated. "Know lot of tings."

"Sorry, not interested."

"You no like Vietnamese wife? She cook, she clean, she very quiet. Do what you say, not like American girl."

"I don't want any wife, American or Vietnamese."

"Why you follow Li?"

Angrily Jack denied it. "I didn't. I just happened to be there."

The man's disbelief was obvious. "You tink about this. You get good Vietnamese wife. She work hard. You no work. She want go stateside, be your baby doll. You tink about this then tell me, Ho Doc Cho. I fix."

"I told you, no wife. I don't need someone to take care of me."

That would change soon, but at that moment, he'd had no idea.

CHAPTER FOURTEEN

As soon as Carrie entered the office Jack saw she was upset, close to tears. For once she forgot to be cool toward him but rushed to his desk and confessed in a rush, "I did something awful. I'm really sorry."

"Sit, Carrie. You look like you're going to faint." She obeyed, her face pale. "Tell me what happened."

"I stole something from that woman's house. I can't believe I did it, but she lied, and I knew she was lying, and then she went to answer the phone, and I found the picture, so I took it."

As she babbled, she fumbled through the small black purse she carried. A pencil and several coins clattered to the floor, and she bent to retrieve the items as they rolled in several directions. "What if she finds out? You'll lose your license, and it'll be my fault. I never would have found it if she hadn't talked so long on the phone. I don't know why I took it. I just did."

When he thought he had the whole story Jack said calmly, "Can I see the picture?"

"Oh." She handed him the photograph, a black and white Polaroid that had curled inward as the developer dried on its surface. Jack looked at it for a moment. "Partner," he said firmly, "you did exactly the right thing."

"But she's sure to notice it's gone, and she'll know who took it."

Jack was still looking at the two people in the picture. "How often do you think a woman like that sits around looking through her old photo albums?"

When Carrie calmed a little, she explained her theory Tate hired Elaine Harris to distract Jim. "She was there to help Tate get away with whatever he pulled."

"A logical theory," Jack responded. "Now we need to either prove or disprove it.

When they showed the picture to the bartender Jack had interviewed before, the man remembered Tate but couldn't say much except that he liked hockey. His comment reminded Carrie that Elaine had met Tate at a hockey game. After dropping Carrie

off at the office, Jack drove to Port Huron and visited the Flags'
ticket office. The clerk there recalled the face in the photograph but
couldn't put a name to it. They'd come to a dead end.

***

Carrie couldn't get over her guilt, and over lunch the next day, she
confessed her crime to Marsha. "Jack doesn't think she'll notice, but
I keep picturing her opening that book and finding a blank spot.
She'll know it was me, because I asked about the guy."

"So what? She doesn't know your name or anything."

"I just feel bad. I've never stolen anything from anybody."

Marsha munched her dill pickle with ladylike enthusiasm.
"Then I suppose we'll have to put it back."

So it was that Carrie's first B & E was not a crime of removal,
but to put something back. Less than forty-eight hours after she'd
stolen it, Marsha drove her to Elaine Harris' house. She remained in
the car, acting as lookout, while Carrie returned the picture to the
album where she'd found it.

Marsha contended it wasn't breaking and entering if Elaine
Harris left her back door unlocked when she went to work, as many
people in small towns did. "It isn't robbery either, so what's the
crime?"

"Entry without permission," Carrie supplied.

"If I'm not mistaken, that's a much less serious charge."

The door was indeed unlocked, not that it made Carrie feel any
better. Though she was frightened half to death, Carrie managed to
remember Marsha's suggestion she look for the photograph's
negative. "People just toss them in a drawer, so who'd notice one
missing? If you have the negative, you can get a copy made."

The house felt different in the darkness, the heavy furniture
seemed threatening, and the silence of emptiness was eerie. Putting
the picture back in place was no problem, and Carrie turned her
efforts to finding the negative. She hoped she didn't have to search
the whole place. It was bad enough to invade someone's privacy by
entering her home uninvited, but she didn't know if she could search
Harris' bedroom.

Listening for the sound of Marsha's car horn, which would signal someone's approach, she finished searching the living room. The flashlight she'd brought lit the corners of the room, casting shadows that made her jump. In the hallway, a desk sat under the wall-mounted phone, and to her relief, one drawer contained a shoebox full of negatives. Frustration at the number of envelopes inside followed.

"Darn it," she said softly, "There must be a hundred here." Remembering the month and year stamped on the picture edge, she dug through the drawer, careful not to make a mess. After a few minutes she found an envelope marked May-July, 1968. Using the flash to light the negatives, she located the one of Elaine and Tate. Taking it seemed less wrong than taking the photo. Or maybe it was simply less discoverable.

Sliding the panel into her coat pocket, she tidied the drawer, closed it, and moved toward the back door, checking to see everything was as it had been.

"Let's go," she ordered, climbing into her friend's station wagon. Though she'd affected nonchalance, Marsha's take-off would have spun the tires if she'd been driving anything other than a Falcon.

Jack was horrified when he heard what Carrie had done, but she surprised him by pooh-poohing his protests. "Nobody saw us and she'll never know I was there, so we've got nothing to worry about." She waved a piece of black film at him. "And now we have the negative."

***

Tuesday and Wednesday were spent waiting for a print from the negative, but on the first of November, Jack was able to take the copy they'd made of Tate's picture to a Port Huron Flags game. He showed it to every employee he could find until one of them said, "He sits in my section, but I don't think he's here tonight. He must have season tickets—same seat every time."

Jack asked the man to indicate about where that was. "I think it's right in here." He frowned at the empty seats. "It's in that row, because I remember he's one back from the front. His seat is somewhere in the middle."

Returning to the box office, Jack saw with satisfaction that the woman at the window was not one he'd already shown the photo to. Leaning an elbow on the ledge he said, "I've never seen live hockey before. I really like it."

The woman smiled professionally. "Good, maybe you'll come and see us again."

"The thing is I got this ticket from a friend of a friend. I'm supposed to pay him for it, but I forgot his last name. His first name is Jeff, and his season ticket is in row B, in the middle." He grinned in his best boyish manner, "Can you help me out?"

At first the woman looked doubtful, but she took in the crutches then shrugged as if thinking, "What could it hurt?" Checking a list on a clipboard that hung from a nail, she said, "Row B, center, huh? The only Jeff is Jeffrey Mancuso. That sound right?"

"Mancuso, that's it. Thanks a lot."

The next morning the office wasn't as cheerful as Jack had hoped, since Li showed up. She flipped silently through a magazine, but her presence caused Jack to tense up and Carrie to look prim. "We have a name," he told her. "Now we'll track him down."

Carrie was fiddling with the thermostat. The building's heating system was old and inefficient, and they turned the heat up and down constantly. "Let me locate him," she suggested. "It should be easy now that we've got a name, and you can work on Crate's case, like you've been wanting to."

It was true Jack wanted to look into what Todd had been looking for. At the same time, he felt he had to work on jobs that helped get the agency established. Since he would never charge Su for his services, their paying jobs supported him and, more importantly, Carrie. They'd been lucky so far, first to get cases, and then to have them turn around quickly. With luck Carrie would locate the fictitious Mr. Tate soon. In the meantime Jack could spend some time looking through the papers and pictures Su had left.

To his irritation, as soon as he opened the manila envelope, Li wandered over and stood behind him. He hated it when anyone did that, but Li could make him angry more easily than most people. Refusing to let her know her presence bugged him, Jack forced himself to look at the stuff calmly. It might have been her closeness and the haunting smell of sandalwood that caused him to recognize, in a group photo of Su and Crate's wedding party, the tattered little man who'd first offered Li as his wife. His clothes were better in deference to the occasion, but the machete haircut remained the same.

"Li, who is that man?"

"What man?" Her face told him she knew exactly which man he meant.

He pointed. "That one." Jack glanced out the doorway. Carrie was on the phone. Noticing, Li's eyes turned cold.

"That Uncle Ho. Not real uncle. He know everybody."

"Why was he at Su's wedding?"

She attempted nonchalance. "Why not? Big party. Everybody come." She moved away. "I go now. This place too dull for me." Picking up her jacket, she left quickly. *Before I can pin her down*, Jack thought.

***

Carrie noticed Li's hurried exit. Though she knew it was none of her business, she was curious about Jack's relationship with his wife. He hadn't said a word to her about Li, never mentioned her name, never showed any emotion when she came or when she left the office. When Li was there, he was controlled, almost robotic. When she left, he became the man Carrie had gotten to know in those first weeks.

Since Li often watched Carrie as if trying to gauge her attachment to Jack, she was careful to be an efficient assistant and no more. Not, she told herself, that there was anything else to their relationship.

It took only a few hours to find a Flint address for Jeffrey Mancuso, but it turned out he'd been gone three months. When Carrie asked the building manager if he could provide his former tenant's new address, the man, whose drawl fairly screamed Kentucky, could not. "They never left a forward. Gave the place up the first of August. He stopped by for a couple weeks to pick up the mail, and after that, nothin'. I tell you, they left in a hurry."

When she reported to Jack, he suggested the best chance of catching Mancuso was to stake out a hockey game. "If he's got a season ticket, he'll show up eventually. We have to be there." He tilted his head. "Do you like hockey, Carrie?"

The look was a little too innocent, and she knew she should say no. The truth was she loved hockey. Not television hockey, which was so gray and grainy it was impossible to see the puck most of the time. But real-life, close-up hockey, where the colors flashed as the players sped by and the frozen moisture flew as skates skidded to a stop, was exciting. Besides, it was business, not pleasure. "Is there any other sport?"

Jack called Su Somers about the man in the picture. Su wasn't sure she remembered him, but since she was coming into town anyway, she agreed to stop in and take a look. Like a bad penny, at least in Carrie's mind, Li showed up after lunch and hung around all afternoon. Her interest picked up when Su arrived.

Carrie noted that Su was polite to Li but not warm, though in her mind two women from the same town in Vietnam, both living in a society alien to them, should be thrilled to see each other. Li became very animated, in fact, and slid her arm around Su's waist in the Asian fashion, switching to Vietnamese. Her comments were rapid and extended, and glances in her direction made Carrie suspect she was under discussion.

Su looked uncomfortable, replying in English and looking apologetically at Carrie when Li continued in their native tongue. Carrie told herself that joy at being able to speak her own language caused Li to forget politeness, but rudeness was by no means unusual for her.

Finally, Su approached the desk. "I'm here to see Jack," she told Carrie with a smile that said she regretted Li's behavior. "He asked me to look at a photograph."

Standing behind Su and in Carrie's direct line of sight, Li stopped cold. She unleashed a flow of Vietnamese at Su, demanding in tone.

"Because Jack asked me to," Su replied. She moved around the counter as Carrie knocked briefly and opened the door to Jack's office. Before Li could follow, Carrie shut the door. For a moment Li looked as if she might push past her and enter, but she thought better of it. She flopped into the saucer chair in the corner so forcefully that it hit the wall with a thud.

CHAPTER FIFTEEN

Jack began by asking if he might serve tea to Su this time. "Are you sure you're okay?" he asked as he fiddled with the small tray Carrie had arranged next to an ancient hotplate. She'd filled the kettle, and Jack, unwilling for her to hear what he and Su might have to say to each other, assured her he could manage from there. "If there's a problem with money..."

"I will be fine." Su provided a litany of proof. "The restaurant will open in one week. Packard's mother will keep the girls, and she is wonderful with them. I have the insurance money from Mr. Green. The house is paid for; it was a rental his parents bought and gave to us when we married." She smiled. "I am a very lucky woman. I was lucky to get a man like Crate, despite...everything."

"I know." Jack's response told Su more than other words would have. He did know.

Perhaps sensing things had gone into dangerous territory, Su changed the subject. "You have a photograph to show me?"

Jack handed it across the desk, and she examined it carefully. "I do remember him. He and my father were business associates of some kind."

"Li calls him Uncle Ho."

"That sounds right, but Ho is a very common name, like Smith here."

"You don't know what he did for a living?"

Su chuckled. "Vietnam is different from here, as you know. People don't always do one thing. I believe this man was useful in getting difficult things done, part businessman, part...I think 'flim-flam man' is the word?"

Jack smiled at her use of a term she must have picked up from the movie with George C, Scott. "Did he have anything to do with your marriage to Crate?"

She seemed offended. "No. Why do you ask?"

"I'm sorry. I wasn't implying anything." The teakettle whistled and Jack scooted his chair over to it, glad to be busy while he told his story. "That man found me one night and offered to arrange a marriage between Li and me." As he spooned loose tea into the pot, the fragrance of it filled the room. Horrified at the American teabag, Li had found loose tea in a shop somewhere. "He knew I was interested in her."

"When was this? I mean, did you know Li then?"

"Not really. Honestly, I was interested in her, but I turned the guy down."

"Then how did you come to marry?"

Jack sighed. Su probably knew most of it anyway. It would be good to tell someone who would neither judge him nor pass the story along to others. "It was after." He didn't say after what, but she nodded understanding. Like Crate, when Jack had been disabled, his view of life changed. "I was in the hospital, and there she was. I don't even remember it very well. I knew I was attracted to her, and...I don't know. It happened." He couldn't tell her everything. He'd never told anyone, not even Todd.

Su's dark eyes watched him, but she asked no more questions. Looking again at the picture, she said, "I will be honest with you, as you have been with me. My father arranged my marriage to Crate to get me out of Vietnam. He fears the U.S. will tire of the war and leave, and we will be defenseless." Her expression turned sad. "He said he was too old to start a new life, but he wanted me to have that chance."

Su's father was probably right. Richard Nixon was campaigning for President by criticizing American involvement in confused politics of the tiny Asian nation. Criticism had succeeded in causing LBJ to refuse a second term, and it was unlikely Hubert Humphrey could overcome the nation's discontent with the Democratic Party's conduct of the war. It might take a year or more, but the U.S. would leave Vietnam. What would happen then to those who had sided with the West?

Handing Su a cup of tea, he picked up Todd's lighter and read the words etched on it once more. The South Vietnamese were fighting for freedom too, but most would not be able to leave the country when they grew tired of fighting.

Su stared into her cup as she continued her story. "Sean Green approached my father and offered to find a GI to marry me and provide for me in the United States."

"Would that be the same Green you spoke of before?"

"Yes. When he returned, he began selling insurance." It was a common transitory occupation for ex-servicemen, who often used old military buddies as clients and contacts.

"What was his job in the military?"

"I don't know. When Packard was in the hospital, waiting to be sent home, Mr. Green took me to meet him, and an agreement was made." She smiled. "I was relieved to find he was a kind man. Packard told me about...having no children, and I was sorry, but he said we'd adopt someday."

"So you married a man you hardly knew."

"As my father wished." Not unusual in Asian society. "Packard feared no woman here would want him after his wound." In unconscious emphasis of the difference between Asian and American women, Su rose and refilled Jack's cup for him, setting the hot drink on the desk before him like an offering. "In time he regained his strength and returned to work. He asked only that I manage our home and care for the children."

"I assume your father paid for this arrangement?"

"I believe so, though Packard never mentioned money. Of course my father did not explain. It was his right to marry me to whomever he chose." She allowed herself a smile. "I had no idea until I arrived here what a difference there is in marriage customs between our countries. Luckily for us, something happened that no one expected. Packard and I learned to love each other."

Tears welled up in Su's dark eyes, but she blinked them back, reaching a hand across the desk as if pleading for understanding. "My marriage was a lie, at least at first, to make the United States government take me in. I don't know if Ho had anything to do with it. I only know about Mr. Green."

"Do you have a phone number for him?"

She frowned. "I'll have to look for it."

"What company does Green work for?"

The frown deepened. "I'll find that out too." She drank the last of the tea and set the cup on the tray. "Mr. Green helped me open an account in the bank in my own name, so I could deposit the money."

Jack still couldn't place Sean Green, but if he was an army buddy of Crate's, maybe they'd talked about whatever was worrying the little guy. "Call me when you find the name and number of the insurance company." After Su left, he sat in the silent office, trying to recall names for the men he'd seen with Crate Somers.

***

There'd been a poker game, organized by Todd, as usual. They were in their tent, a GP medium-purpose structure designed to house sixteen men. They'd pulled a footlocker between two cots to serve as a table, and there was for once cold, at least, slightly cold beer. Someone had obtained some non-potable ice, usable only for external cooling but valuable, nevertheless.

A guy on a bunk in the background was teaching himself the guitar, moving with agonizing slowness from one chord to the other of "House of the Rising Sun." Around the makeshift table sat seven men, as he remembered it. Who were they? Todd, Jack, and Crate. Who else? Marconi, nicknamed "Wireless" by Todd for obvious reasons; Parrott, a thick-headed slob who said very little and nothing worthwhile, dubbed "Polly" in Todd's book; Kelly, a big Irishman with hands like meat hooks; and Corfa, called "Greek" or sometimes "Freak," the former due to his heritage, the latter to his compulsive cleanliness.

In a country where either dust or mud was a constant, Corfa struggled to keep his possessions spotlessly clean. Everybody was careful about their feet, socks, and boots, but Corfa amused and annoyed everyone by washing out his clothes each evening and stringing a line from bunk to bunk to hang them. It didn't matter to him that they often didn't dry in the overpowering humidity of Southeast Asia. It was his requirement they be washed, not dried. Because of that, the area around Corfa's bunk always smelled like mildewed laundry.

When the deal came around to Crate, he called Indian for the third time, much to the disgust of the others. Crate thought it was funny to see grown men each holding a card to his forehead. "Come on, Crate," Wireless moaned.

The Greek was more aggressive about it. "Listen, Somers, you call Indian again and you're out of here."

Crate had had a few beers, which made him brave enough to talk back, especially with Todd next to him. "Dealer calls the game. If you don't like it, you're out of here."

Always the peacemaker, Todd suggested they play one more hand of Indian and Crate would choose a new game on his next deal. After Indian it was Todd's turn, and he called Blind Baseball. Todd liked to do a running commentary as he turned the cards up. "Pair of sixes for the Joker, not much to bet on, Buddy. The Freak gets three clubs, possible flush. Kelly has queen high; Wireless has threes and tens, maybe a full house there. Parrot has nothing much showing." On this occasion, his patter irritated the Greek. "Shut up, Sex. We don't need your smart-ass comments."

Jack was a bit surprised. Though everyone got irritated at Crate, few people gave Todd any grief. When Todd didn't respond, the moment passed. Next was Jack's deal. He always played straight poker. After his game Kelly took the deck. "Three-card draw, gents: Jacks or better to open, trips to win, aces and tens are wild."

There were moans all around the table, and Wireless cracked his knuckles nervously. "Geez, Kelly, if I'd known you were gonna get complicated, I wouldn't have had those last three beers."

"Gotta keep people off balance if you're gonna get ahead," was Kelly's response. "You'll always win if you can dazzle 'em."

He was right, that night anyway. He bluffed everyone out of the first round except Jack, who stayed in with a pair of tens simply to make a point. "Good for you, Joker," Todd crowed. "Keep him honest."

"Ain't nobody alive can do that," Kelly averred, then added, "Damn!" when the hand he drew didn't fill his own requirement for three of a kind or better.

It was a game that would have gone on and on but for a cry of "Incoming!" Cards and money scattered as seven men jumped in alarm. Jack was right behind Todd as they hit the bunker, where they crouched, waiting until the scream of the mortar round ended in an ear-splitting roar twenty yards away. He remembered Todd's gaze on him as the flash lit the sky, his eyes seeking Jack's as if seeking assurance they'd survive. That was the thing. You never got used to waiting to see if you would.

When calm settled again, they returned to the tent. Cards lay all over the floor of the tent, but the pile of money that had laid atop the footlocker was gone.

CHAPTER SIXTEEN

Carrie was surprised at how much she liked her job. Though Li Porter made it uncomfortable at times, there was also a satisfaction she'd never had before. Jack didn't expect her to do anything he wouldn't do himself, and even tried to type sometimes in a non-rhythmic, two-finger method he'd developed in Vietnam when required to submit reports. Beyond that they both did research and conducted interviews, afterward talking over what they'd learned to build a base of shared information.

Jack kept careful notes, and she learned to do the same, finding that days later the mind can't be trusted to remember things well or at all. Carrie also discovered that written information sometimes struck her later in a different way, sending her in a new direction. She'd even enjoyed her brush with danger at Elaine Harris' home, and the picture had moved the case forward. She felt fulfilled, the way women on the news said she should. Still, the feeling didn't come from simply having a job. It was doing the job she wanted and doing it well that made her see herself differently.

Of course there was her mother to contend with. Unhappy with Carrie's new career, Onalee talked about the "big risk" she'd taken and asked probing questions about the relationship between her and Jack.

"Two people in an office all day. He could be planning something," she declared.

"He's not that kind of man, Mom." Since Marsha's comment about Mom's possible motives, Carrie had begun to see Onalee in a new light. Her frequent reminders of the dangers of rape and seduction came as much from fear of her daughter's new independence and lessening susceptibility to manipulation than from maternal concern.

This knowledge resulted not in anger, but in sympathy. Carrie was less susceptible to Onalee's barbs these days, and she felt sorry for her shallow, pretty mother.

Understanding didn't change the carping she had to endure. "You just don't have enough experience with men to judge their motives."

Carrie's grip tightened on the phone despite her resolve. "Mom, I know about wolves and perverts." Not that she'd ever have shared that part of her life with Onalee.

"Well, that man wants something. He wouldn't hire you—"

"For myself? Mom, I'm good at what I do."

"I'm sure you are, dear." The placating tone implied Carrie was inept, naive, and hopeless. "Be careful, is all I'm saying. Men take advantage of girls like you all the time." When the call ended, Carrie wondered why, according to her mother, girls like her were supposedly more prone to seduction than others. She supposed Onalee would say their desperation showed plainly on their plain faces.

Jack did like her, and she could see he wasn't happily married. Though he gave Li every consideration, he treated her with cool politeness, not affection. In return Li flaunted her position, being rude to Carrie when she could get away with it, though she was careful when Jack was around. The worst thing for Carrie was being watched. Everything she did, everything she and Jack said to each other, was taken in by that beautiful, hostile face and judged in a way that wasn't in the least complimentary.

On the other hand, Carrie liked Su Somers very much. On Tuesday she volunteered to return the packet of pictures and papers Su had left with Jack, but the drive out to Gooderich turned into an adventure of sorts. An early storm made the roads slick and the visibility low, and the truck fishtailed if she pressed the accelerator too hard or too quickly. By the time she arrived, Carrie's hands ached from gripping the steering wheel.

Su insisted she come in and have coffee. They sat in her cozy kitchen at a glass-topped table surrounded by captain's chairs. Su served coffee from a drip coffeepot she reheated briefly on the avocado green gas stove. It was too strong, and Carrie noticed Su didn't have any. She'd made it for her guest as a courtesy.

"I start work in a few days," Su told Carrie. "I will be glad, for it's hard to be here all day, thinking about the past." She glanced at the twin three-year-olds playing in the living room. Of mixed race, with golden skin and liquid eyes, they were beautiful, and they had every piece of furniture and square foot of floor strewn with toys. "Of course the girls keep me busy."

"I know what you mean though. Something outside the house to keep your mind occupied for a few hours every day." After her dad's death, work's demands had required her to push her grief to the back of her heart, where healing begins.

The telephone on the counter rang and Su excused herself. "Hello?"

Carrie immediately saw that the call was upsetting. "Packard isn't—He is—He died," Su finally got out.

The caller became upset, so much so that Carrie heard both sides of the conversation. "Dead?" a voice said. "Crate's dead? Oh, God! Now what do I do?"

"Who is this?" Su asked.

"We were in the army together." The man sounded as if he'd run a long way. "He was going to get in touch with someone for me."

Su looked at Carrie. "Do you mean Todd Sachs?"

"Yeah." The man seemed surprised that she knew.

Carrie pointed to herself questioningly, and Su nodded. "There's someone here right now who can tell you about Todd. Will you speak to her?"

Su handed the phone to Carrie. "This is Caroline Walsh. I work for Jack Porter, Todd Sachs' partner in the Eagle Detective Agency." She thought it best not to mention Todd's death yet. "Is there something you want them to know?"

"They killed her, and now they're trying to kill me!" The words were a moan of despair.

"Can I get your name?" Carrie got a notepad from her purse, and Su provided a pen.

"Bartkowski, Stan Bartkowski. I was in Crate's squad overseas."

"And where are you now, Mr. Bartkowski?"

"Chicago. A motel on the east side." He went on in a rambling tone, "The cops say it was an accident, but it wasn't. Jen never drove over forty. She was afraid to, so how could she hit a tree hard enough to kill her? She saw that damned ghost, and he knew Jen and me would figure out their scheme."

"What scheme, Mr. Bartkowski?"

He was beyond answering her questions. "I've been hiding, but they're going to find me!"

Carrie struggled to make sense of the rapid pace and half-explained sentences. A ghost had tried to kill him? It had killed his wife?

"The police think your wife's death was an accident?"

"Idiots!" His tone dropped to a rumble. "The cop says, 'Mr. Bartkowski, have you and your wife been getting along recently?' They think she was leaving me, but Jen wouldn't do that. They killed her, the bastards!"

Carrie twisted the phone cord around her fingers, quelling her natural tendency to fill a conversational void. Jack got information from people by listening, often letting long silences develop in order to draw them out. Finally the caller went on.

"They came after me, but by some miracle I survived the fire. Then Jen told me she seen Sean downtown."

The operator interrupted to ask for more money, and Carrie heard the sound of coins being dropped into the slots. When she had thanked Bartkowski, he went on. "I called the company, and that's when I knew I had to get away."

"You said she saw a ghost? Who was that?"

"I don't know the ghost's name. I only know Sean."

He called the company? A ghost? None of it made sense. The man sounded paranoid, but the death of another person associated with Todd and Crate was odd. Two vets who'd known each other and now the wife of a third vet was dead as well?

"Mr. Bartkowski, I'm sure Mr. Porter will want to know more. Can you call his office if I give you the number?"

"Haven't got any more change."

"Then give me a number where he can reach you."

"This ain't Howard Johnson's. There's only the pay phone." He read off the number and Carrie wrote it down. "I don't know if I should stay around. I'm out in the open here."

"What's the address where you're staying?"

She copied onto her notepad.

"I'll get this information to Mr. Porter right away. Can you stay there for an hour? He could call by then."

"I guess so. I don't like sitting around out here in the open though." The man seemed paranoid, possibly delusional.

"I'll hurry," Carrie assured him. She hung up. "I've got to go, Mrs. Somers."

"Please call me Su." She rose to get Carrie's coat from the hallway rack. "You can call Jack from here. The long-distance charge will not be much."

"I'd like to be there when he talks to this man. Together we might figure out what he's talking about." Carrie took her coat, removing a pair of soft gloves from the pocket and putting them on as she spoke. "Su, do you know Stan Bartkowski?"

"From his voice I think he is the man who called before."

Carrie sat down to put on her boots, and Su paused for a few seconds before asking, "Miss Walsh, why does Li Porter spend her days in the office?"

"Call me Carrie," she urged. "I guess she doesn't have anything else to do. Why?"

"Oh, nothing," Su said a little too quickly.

Carrie met her gaze. "I get the impression you're not fond of Mrs. Porter."

Su seemed to choose her words carefully. "Do you know the circumstances of my marriage?"

Never good at answering a direct question with a lie Carrie answered, "Jack told me, but only because of the possibility that your husband was murdered."

"I have no reason to dislike Li, but when we came to this country together, it seemed she looked bad—looked down on me." Su corrected herself as she recalled the proper idiom. "I thought it was because I married a man I did not know so I could leave Vietnam. That was not fair."

Finished with her boots, Carrie stood. "You were a good wife, I can see that."

"That's not what I meant," Su said as they walked to the door. "She has no right to look down on me because her marriage to Jack was arranged, the same way as ours."

Carrie could hardly find the words to make a polite goodbye to Su Somers. What she'd said explained so much, yet it created a whole new crop of questions. Why was foremost, and she returned to the truck repeating it unconsciously as she went. Why? Why?

Snow had stopped falling, and a county truck had scraped the roads back to navigable shape. At the office Carrie caught Jack up on what she'd learned, at least most of it. All the way back to Flint she'd pondered Su's words. Jack's marriage was arranged? He didn't seem the type to marry a woman he didn't know, to make a deal that provided a man a submissive wife and a woman a ticket out of a war-torn country.

Had he and Li gotten what they wanted? Li didn't seem happy, and Jack didn't either. Carrie decided she probably couldn't understand the pressures that acted on people in the conditions they'd faced. Maybe someday Jack would trust her enough to tell her about it. Until then, she'd keep her mouth shut.

Jack was very interested in Bartkowski's call and tried to return it immediately. There was no answer, so while he waited a few minutes before trying again, he had Carrie carefully repeat everything Bartkowski had said.

"He said 'they' killed his wife and were after him too."

"But he didn't give a reason?"

"He was almost hysterical. There was something about a ghost."

Jack shook his head in frustration. "I wish I could reach him. Someone he served with might be able to figure out what happened—or what he thinks happened."

***

The doctor's office had called while Carrie was out with the news that her items were in. While Jack continued to try to reach Bartkowski, she took the truck again and drove out Court Street to Miller Road. Having had no lunch, she treated herself to a meal at Bill Knapp's before heading to her final fitting with the optician. Jack insisted she draw a generous salary from the agency, claiming an associate should earn more than a secretary. She suspected he put in personal funds to cover her wages, but she consoled herself with the thought they were getting cases. That meant he'd be able to pay himself back soon.

Carrie had chosen glasses with a rounded frame, avoiding the "cat eye" look that was fast losing popularity. The optician put the glasses on her, testing their fit by running his fingers along the bows and into her hair. The plastic lenses felt lighter and were less distorting than her old glass ones. The frames blended with her facial shape and coloring rather than overpowering it the way the oversized black ones had.

"They look really good," the young man said. "You look...really good."

He was cute: young, with a tan just starting to fade, regular features, and brown eyes that didn't require correction. Looking closer, Carrie revised her conclusion. He was wearing contacts. From longer-than-usual eye contact, she also realized the guy was flirting.

Glancing at the mirrors that surrounded her on three sides, Carrie blushed to acknowledge the reason. The little navy dress with an empire waist Marsha had whipped up literally overnight showed her slim figure to advantage. The hairstyle, as easy to maintain as Jillian had promised, suited her face and gave her a gamin-like quality. Her glasses no longer detracted from her looks. They fit her facial structure and toned down the pert hairstyle, creating a balanced effect.

After the new frames were adjusted to fit properly, Carrie got her first lesson on contact lens insertion and care. Her lenses were surprisingly small hard plastic discs, the right one marked with a blue dot so she wouldn't put them in wrong.

She learned how to clean the lenses, how to store them at night, and how to insert and remove them. The process of putting something on her eye seemed repellant at first, but Carrie was surprised at how easily she learned to do it. It wasn't comfortable, however, and she blinked constantly as her eyes tried to expel the foreign objects. The doctor only left them in for fifteen minutes the first time, but even so, it was a relief to take the lenses out by "popping" them off her eyeballs with her eyelids.

The optician, hovering behind his boss in his eagerness to help, put the plastic lens case into a metal sleeve and gave Carrie a schedule. Each day she'd wear the lenses for a bit longer until in about two weeks her eyes would adjust, and she'd be able to wear the contacts twelve hours a day. At other times she'd wear the glasses.

The whole experience was interesting, and before she left, Carrie had a date for dinner with the pleasant optician, whose name was Ben.

CHAPTER SEVENTEEN

Before she returned to the office, Carrie put her old glasses back on, suddenly self-conscious. What if Jack thought she was changing her looks so he'd notice her? What if Li did? If Li became jealous and told Jack to fire her, would he do it? Carrie didn't think so, but why put him in the position of having to choose between his wife and his associate? She decided she'd wear the new glasses tomorrow.

Li wasn't there, and Jack was having no luck reaching Bartkowski. "Maybe I copied the number down wrong," Carrie suggested.

"He probably had to leave for a while. I'll try again in a few minutes."

At five, as Carrie clicked the deadbolt lock into place on the front door, Jack reminded her, "Don't forget you're working tonight, Walsh. Wear something sexy."

After a second, she remembered: the hockey game. It had sounded like fun when Jack proposed it, but what she'd learned from Su Somers made her reluctant to spend time after hours with him. She was dying to know why Jack had married Li, but she couldn't ask. Could she keep her questions from bubbling out through a whole evening with him? Worse, her mother had called with the rare proposal they go to a movie together. She'd had to tell her she was busy, which led to all kinds of questions. Carrie pictured Onalee's raised eyebrow, the one that said so much. Still, Jack needed her help. They planned to contact Tate—or rather Mancuso. She was the bait.

Jack picked her up at her home. The pickup was encrusted with white from the salt spread on the roads to melt the ice, and seeing it brought to mind one winter when her father, determined to fight the curse of Michigan vehicles, had every afternoon hauled a bucket of warm water out to his car and swabbed the salt off the metal wheel-wells and fenders. Another year he'd paid for undercoating, though any chink in the "armor" meant decay. In the end he'd accepted that any Michigan vehicle driven in the winter would be corroded by salt.

The drive from Flint to Port Huron on I-69 was mostly silent. Jack wasn't one for small talk, and Carrie was apprehensive about the evening ahead. She'd been slightly alarmed when he suggested she wear something sexy. Owning no clothes that fit in that category, she chose from her wardrobe things she felt vaguely uncomfortable in: an emerald green mohair sweater she'd gotten for Christmas the year before and never worn. It was clingy and low-cut, and she'd had to resist the impulse to put a turtleneck under it. With it she wore a pair of jeans that had become overly snug when washed. She'd tied a silky scarf of green and navy-blue hound's-tooth print in her hair and used make-up again. Then it was time for a decision on eyewear. She wasn't ready for hours of contact-wearing, and the new glasses looked good, but with the unfamiliar clothes and the new hairdo, she felt like an alien. She put on her old glasses and felt like herself again.

They pulled into the arena parking lot with plenty of time to spare. Carrie wore boots, since the weather was sloppy, but she left them in the cloakroom and pulled a pair of loafers from a shoe bag. She was pleased when, after hanging up her coat and running a brush through her hair, she faced Jack and he grinned appreciatively. "You're bound to attract a wolf or two," was his comment. Jack had taken the nearest seats he could to Mancuso's, and Carrie noted he'd cleverly reserved three. Directing her to the one on the aisle, he left an empty one between them. The last thing he did before sitting down was reach over, take her glasses, and slip them into his jacket pocket. As Carrie touched her face in confusion he ordered, "Just yell when I yell."

A few minutes after the game began, a man who was a blur to Carrie entered their row, dumping a few kernels of popcorn onto her lap as he passed. He apologized so profusely that she recognized his ulterior motive. Looking in his general direction, she smiled sweetly. "That's all right. Pretty tight quarters in here."

"Yeah, but I love it, don't you?"

Deciding not to be too friendly at first, she said primly, "I enjoy hockey very much."

"I haven't seen you here before."

She looked him in the eye—at least where she thought his eye was. "I'm new to the area."

"Is that why a sweet young thing like you is here all alone?"

Carrie forced herself not to look at Jack. "I guess so."

Mancuso stood over her, his knees almost brushing hers. "Do you mind if I sit beside you?"

"I can't stop you." That didn't sound right so she added, "You look pretty strong to me."

For the rest of the game Jeffrey Mancuso leaned against her, patted her arm, and talked, talked, talked. At first it was hockey talk, and she could hold her own there, thanks to her father's influence. They discussed Guy Jamison's play and the addition of Geoff Pollis to the team and what it might mean for their prospects. From there it became more personal, and Carrie concentrated on finding out everything she could.

It wasn't difficult, since Mancuso was brash and self-absorbed. He dropped information into the conversation that inflated his importance. Possible truths emerged, but there were lies too. He claimed he wasn't married, which was a lie. His name was Jeff Owens—another lie. He owned a business in Saginaw that made circuitry parts for GM—possibly true.

Between periods Carrie turned to her new friend, doing her best to look innocent. "I need to find a lawyer in the area. Do you know any good ones?"

Mancuso's tone changed. "I can tell you some to avoid."

"You mean dishonest ones?"

"Maybe not dishonest, but they're no good."

"Which firm?"

"Callender, Callender, and Callender."

Carrie laughed. "It'll be easy to remember that name."

"Take my word for it. They take advantage of people."

She widened her eyes. "Did they cheat you?"

"I hear things." It sounded final. "The Marley firm in Saginaw handled my divorce."

"Oh, I'm sorry," Carrie murmured.

"Actually, it was my second divorce." Mancuso grinned as he

delivered the punch line to an obviously favorite joke. "I've decided that next time I feel like getting married, I'll find a woman I don't like and buy her a house instead." Pressing Carrie's arm with his elbow, he leaned in close. "Unless someone like you comes along, of course."

Carrie giggled appropriately. "Thanks for the tip on the lawyers."

"Anything for a lovely lady." He was back to sleazy mode. "Can I call you some night? We could get some dinner, talk about hockey—maybe give Coach Tarwin the benefit of our combined expertise."

Carrie thought fast. "I don't have a phone yet. The waiting list is huge, I guess. Maybe I could call you?"

He hesitated. "I'm pretty hard to catch up with. Are you coming to the game on Tuesday?"

"I guess I could."

"How about if I meet you somewhere? We could have dinner in Flint and then drive over here together." Mancuso touched her hair in a practiced gesture of casual flirting. "You don't know how nice it is to meet a girl who likes hockey as much as I do." She wondered if Elaine Harris had heard the same line.

"It's nice to meet someone from the area. I've only met people at work." Oops, that was a mistake. Now she had to invent a job. "I'm a social worker for the Mott Foundation." It was the first thing that came into her head.

"Well, well. A do-gooder, huh?" His voice was slightly mocking, but she guessed he didn't really care what she did for a living. "So how about next Tuesday?"

Carrie agreed, though she had no intention of keeping the date. They watched the rest of the game, at least Mancuso did. Carrie gazed at the ice, seeing only a blur of movement. Before the final buzzer she left, making the convenient female excuse of the ladies' room. Jack had collected his crutches and moved out earlier, and she figured he'd be waiting in the coatroom. It took a while to find him, since he still had her glasses in his pocket. He handed them to her, and she put them on. It felt good to have her part done and to be able to see again. "You heard?"

"Most of it. Are you sure you haven't practiced flirting before?" He sounded almost irritated, and Carrie was surprised at how good that made her feel.

"I couldn't get a phone number, though."

"That's okay, because we're going to follow your new boyfriend home."

"We are?"

"I figure the reason he didn't ask you to go somewhere with him tonight is he has to plan his tête-à-têtes ahead of time. Come on, we have to hurry."

They crossed the parking lot to the truck, Jack moving through the wet slush smoothly but carefully. Throwing them behind the seat, he climbed in, started the pickup and pulled off to one side of the main door, shutting off the headlights. They watched the crowd of noisy, laughing people burst from the arena doors, among them Mancuso, who stopped on the steps and lit a cigarette. He waited around for a few seconds, possibly looking for Carrie, then finally made his way to a blue Camaro.

"Hope we can keep up," Jack muttered as he put the truck in gear and pulled out behind the Chevy. It was difficult at first to keep sight of Mancuso in the crush of cars fighting to nose their way out of the parking lot. Once the traffic spread out, they had to stay back to keep their quarry from seeing he was being followed. When they turned north onto I-75 Jack observed, "Guess he wasn't lying about living in Saginaw."

The road was wet but clear. Mancuso drove a hair over 70, too fast for winter roads to Carrie's mind, but Jack pressed the gas pedal. The truck groaned a bit but kept pace.

When Mancuso turned on his blinker at the Mt. Morris exit, Jack followed without using his. Ordering Carrie to crouch down, he pulled into the right turn lane beside the Chevy, which turned left. Jack made a right but immediately pulled into a driveway and did a quick U-turn, catching up with Mancuso within a minute.

They traveled several miles at a good distance back from the blue car, which then turned down a side road. Jack drove by it, pulled over, and turned off the lights. They watched the car move away until Jack deemed it safe to follow, pulled another U-turn, and started down the road without lights. They drove in almost complete darkness for a while, following Mancuso's taillights. Finally, the car turned again. Slowing to a crawl, Jack drove until Carrie said, "There."

Mancuso was coming out of a garage that sat beside a one-story house. Jack stopped the truck several hundred feet back, rolled his window down, and looked through binoculars Carrie handed him from the glove box.

The house was ranch style, with brick halfway up and a light aluminum siding on top. The porch light was on, but the house itself was dark. Carrie heard the rattle of a chain as Mancuso closed the garage door then went up the sidewalk to the front. In a few seconds interior lights came on. They followed his progress as he went from room to room, finally settling in an area where there was a television. "He set a can of beer on the table by his chair," Jack reported. "He's in for the night."

She'd been writing down the roads they'd taken since leaving the freeway. "Can you see a house number?"

"I'll pull up by the mailbox and get it from there." He read off the number as she wrote it down, then continued down the road far enough to be out of sight before turning around yet again. As they came back out to Mt. Morris Road, Jack stopped at the corner. The house was on Alberta, which completed the address.

"Jeffrey Mancuso, 2133 Alberta Road, Mt. Morris."

"Once again, good work, Miss Walsh," Jack said. "Though I don't know why you agreed to go out with him."

Carrie chose to ignore the comment, since she didn't intend to keep the date. She put the binoculars back into the glove compartment and snapped it closed. "The question is what did the guy gain from his shenanigans at the law firm?"

"I don't know. He said they take advantage of people."

"That's true. Brad and Peter Callender would scalp anyone, and Jim—Jack, what if Jim had one of his flings with Mancuso's wife?"

"You did say he's one for the ladies."

"Half their fights are about his unethical liaisons with clients."

"So if Mancuso's wife was playing around with Callender, he got back at them by running up a big tab and stiffing them?"

"But then he tries to pick me up at a hockey game." Carrie's tone was disgusted. "And he had that thing with Elaine Harris too."

Jack turned onto Court Street. "I don't claim to understand the rules between husbands and wives, but it looks like Mancuso thinks what's good for the gander is a no-no for the goose."

"Men!" Carrie brushed at her shoulder as if to clean the spot Mancuso had touched.

"There are women who only want things their way too." She wondered if they were still talking about the Mancusos, but Jack's next comment revealed something else entirely. "Anyway, I don't want you dealing with this guy anymore. He's a jerk." Odd coming from the man who'd set her up as bait!

"But—"

"We were hired to find the missing client, and we've found him. What the Callenders do about it is up to them."

"But I wonder why he did it."

"Lots of times you do. Why did a guy go AWOL? Why does a competent nurse suddenly lose it and smash every medicine bottle in the supply tent? You can go nuts trying to answer everybody's questions. We each have enough of our own."

Carrie heard the strain in his voice. Jack only let himself care about a few causes, a few people. She'd become one of those people, possibly because she came along just after he lost his best friend. Whatever the reason, Jack was protective of her. The thought was comforting, but it didn't change her mind about Mancuso. She still wanted to know why.

CHAPTER EIGHTEEN

At 8:50 Monday morning, Marsha seemed surprised and pleased to find Carrie waiting when she arrived to open the Callender law offices. "You look great!" Carrie complimented, and Marsha twirled, showing off the suit she'd made. A straight black wool skirt stopped an inch above her knees, and the matching jacket had a Nehru collar. Under it an azure blouse with wide cuffs and a high neck brightened the ensemble. She looked every inch the efficient, stylish secretary, and Carrie made a mental note to ask for something similar. She liked the way people reacted to her developing sense of style.

That reminded her that she'd have to buy something if—if she was going to meet Mancuso for dinner on Tuesday. A silky blouse and a pair of those new palazzo pants would look stylish. What Jack didn't know couldn't make his handsome face turn sour.

"So what's up, kiddo? Did your cute new boss dump his wife in favor of your charms?" Marsha had decided Jack and Carrie were meant for each other. She'd told her friend about Li to shut her up, but it had only made things worse.

"I have some things to tell you about the Tate case." Carrie filled her in on what they'd learned about Jeff Mancuso. "I need to know if Mrs. Mancuso was ever a client."

"Come on in." Carrie entered, feeling odd when Marsha took the place behind the desk that used to be hers and opened files she had once maintained.

"It's right here," Marsha cried triumphantly. "Anabel Mancuso." She pulled a manila folder from a metal file drawer and banged it closed with her hip, "She came to have her mother's estate settled in March of last year. You noted four—no five visits."

"What was the mother's name?"

"Kilborne."

"Now that I remember. The mother was a client for years, so Anabel had us handle the probate. And the partner who dealt with it was?"

"Rat Fink." Marsha looked up from the file. "You think she's one of Jim's 'ladies'?"

"It's beginning to look that way. The Mancusos left Flint suddenly in August. We think Mr. figured out that Mrs. was involved with Jim."

"He moves her out of town then plots revenge," Marsha said dramatically.

"Don't say anything about this to the Callenders yet. One more day won't change anything, and I'd like to find out the rest of this story."

"Sure thing," Marsha replied, "as long as you let me in on all the dirt eventually."

As she descended the stairs from the law office, Carrie saw Bea sweeping the foyer. "Miss Walsh, you looking fine, girl!"

"Thanks, Bea. I had my hair cut at a salon."

Bea laid a work-roughened hand on Carrie's arm. "I always said you was a pretty thing. Glad to see you're out of this place, Miss Walsh. Them men's no good."

"How do you get along with Marsha?"

"She fine. Doesn't stop and chat like you used to do, but she got kids, so I understand. She'll whip those Callenders into shape, though—believe it."

Carrie felt a little deflated. Why hadn't she been able to "whip those Callenders into shape"? Not assertive enough.

At the office she found Jack already at work. When he saw her, his eyes lit with appreciation. She'd worn the new glasses, convincing herself it was silly to have them and not use them. In moment of recklessness at J.C. Penney's she's also bought a winter coat. Advertised as a "fun fur" (meaning fake), it was soft, white, and luxurious. She felt downright adorable in it.

Jack glanced over her shoulder, and the light in his eyes died away. Turning, Carrie saw Li enter the office, a svelte leather coat belted over her jeans. Standing next to Jack's petite wife, Carrie suddenly felt clumsy and oversized. Jack went back to work, apparently having nothing to say to either of them.

At noon Carrie managed to think of a reason to use the truck and located the address where Mancuso and his wife had lived until

August. She was surprised at how easy it was to get people to say unkind things about others. With only the flimsiest of excuses for doing so, neighbors gossiped there had been a noisy argument in mid-July when Mancuso accused his wife of all kinds of things. Shortly afterward, they'd moved out of the city without a word to anyone. One man reported hearing him shout something about "shysters" and "whores," which he recalled because it seemed an odd combination.

Driving back to the office with a chocolate milkshake from the Varsity so thick it wouldn't come through the straw, Carrie put a different interpretation on a period of several weeks in September when there had been quiet at the law office. Jim had neither taken long afternoons off nor fawned over females who came to consult them. She had naively concluded he'd finally grown up, but his good behavior lasted only until the girl with the red Mustang entered the office.

Carrie phoned Marsha when she got back to work, telling her they'd been successful. "Before we tell the Callenders, I think Jack and I need to speak with Jim alone."

"So what do I do?"

"When you can get Jim alone, ask him—no, tell him—to come to Jack's office. We'll handle it from there."

"That Jim is something else. He tried to put the moves on me the first week I was here."

That was a shock. "He never tried anything with me."

Marsha's voice became muffled as she apparently held the phone with her shoulder so she could type. "Guys like him like 'em married. Part of the fun is taking what belongs to someone else."

"Marsha, I'm sorry I got you involved with these creeps."

"We've come to an understanding."

"You didn't send them to their offices again."

"Well, they started in again, so they got the Mom Talk." The typewriter platen let go with an abrupt grind as Marsha pulled her work free.

"And that is...?"

"Like when I told my oldest he should leave home, since his parents are unfair. I offered to help him find a place, get a job, work out a budget. He was ten, and I scared the daylights out of him."

"And the Callenders?"

"I explained they'd each have to rent a whole office, rather than sharing one. They'd have to split their clients equally, as well as their assets. I threw in everything I could think of, including the fact that I, of course, was quitting so they'd each have to find a new secretary. I said with moving costs and everything else, they might recover from the break-up in three years—maybe five."

"Marsha!"

"Brilliant, wasn't it? In their grimy little hearts they know they need each other, because who else would put up with them? In the end they went to their offices without being ordered to."

Carrie burst into laughter, picturing the three pompous lawyers being chided like naughty schoolboys. Marsha joined in, and when she could breathe again, she pointed out, "Well, they act like children."

"What was the end result?"

"They held some sort of council in Peter's office. I heard whispering, a few growls, and more whispering. Finally, Jim came out to ask me to please stay. He promised I'll never have to listen to their fights again."

"They'll have to rent a room when they feel a fight coming on," Carrie chuckled.

"A boxing ring is more like it." Marsha snorted another laugh. "Now if you could make Jim give up his work-related affairs, it would be great."

"We'll do our best," Carrie promised.

CHAPTER NINETEEN

After Carrie told him her plan and returned to her desk, Jack gauged the changes he'd seen in her over the short time they'd known each other. Lately she was confident enough to work without him, to finish what she'd started then lay it in front of him, a *fait accompli*. His encouragement, Marsha's support, increased responsibility at the agency, and even the competition Li represented had brought Carrie out, showing her she wasn't someone doomed to counting flowers on the wall. Jack reminded himself the changes could bring him gratification for a co-worker's happiness, nothing more. Li's presence in his life made anything else impossible.

It was mid-morning when Jim Callender came into the office, accompanied by his usual cloud of aftershave. A man just past his prime, with sun-damaged skin and muscles that had begun to turn slack, he nevertheless complimented Carrie lavishly on the office decor and introduced himself to Jack with an air of noblesse oblige. Eyeing him warily, Jack invited him to sit. "We asked you here, Mr. Callender, because we found Mr. Tate."

"Oh, good for you."

"The question might be is it good for you." At Jack's tone, Callender's brows rose.

"If we have a chance to recoup the money he owes for our services, it must be."

"Mr. Callender, do you know—" Jack consulted Carrie's note— "Anabel Mancuso?"

Jim's expression turned blank. He doesn't even remember their names. Finally, his face cleared. "Oh, Annie, yes. We're acquainted."

"She is married to one Jeffrey Mancuso, the man you know as Jeffrey Tate."

His high brow furrowed. "Tate is Annie's husband?"

"We think your...acquaintance with his wife made him angry," Carrie explained. "He got back at you by running up a big bill and sticking you with it."

"Why, the gall of someone to—"

"Some men become unreasonable when they find out their

wives are sleeping with their legal representative," Jack commented dryly. "You're lucky you didn't get involved with the woman who pretended to be his wife. Your brother's intervention saved you considerable embarrassment, perhaps disbarment."

"You mean she was—"

"Planning to provide proof that you seduce your clients, Mr. Callender." Jack's tone was harsh. "Your behavior is highly unethical." Jim gasped like a landed trout, but Jack went on. "The question is what do we do with this information? If your partners find out—"

"That cannot happen!" Jim jumped to his feet, almost upsetting the planter beside his chair. "There's no reason to tell them about this, none at all. We'll say you couldn't find the man."

"That would make your partners think we can't do our job," Carrie stated flatly. "Since we'd like a good working relationship with all three of you, we're giving you a chance to make this right."

"How would I do that?" Jim asked, though it was plain from his face he had an idea.

"You'll pay the money the fictitious Tate owes the office."

"Why should I?"

"Because your behavior brought the problem about." Carrie surprised Jack with her frankness. "You've put your firm's reputation in jeopardy, over and over, by fooling around with clients, clients' wives, even daughters of clients." Jim sputtered something incomprehensible, but she ignored the interruption. "Mr. Porter is correct. It's unethical—in fact, it's disgusting. Now you have to pay for it, and what's more—" She raised her voice slightly as Callender again tried to say something. "—it's time you stopped messing around. You're a married man. Besides betraying your wife, you take advantage of your position in the worst possible way."

Jim's mouth flapped a couple of times as he tried to respond. His feet shuffled on the floor as if he meant to rise and walk out on them, but he couldn't do it. Finally, his head dropped to his chest and a single tear flowed down each of his cheeks.

Carrie's eyes met Jack's, and he saw both pity and vindication there. She hadn't expected Jim to collapse so completely.

After a moment Callender spoke, his head still low, "I'll pay the firm what Tate owes if you promise not to tell my brother the details."

"We'll let you decide what to tell them," Jack agreed. Catching Carrie's eye he added, "There are counselors, you know. People who can help you."

There was a silence as Jim pulled himself together and left the office, hardly aware of where he was going. As the door closed behind him Jack turned to Carrie. "You were pretty straight with the guy, and you're going to start feeling like you were too hard on him. But understand this: some people can't be reached by kind hints and hopeful thoughts. They need it laid out for them. You probably did more to help Callender grow up today than his parents ever did."

"Thank you for saying so," she murmured.

Jack reached into his desk drawer, pulled out a Nerf ball, and tossed it at her. "Here, take out all that extra adrenalin on this." The ball hit her on the shoulder and bounced off harmlessly, but she scooped it up from the floor and squished it a few times. She tossed it back at Jack, who batted it back in her direction, making her laugh as she flailed to keep it from hitting the floor.

Having lightened the mood, Jack brought up a new subject. "Our message service had a call last night from Bartkowski. He left a new number. I tried to reach him several times, but there's no answer. Finally I asked the front desk guy into knocking on the door, but he got no answer. He thinks Stan's gone out."

"But you don't agree?"

"His message said to call first thing in the morning. It's now almost eleven there."

"So what do we do?"

He sighed. "We could try the Chicago police and see if they'll make a run out there and check for us, but I'm not sure they'd do that just because a guy we don't know isn't answering his phone. I thought we might go there ourselves."

"Us? Go to Chicago?"

"If he's as skittish as you say, Bartkowski might trust a woman at his door more than he trusts a man." Jack retrieved the football, which had bounced into a corner, and squeezed it to half-size. "It's my hometown. I'll show you the sights." He raised a hand in a mock vow. "And I promise, separate rooms."

"I would expect that," Carrie said, a little primly. "But is it wise for both of us to go and leave the office closed?"

"I thought about that too. Li can answer the phone for a couple of days. It's time she earned her keep."

***

A trip to Chicago? Carrie had hardly been anywhere, and the thought of the city was both appealing and scary. But Jack would be with her, and he knew his way around. She hadn't considered traveling with her partner, but it was business. And he had specified two hotel rooms.

Carrie reserved two seats on the train to Chicago that evening at 8:04, causing her to wonder why train schedules were always at odd minutes. Why didn't they leave at 8:00 or 8:10?

As the noon hour neared, she mentally packed a small bag, thinking it was the first time she'd needed the little suitcase her dad had bought for her high school graduation. He'd wanted her to travel, but it hadn't worked out, at least until now. Until Jack.

The bell over the door sounded, and Carrie looked up to see her mother entering the office. What was she doing in town in the middle of the week?

"Hello, darling," Onalee called loudly enough for anyone within a block to hear. "I brought a friend into town for some medical tests, so I thought I'd drop in to see my little girl."

"Great!" Carrie assumed enthusiasm she didn't feel. Onalee was there was to look Jack over for herself. What fault would she find with him—what reason why Carrie should quit this job and get something more respectable?

As if on cue, Jack rolled his office chair into the doorway. His eyes sought Carrie's first, gauging her reaction. "Mom, this is my boss, Jack Porter. Mr. Porter, I'd like you to meet my mother, Onalee Walsh." She hoped that was right—you were supposed to speak to the older person first. Or did you introduce the older person to the younger?

Jack spoke warmly. "Mrs. Walsh, it's nice to finally meet you."

Onalee was on her high horse. She regarded the office critically, wrinkling her nose as if she smelled a mouse. "Mr. Porter, I'll be frank. I've come to see what goes on here and if it's a proper place for a young woman to work."

Carrie's heart sank even further. If she'd told her mother half of what went on at the law firm, Onalee would have been shaking her finger under the Callenders' noses once a week. "Mother." It was a warning.

"It's all right," Jack said calmly. "What's going on, Mrs. Walsh, is a professional operation in which your daughter plays an important part. She handles customer relations, research, and tasks I'm not able to handle right now." He glanced down at his missing leg.

"Oh, I'm so sorry," Onalee breathed.

Jack gave a brief nod to acknowledge her sympathy. "I've come to depend on Carrie's sense of responsibility and integrity, and I guessed her mother was a real lady. You can always tell good parents by their children's behavior."

Carrie stared open-mouthed. In addition to the fact that it was more than she'd heard Jack say at once in all the time she'd known him, he was charming the socks off Carrie's mom.

Onalee's disapproval vanished, and instead of the haughty beauty she'd obviously intended to play, a simpering belle appeared. "Thank you, Mr. Porter. It's nice to meet a real gentleman." She patted Jack's shoulder, rather like he was a collie, Carrie thought. "Many people don't appreciate a girl like Carrie, whose good qualities are intrinsic, so to speak." Leave it to Mom to jab me, but at least she likes him.

Jack's appearance had improved since the business opened. Carrie had insisted on professional attire when he'd argued for jeans, and they'd compromised on chinos with Oxford shirts and a tweed jacket. Though he looked more like Professor Fournier's friends than Sam Spade, he'd do. A recent haircut had tamed his thick curls, so the overall picture was respectable, and, she admitted, darned attractive.

Knowing Onalee's sensitivity for the feelings of others might be compared to that of a lioness in a herd of gazelles, Carrie stepped in before her mother could comment further on Jack's injury. "You're just in time for lunch, Mom."

"Mr. Porter might like to come along, Carrie. It's rude not to ask."

Jack gave her a charming but completely artificial smile. "I'd love to, Mrs. Walsh, but I have an appointment. Maybe next time."

Carrie practically dragged Onalee out the door, throwing Jack a look that was both pained and amused. She could already play the lunch-time conversation in her head. Onalee would wonder aloud why Carrie hadn't mentioned that her boss was a cripple. She'd comment that it made working for him safer, and she'd exclaim over his good looks and his wonderful personality. Anyone who flattered Onalee Walsh was obviously a discerning, intelligent man.

After lunch Onalee seemed reluctant to leave, but Carrie gently reminded her that her friend was probably finished with her tests. She was uncharacteristically silent, but Carrie took that as a sign of disappointment, since she'd found nothing to criticize at the agency.

She returned to the office to clear up what couldn't wait until Friday. One item was what to do about Mancuso. It was Tuesday, and she'd promised to meet him for dinner. Jack didn't want her to go, didn't consider it necessary, but Carrie saw closure in letting the guy know someone knew about his nasty little plan. Besides, she thought Mancuso could use some of the same straight talk Jim Callender had received. A man who so casually picked up women should be aware that his anger at his wife's affair was less than righteous. With new self-confidence that blended with her ever-present sense of justice, Carrie appointed herself the messenger Mancuso needed. She could make dinner, say her piece, and still get to the train station by 7:30.

At her apartment, Carrie stopped before going upstairs to tell her landlord she'd be gone for a few days. Dr. Fournier was bent over the stove, stirring something that smelled tempting. His completely hairless head lifted when she rapped on the back door, and he smiled when he saw who was there.

"Carrie, come in! You have to try my fondue. I'm having a few people over, and I thought, why not? It's all the rage, and I'm expected to keep up, even at my advanced age." Once she'd gotten used to Fournier's dramatic manner, Carrie had become quite fond of him. She'd heard a few disparaging remarks from other students about old queens, but she figured his private life was none of her business.

Fondue was interesting, after several samples she decided it was a lot of bother to go to for bread and vegetables. Still, she was sure it would be a hit. "I stopped to tell you I'm going to Chicago for two days on business."

He gave her a brief but enthusiastic hug. "Chicago! Oh, Carrie, you'll love it. Be sure to see the Hancock Building—best view of the city."

"I don't think I'll be sightseeing. We're going there to interview a man who says his wife was murdered."

"I hope you at least get to ride the El and see the Sears Tower."

"We will. I might get some free time. Since it's his hometown, I suppose Jack will have people he wants to see while he's there."

"And how is the dreamy Mr. Porter?" Fournier had seen Jack one day when he gave Carrie a lift home and had not stopped urging her to "take her chance" with her boss, even when he learned about Li. "Free love, Carrie," he told her for the tenth time. "It will make you happy." Giving Fournier a quick kiss, she left him to his fondue pot and went back outside, where an exterior stairway led to her apartment and several tasks she needed to get done before getting on the train.

CHAPTER TWENTY

Jack sat at his desk for a long time after Carrie left, flipping Todd's lighter open and closed. With sudden decision, he picked up the receiver, found a number, and called his doctor in Chicago. The receptionist remembered him and sounded pleased with his request, though it still galled him to hear the tone of practiced kindness in her voice. Encourage them, he could almost hear them telling each other. They're vulnerable, and they doubt themselves, so be kind. He wanted none of their false cheer and their rap groups where everyone sat in a circle and got in touch with their feelings. But he did want something from them now, and he'd do whatever it took to get it.

Jack considered the conversation he'd have with Li. While he'd been nonchalant with Carrie, he didn't look forward to telling Li that he and his associate were going to Chicago without her.

He could have gone alone; it was true. Reluctantly he admitted to himself that he wanted to spend time with Carrie, wanted to show her his city and give her a taste of life outside Genesee County. Still, being left behind was bound to make Li angry. Her jealousy where Carrie was concerned was something Jack didn't get. He treated Carrie formally, even coolly, when Li was around, and she responded with equal coolness. But Li had always had a sense for undercurrents. She knew Jack found Carrie appealing, and she wouldn't be happy with his plan. He was going to get an earful.

***

VIETNAM, 1967

After eight months in country, it had become eerily normal to exist in the middle of a war. Mundane daily tasks—showering, eating, driving—didn't stick in Jack's mind any more than they would have at home. He and Todd were traveling down a road that was for once clear of hanging clouds of dust. It was early in the morning, and they were delivering a young private accused of assault to the provost marshal's office for possible disciplinary action. The private was depressed and hung over, so he wasn't saying much.

Jack focused his mind on taking a shower—how good it would feel after the night's work. Of course the feeling never lasted long in the heat—that had been his thought when it happened.

There was a roar of sound and the surreal feeling of rising slowly into the air as the mine exploded beneath the jeep's left front tire. Things seemed to speed up, and he felt his body separate from the jeep. Then he knew no more.

When he awoke, he was in a room where everything was white. They said he was lucky to have survived; the private hadn't. They said he was lucky to be going home; his war was over. They said he was lucky to have escaped with one good leg when the jeep fell on him. They took shrapnel out of his scalp and told him he was lucky it had caused only a mild concussion. They kept telling him how lucky he was, but Jack didn't believe them for a second.

Sleep saved his sanity those first days. The combination of drugs and shock helped to shut his mind down, and he thought of nothing. He would wake briefly to some cheerful face and stare at it, unable to respond. Finally he would let himself drift away again. Sometimes he awoke in the depth of night and lay listening to the muted sounds around him, telling himself he was in his tent, and it had all been a dream. Memories of the aftermath flickered from time to time, unclear and unreal.

Once he saw Todd leaning over him anxiously and somehow knew that Todd, who'd been thrown clear, had kept him alive until help came. There were other images, too. The oddest was the Vietnamese girl he'd followed that day in Phu Bai. He thought she was in the room, that she examined him dispassionately. It must have been a dream.

And then there was a vaguely familiar face, a Vietnamese fellow who kept repeating, "You a cripple now, Porter. You need someone help you do tings. I fix. You listen? I fix." He drifted then, but later, both the girl and the man were there, along with a man he didn't know who spoke sternly to him. He said yes to something important.

When he finally came back to full consciousness, Ho explained he now had a wife. When Jack objected angrily the little man shushed him, looking around to see that no one was paying attention.

His tone turned less friendly. "You cripple now. It is hard, even in United States, to be cripple, I tink. Vietnam girls best wives anywhere. They do what you say. They take care you. They don't even care if you screw around."

"That's not the point."

He continued as if Jack had not spoken. "Li much beautiful girl. You like her, yes?" Jack looked away, unable to deny his interest. "There, see? You say to me, I want Li. I get this done, very legal. You go State-side soon. She will follow when papers are in order." Drawing himself to his full five feet he finished, "You take back what you say to me? I will tell Li you no want her. You no get beautiful wife. You no have help with gone leg."

Just then Li had appeared in the doorway, all in white and looking like an angel.

"It's okay," Jack told the man. "I'm not backing out."

***

Li came into the office around four. "I have to go to Chicago for a couple of days, and I need your help." The look she gave him was eager, almost joyful, and he realized he'd begun all wrong. Damn! Even when he planned ahead, he still said the wrong thing. Shuffling the papers on his desk nervously, he hurried on to his request. "Can you watch the office for a few days?"

Realization dawned in her eyes, and she snarled, "So you can take your little blind mouse with you? I think no."

Ruffling his hair, Jack told himself to stay calm. "Li, why are you jealous of Carrie?"

Her voice turned shrill, and her nostrils flared. "I not jealous. You married to me!"

In Li's world, feelings didn't matter. Ownership mattered. "There is nothing between Carrie and me, Li. She works for me, and she's good at the job. I need her help in Chicago."

"Why you go Chicago?" Li demanded.

"There's a man there, a vet, who claims someone killed his wife. I think it's connected to the other matters, Todd's death and Crate's."

Her eyes narrowed. "You believe Su? Crate was murder?"

"Maybe. It's odd that all this happened at once."

Li's face took on an expression Jack couldn't decipher, though he knew most of her moods. "All right, I stay here. You go. Take your mouse." Jack felt his shoulders relax. He said no more about the matter in case Li changed her mind.

***

Jeffrey Mancuso waited at the bar when Carrie entered, a beer at his elbow. The place he'd chosen for their date tried for upscale, but there was no denying the old-beer-and-cigarettes smell that hung in the air, waiting to sink into hair, clothing, even pores.

With sleazy gallantry Mancuso ushered her to a booth in a corner, which he had reserved by leaving his coat and hat on the bench seat. "What are you having?" he asked as a waitress moved toward them.

"A Coke will be fine." A slight frown puckered his brow momentarily, but Carrie was done playing a role. He repeated the order to the waitress, and as she moved off, Carrie began, "I have something to tell you, Mr. Mancuso."

He realized right away he'd been had. "Who are you?" he sputtered. "Did Anabel—"

"Your wife knows nothing about me, and she doesn't ever need to. I'm here to tell you the Callender law firm knows your identity." At mention of the name, Mancuso's expression turned belligerent, and Carrie held up a hand to stop his objection. "You had some provocation to do what you did, but you could still be in big trouble. Using a false name to defraud is a crime, and while the Callenders don't intend to prosecute, they could. In the future I suggest you stay well away from them."

Mancuso looked both angry and aggrieved. "I don't want anything to do with vermin like that anyway." Reaching into his shirt pocket, he pulled out a pack of Pall Malls then fumbled in another pocket for a lighter. Obviously brooding on past injuries, he lit up and sucked a strong draft of smoke into his lungs. It was time for Round Two.

"I've spoken to Elaine Harris." Carrie batted smoke back in his direction. "From that and my own experience, I'd say you have little to criticize your wife for."

"Now listen here—" Mancuso growled.

"I don't have to," Carrie said in a matter-of-fact tone. "You're lucky any woman will live with you, Jeffrey. Whatever your wife's reasons for staying, I suggest you think about her the next time you feel like flirting. Remind yourself you made a vow to her."

With that Carrie rose to leave. Mancuso rose quickly and bumped into the waitress who approached with the now unnecessary Coke. Distracted for a moment, he grabbed the woman to keep her from falling. Carrie headed for the door, stopping only to pick up the overnight case she'd set in the cloakroom on her way in.

She left the restaurant, feeling a rush of adrenalin. *I did it!* Whether speaking her mind on wayward husbands had done any good or not, Carrie believed she'd struck a blow for women-kind. Turning left, she left the well-lit parking lot and headed for the bus stop two blocks down.

Near the end of the first block, the streetlamp's bulb was either burned out or broken. Somewhat nervous in the darkness, Carrie turned to glance backward and gasped sharply. Jeffrey Mancuso had left the restaurant and stood on the sidewalk, looking around him. When he caught sight of Carrie, he started in her direction, his head leaned forward in obvious agitation.

Fearfully Carrie sorted her options, Should she run? Fight back? Scream for help? Making her decision, she turned to face him, feeling shaky but determined. He wouldn't dare to attack her on a public street—she hoped.

Mancuso stopped abruptly several feet back, looking beyond her at something unexpected. For a moment Carrie wondered what had stopped him, but suddenly, strong arms grabbed her from behind. She yelped in surprise and turned to see two men with hats pulled low over their faces. She twisted wildly, trying to free herself from the larger one, who held her with a grip like pincers. There was a clatter as her suitcase hit the sidewalk.

Twenty feet away Mancuso grunted in confusion, and the men paused, seeing him for the first time. Overcoming his shock, Mancuso chose his path. "Hey! Let her go!"

Surprisingly, they obeyed, releasing Carrie and ducking into the alley they'd apparently come from. The incident was over so quickly she wasn't sure what had happened.

Mancuso was equally at sea. "What was that?"

"I don't know," she replied, "They came from nowhere."

He peered into the alley. "Guess I'm not the only one mad at you."

She gave him a shaky smile. "I'm glad you were mad enough to come after me."

"What else would a gentleman do?" Mancuso's teeth flashed white in the dim light, "I'll offer you that drink again now. We could both use one."

"I can't. I—" Carrie swayed a little as a nervous reaction set in.

He took her arm. "We should call the police."

"I didn't get much of a look at them. Did you?"

"No. Their faces were covered."

She recalled Stevenson's lack of confidence in solving random crimes. "It won't help then. Besides, I have a train to catch."

"Tell you what," Mancuso said. "If you trust me to behave myself, I'll drive you to the train station." Carrie hesitated but he went on, "Let me prove I'm not a total jerk." Sensing her acquiescence, he took up her suitcase. "Did you ever ride in a 396 Camaro SS?"

The train left at 8:04 precisely, which convinced Carrie there had to be a reason for it somewhere. She'd arrived a little later than planned, but Jack didn't notice. Carrie decided to add the incident to the list of things she wasn't telling her partner. Instead she mentioned she'd never been on a train before. Jack made a rueful grimace. "Not enough people travel by train to make it profitable, but it sure beats driving in Chicago traffic."

The train made sounds that signaled departure, huffing and hissing busily as a loudspeaker muttered indecipherable predictions of stops and times. They made themselves comfortable at the end of a compartment where they could sit facing each other rather than side by side. The car was only half full and no one joined them, which meant they had plenty of room to stretch out. Soon the train was on its way, rocking gently side to side with a comforting click that was unobtrusive and hypnotic. The ride was pleasant though not scenic, since the large windows revealed little that was cheerful. Carrie had never imagined how poor the neighborhoods trains ran through would be. Most of the ride was in darkness though, so they passed the time trying to put together the bits and pieces of their puzzle.

"We have three deaths that might be related," Jack began.

"Probably are," Carrie corrected. "The fact that the victims were in contact shortly before their deaths is suspicious."

"Two of them are guys I served with in Vietnam."

"And the third was married to a vet." She chewed at her bottom lip. "I'm not sure how that ties the victims together."

"Bartkowski said they were after him, whoever 'they' are. Maybe she got killed by mistake."

The conductor made his way along the aisle, joking with his regulars and checking tickets. They halted their conversation briefly to prove their legitimacy as passengers and resumed after the man slid the rear door closed with a grinding rattle that ended in a slam.

Jack frowned. "I wish I could place Bartkowski. I know he wasn't in my immediate circle, but Todd was connected to a lot of people. I probably met him at some point and didn't pay any attention."

"He kind of sounded wild on the phone—out of control."

Jack's expression was serious. "Some guys can't get their heads right after being in-country. He might be one of them."

Carrie had done some reading on Post-Traumatic Stress, which the conflict in Vietnam was bringing to public awareness. Called "shell shock" in earlier wars, it had long been recognized by physicians, but the nation was beginning to understand it better as veterans of the unpopular war struggled with drug addiction, alcohol abuse, and mental breakdowns.

"But you believe Su's husband was murdered."

He nodded. "The little boy said a man was up there earlier. I think the killer pulled something loose, a shingle or a piece of flashing, so Crate had to climb up and fix it. He could have waited on the other side of the roof until Crate got up there and pushed him off."

"That's kind of a big chance to take, don't you think?"

"It was a weekday morning, cold enough to keep most people inside. It was pure chance the kid saw "G.I. Joe," which could have been a guy in a fatigue jacket, from his bedroom window."

"He could have waited on the ground and pulled the ladder out from under Crate when he started back down."

Jack gave Carrie a look of assessment. "You like following leads and concocting theories, don't you?"

She felt herself blush. "I do. I like putting the pieces together. I like helping people. I like...all of it." She'd almost said, *Talking with you about it.* That was too much.

"That's good." Jack pulled a packet of waxed paper out of his duffel bag that smelled of cinnamon. Carrie guessed it contained his favorite snack, doughnuts, and she was correct. Handing her one, he finished his thought before taking a bite of his own. "We've got a lot of pieces to assemble before this ride is over."

CHAPTER TWENTY-ONE

The address Stan Bartkowski had given Jack was a motel off the interstate between Chicago and Gary, Indiana. It was a long taxi ride from their hotel near the Loop, which made Jack wish he'd driven the truck after all. The place was not luxurious by any means, but it was well-kept and cute, if you didn't mind pink. The outside was pink, the sign was pink, the lobby was pink, and the curtains that showed through the front windows were pink, with seahorses. Dean Martin crooned about *amore* from a hi-fi, his voice quavery due to an unbalanced turntable.

The woman behind the desk wore a faded, shapeless, almost-pink dress that didn't hide her flabby figure in the least, dirty-looking felt slippers probably meant for a man, and at least thirty rollers in her thin blonde hair. They were the metal kind with bristles, held in place by three-inch pink plastic pins. Jack wondered about women who wore curlers in their hair all day. What was going to happen to them that evening that was worth twelve hours of looking tacky?

Unhappy to learn they weren't signing in, the woman stared rudely at Jack's missing leg and managed to imply with a look that giving them Stan's room number was a huge imposition. She knew nothing about her guest except that he'd paid cash for a week. They should ask him anything else they wanted to know. She was back to Photoplay magazine before they were out the door.

Bartkowski was in Room #12, farthest from the office. Watchful for patches of ice, they made their way down the row, Jack's crutches clicking as his weight shifted on them. At the door he knocked several times, calling out his name to allay Stan's suspicions, but there was no answer. Carrie returned to the office and convinced the woman to get a passkey. Muttering about cops and nosy visitors, Pink Lady unlocked the door and pushed it open.

The musty smell of seldom-used motel space greeted them, along with a mix of other unhealthy odors Jack tried not to identify. The room was a mess, but that was apparently Bartkowski's living style. Clothes lay scattered over pieces of furniture, cardboard take-out containers littered the dresser, and used towels had been hung around the room to dry. Jack stepped inside, telling the women to wait. He moved through the room, absorbing every hint to the occupant's personality. The bathroom door was closed, no answer when he knocked. Turning the knob, he looked in and confirmed his worst fears. A man lay in the bathtub, his body slack. From his age and the fatigue jacket tossed over the toilet lid, Jack concluded it was Bartkowski.

Checking the carotid, Jack turned to the motel owner. "Call the police. You have a dead body in here." She left without a word, her slippers squishing on the wet sidewalk.

"Jack?"

"Don't come in, Carrie. Observe the room. Memorize everything." He did the same for the scene before him. Bartkowski wore only boxer shorts. He hadn't shaved in days, and his hair needed cutting. He showed signs of being a chain smoker: nicotine stains on his fingers and small lines around his mouth. He was Jack's age but looked older—Rode hard and put away wet, Jack's granddad would have said.

Next, he circled the room itself, taking a second and then a third careful pass through the clutter. Smells separated as he moved: the pine-like reek of gin, the rancid odor of old French fries, and the stink of old shoes and dirty socks.

There was a wallet on the nightstand. Using a pen to open it, Jack examined the driver's license, checked the money slit, refolded it, and left it where it was. Finally, he backed out of the room.

They waited outside, their breath making clouds in the air. The Pink Lady peered out her door every few minutes, obviously dying to know what was happening. Carrie suggested they could go into the motel lobby to wait, but Jack preferred to stand outside the room in the frosted sunlight, a single, imperfect honor guard for a fallen comrade. He was faintly aware he wore the "thousand-yard stare," a look soldiers often exhibited when they'd gone beyond what they were able to stand. Things got a tiny bit better when Carrie said the sunshine was nice, and she'd stay too.

When the first officers arrived Jack pulled himself together, answering their questions in a calm voice. He kept his hands in his pockets, sure their shaking was not only from the cold. After   the patrol car came an unmarked unit, and a detective took control of the scene. He seemed pleased the scene was undisturbed, and he told Jack and Carrie he'd like to hear their statements separately, to ensure accuracy. Jack knew he'd look for discrepancies, but the guy would soon figure out they'd had nothing to do with Bartkowski's death. He'd been dead at least a day, maybe more.

Carrie suggested Jack go first, and the detective led them into the lobby and claimed a small table off to one side. When he sat, Jack let out an unconscious sigh of betrayed fatigue and stress. Carrie went over and spoke to the owner, who had moved behind the counter to get her record book for one of the patrolmen.

Stan Bartkowski had drowned in the motel room's bathtub. The detective, Matt Molineaux, agreed with Jack that the death had occurred some time ago. Thirty-ish with dark hair, smoky eyes, and a five o'clock shadow that was apparently with him all day, Molineaux was young for a detective. His leather holster creaked each time he moved, betraying its newness. Still, his demeanor was that of one who'd seen too much already. His gaze was penetrating but not unkind, and he listened as Jack told how they'd come to be in Chicago that morning.

Jack reported the phone calls from Bartkowski. "His face is familiar from my tour in Vietnam, but I can't say I knew the guy. My buddy Todd called him Stosh. He invited him to a couple of our poker games."

A soft cough behind him made Jack turn, and he saw Carrie standing diffidently several feet away with a tray in her hands. "Ovaltine," she said diffidently. "There's a kitchen in the back, and I thought it would warm us up."

The aroma of chocolate wafted toward him, and Jack realized he was cold to his core. It might have been the wait in the November weather, but there was shock too. A third vet dead, another comrade who'd lived through Vietnam only to die violently and without explanation, back at home. Carrie had seen his distress and countered it the only way she could—with Ovaltine.

"That sounds great, Carrie. Sergeant, does something hot sound good to you?"

Molineaux said in a slightly surprised tone, "It does. Thanks."

As she poured three cups from the battered saucepan she'd used to heat the milk, Jack took his portion and gave her the chair so the detective could speak to her alone.

Carrie told the detective about the phone call in which Stan said he feared for his life and suspected his wife had been murdered. Molineaux asked a few more questions to clarify things in his own mind then went off to make some calls. A few minutes later he spoke to them directly, setting the cup down carefully on the slightly uneven tabletop before he began.

"Mr. Porter, Miss Walsh, I appreciate your help, but I'll be honest. From what I've been able to learn, Mr. Bartkowski was, uh, disturbed since he returned from Vietnam. His sister claims he was a heavy drinker who couldn't hold a job for long. He and his wife fought a lot, according to the neighbors. It's likely she was leaving him when she lost control of her car on a slippery road in Wisconsin and died."

"He insisted someone killed her," Carrie put in.

Molineaux held his face carefully expressionless, but the scrape of the chair as he shifted position spoke volumes. "The guy is despondent and, uh, mentally fragile. He doesn't want to think it's his fault his wife died, so he invents an attempt on his life."

"He did say it was a ghost," she admitted. "That's pretty crazy."

Molineaux spoke directly to Jack, apparently fearing he'd be offended by an easy dismissal of Bartkowski's claims. "He drinks himself into a stupor and drowns. Could be an accident, could be suicide. It's hard to accept that a friend would do such a thing—"

"I hardly knew the guy," Jack objected. "But two men he told his story to are dead. Is that a coincidence?"

"You said one was an accident."

"And the other was murder."

"Robbery, the Flint police think." Molineaux was thorough.

Jack saw Molineaux push away the easy answer, a derelict who'd "bought the farm" rather than face his demons for another day. "We'll follow up on everything you've told us." He was a good cop who tried not to make assumptions. It was all they could ask for.

The detective asked a patrolman standing in the doorway to arrange a ride back to the hotel for Jack and Carrie. Jack thanked him, rose, and set his crutches in place, but he wasn't finished with Molineaux yet. "When the autopsy's done, I'd like to know what drugs are present."

"Sure," he drained his cup, which had to be cold by now, and set it on the tray Carrie had brought in. "Thanks, Miss Walsh. Somewhere along the line I missed lunch, and that took the edge off." To Jack he said, "Leave your address and I'll contact you."

"Is there any way I can get more information on the wife's death?"

"I can find out where in Wisconsin it happened and let you know."

"Thanks." Jack gave him a business card, and they left with a baby-faced patrolman who was so busy watching Carrie that he forgot to stare at Jack's leg. Despite everything, Jack smiled. His partner was starting to turn heads, and she was totally unaware of it.

"That detective doesn't believe it was murder, does he?" Carrie asked when they got back to the hotel.

"To him Stan's another crazy vet, and there are getting to be a lot of those." Jack massaged his knotted forehead. "You and I know another death is no coincidence." He counted on his fingers. "Todd starts looking into something for Crate, and he's knifed in an alley. Crate knows something about it, and he falls off his roof. Mrs. Bartkowski tries to leave Chicago and has a car accident." He raised his hand as he raised the fourth finger. "Stosh calls us for help and then becomes suicidal?"

His hand dropped to the ruined leg and he kneaded the muscle unconsciously. "The problem is the crimes, if that's what they are, are spread out. No one police agency is seeing the whole picture. By themselves, they look like isolated incidents. Together, it looks like someone is killing vets."

"But Mrs. Bartkowski wasn't a vet."

"Whatever happened to her is related to the others, I'm sure of it. The question is who gains anything from killing these people? Su got a small insurance settlement. I got Todd's truck and some odds and ends. I bet the Bartkowskis had zero to leave anybody."

Jack repositioned his leg, wincing as he did, and Carrie wondered how much it pained him. He never said, never asked for special consideration, but she saw lines of fatigue around his mouth and eyes. How long had it been? Six months, no more. And how much more grief had been laid on his shoulders since the loss of his leg? Of course Jack didn't discuss it, at least not with her.

"Could we talk to the sister?"

With a grin that said he liked her idea, Jack picked up the phone and dialed the number on the card Molineaux had given him. "Hello, it's Jack Porter. I'd like to express my condolences to Stan Bartkowski's sister, and I wondered if you have a phone number where I can reach her." Copying it down on the back of the card, Jack clipped his ball point pen inside his jacket. "Thanks." Turning to Carrie he asked, "Shall I call or you?"

"You, I think. As an old army buddy, you'll have credence."

Jack seemed rejuvenated with something constructive to do, and Carrie called a taxi and picked up flowers in the hotel gift shop. Within two hours, they were seated on a sectional couch in the home of Verna Symons, nee Bartkowski.

Verna resembled her brother: square body and face, light coloring, and a flawless complexion. Her house was old but well-maintained, the yard small but neat. A pressure cooker hissed somewhere in the back, and the blend of food odors told Carrie supper would be cabbage, potatoes, rutabaga, carrots, and sausage steam-cooked to a delicious blend: boiled dinner.

Verna wore a flowered housedress with a full apron over it. In such households, having company stop by required not removing one's apron, but putting on a clean one. They first assured their hostess it was impossible for them to stay for supper, since they had plans. Though the invitation seemed sincere, she didn't offer a second time.

Verna was sad but not surprised at her brother's death. "He wasn't doing very good," she told them once coffee had been served and a plate of freshly baked molasses cookies set close to them in tacit invitation. "Stan was always a little wild, but Vietnam made everything worse. He came back different." Her Polish heritage brought an eccentricity to her pronunciation of certain words, discernible in emphasis on some consonants and the replacement of initial *th* sounds with *d*'s.

"Different how?" Jack asked.

"Oh, you know, like they say. He had nightmares. He drank too much. God knows what else. He couldn't settle down and hold a job. I felt sorry for poor Jen. She tried to be a good wife, but Stan was—" Words failed, and she lapsed into silence.

"He called a friend of mine a while back and said some pretty strange things," Jack told her. "Do you know anything about an attempt on his life?"

Her smile was tinged with doubt. "He told me someone tried to kill him, but he was drunk or high or both. He said it was a ghost."

"That's what he told me, too," Carrie put in. "He said his wife saw the ghost with Sean, so they killed her."

"Yeah. Sean was Stan's insurance man." Verna crossed her arms over her full chest. "My brother believed a ghost and some door-to-door salesman was gonna kill him and collect his death benefit—all one thousand dollars." Her tone revealed how absurd she found that.

"A thousand?"

"I saw it myself. Now who sets up some complicated scheme to kill some broken-down drunk for five hundred dollars apiece?" She straightened the collar of her dress. "They'd be better off running for Congress. The crooks there make more money, and they don't have to kill anybody, at least not personally. They send the poor slobs off to the jungle to go crazy or die." She turned her eyes away, angry at the politicians, angry at Stosh, angry at life and at death.

They were silent for a while as their taxi made its way back toward the Palmer House. Carrie wondered if the visit to Bartkowski's sister had made Jack feel more confident or more confused. She was leaning toward the latter, but Jack had apparently put the day's questions aside. Leaning toward her he asked, "Do you like Greek food?"

"I don't know. I've never tried it."

Jack grinned. Leaning forward he gave the taxi driver an address then said to her, "Greek it is for dinner."

Carrie entered a dimly lit restaurant where the waiters spoke to each other in loud, incomprehensible bursts and hurried through the room with trays of intriguing items. Familiar and unfamiliar smells mingled, and over the next hour she tried foods she'd never tasted: lamb with goat's meat gravy, olives the size of golf balls, and dolmades, grape leaves stuffed with a blend of delicious items. With it came ouzo, the licorice-like liqueur Jack suggested was safest for the neophyte when mixed with water. After all that they had baklava, sticky and sweet. Everything was delicious.

As they ate, they agreed with Verna Symons that Stan's story made no sense. "Even so," Jack muttered, "We've got too many deaths to ignore what he said."

When they'd eaten, Jack said rest and time would help them see things more clearly. Carrie suggested taking a taxi back to the hotel, claiming she was too tired to walk a step farther. She could easily have made it, but she knew Jack was suffering despite his determination not to show it. As they parted at the elevator he said, "You can sleep in tomorrow. Our train isn't until afternoon, and I have some things to do here in town. I'll call you when I get in."

Unable to sleep in, Carrie was tired of her hotel room, nice as it was, by eight o'clock the next morning. She decided to enjoy the ambiance of the Palmer House until the stores opened then do some shopping. Exploring, she found a small restaurant off the lobby where she had breakfast. It was partitioned with glass, which was how, as she sat drinking excellent coffee served at exactly the right temperature, she spotted Jack moving smoothly on his crutches through the lobby. She guessed he was off to visit friends, or even family. Since he hadn't shared that he had a wife, he might also have a dozen siblings or several dozen cousins.

Shopping on Michigan Avenue, she considered buying something at Sak's Fifth Avenue—until she looked at a price tag. At Marshall Field's she found a little black halter dress that fell three inches above the knee and made her feel modern and even sexy. The price was steep but not impossible. Carrie wavered for a few minutes. She had no place to wear a dress like that, but what could it hurt to have one in the closet, just in case?

They checked out of the hotel at eleven, leaving their bags with the bellhop while they had lunch at Trader Vic's. Carrie liked the themed décor, different from the run-of-the-mill restaurants at home, the attentive waiters, and the excellent food. As they picked up their bags and left the hotel, she stopped to take one more look around and to listen to the sounds of Chicago. She liked it here, liked the el trains rumbling overhead and the feeling that everyone was in a hurry to get somewhere. She didn't even mind the bitter wind that pushed them on their way.

Jack had strapped the army back-pack he'd brought along on his back, and from it protruded a long box wrapped in brown paper. It had no markings on it, and Carrie kept her curiosity to herself, figuring he'd mention it if he felt like it. He never did.

CHAPTER TWENTY-TWO

They finished out the workweek at the office. Though Li didn't appear, she'd taken two messages while they were gone. The first number led to a man interested in locating his ex-wife, who had taken off with his three children. The second call was from Su Somers, and Jack called her to fill her in on Bartkowski's death. Su was quick to suggest it might be another murder, and he didn't disagree, though he mentioned the police theories of suicide or accidental death.

When Carrie got the mail, she found a check from the Callenders for closing the Tate case and a letter from the detective in Chicago, Sergeant Molineaux. She took it to Jack, who commented wryly, "And here I thought he promised help just to get rid of us."

The letter contained information on Jen Bartkowski's accident, typed by the Sergeant himself, Carrie guessed from the numerous errors as she read over Jack's shoulder. He'd spoken with the Wisconsin State Police. Mrs. Bartkowski's cause of death was head trauma from striking the steering wheel when the Corvair she was driving struck a tree. "Those things are death traps," Jack muttered.

Carrie took the letter and read it a second time. "Look at the physical characteristics." Handing it back to Jack, she ran a hand across her forehead, as if to encourage something that lay below its surface.

"Four feet, six inches, black hair."

"Asian."

Jack looked up at her. "Vietnamese?"

"I'd bet on it. Remember what I told you Todd tried to say?"

"Yeah. Namwise and kali something shur enz."

"I notice you seldom call it Vietnam. It's just 'Nam."

His face showed understanding, "'Nam wives. He was trying to say something about Vietnamese wives."

"And we've got a dead one, plus two husbands."

"But not Todd."

"No," she agreed. "Either he stumbled onto something he wasn't supposed to, or—"

"Or what?" Jack demanded.

"Or they were after you."

He thought about that for a while then nodded at his crutches. "That's not likely, since I'm pretty easy to spot with those. I think your first idea is closer to the truth. Crate's call sent Todd looking for something. When he found it, somebody killed him."

"But we don't know what Todd found."

Jack stared into space, recalling the last conversation they'd had. "He said he was going to search some records. What does that tell us?"

Carrie brushed some lint from her box-pleated skirt. "The courthouse has records of military service and marriages."

"Right. So we look up the names of our dead GIs."

"Shall I do that?

Jack shook his head. "I might see something that rings a bell. Plus I've got to start working with this." To Carrie's surprise, he stood up, wearing a sheepish grin and displaying two legs and two shoes.

"Jack!" she exclaimed. "You're trying the prosthesis."

"They fitted me for it when I came home, but I wasn't ready to deal with it." He seemed ashamed of himself. "I stormed out one day when they were trying to teach me to use the thing, told them I didn't want it. Todd wasn't happy with me for giving up, but I told him to shove it. It was as close to a fight as we ever had."

"I'll bet Todd understood."

"He wanted me to get on with life. I was too busy feeling sorry for myself."

Carrie had to resist the impulse to touch his shoulder. Instead she said briskly, "Well, you're past that now."

Jack immediately turned practical. "I'm a little shaky yet. The crutches will help with balance until I get the hang of it."

Carrie matched his light tone, gesturing at the snow falling outside the window. "That's wise, since it looks like winter's decided to settle in for a while."

***

Jack was gone for the rest of the morning, and in his absence, Carrie began the search for their client's missing ex-wife, Madeline Cabot. She'd left Genesee County without telling anyone where she was going, taking their three young children. Through court documents, Carrie learned the husband did indeed have visitation rights and had been faithful in paying child support. Talking to people Madeline had worked with at a small office-supply house, she began to suspect the woman had gone south.

"Maddy hates winter," said the clerk who answered the phone. In the background Carrie heard the hum and subsequent rattle of an adding machine as the woman totaled a purchase as she spoke. "She always talked about living where it's warm, but her in-laws were here, and Art wouldn't even discuss moving away from his mom and dad."

Madeline's boss recalled her mentioning Florida once. "I don't know what we were talking about, but she said she had a friend in New Port Richey. Oh, yeah, I wanted to do some deep-sea fishing, and she said it was easy to charter a boat there."

Armed with that information, Carrie used one of the many phone books Jack and Todd had collected to assist in such searches and began calling schools in the vicinity of New Port Richey, Florida. After three calls she found a secretary who cautiously admitted the Cabot children were enrolled at the school. That's all she'd tell a stranger.

Undaunted, Carrie called new number information and asked for M. Cabot in New Port Richey. No listing. Consulting a Florida map, she asked for M. Cabot in surrounding towns. Nothing. Finally, she asked the operator to check New Port Richey again, this time for Mrs. Cabot's maiden name, Madeline Jessup. That was under new listings, and the operator read off the number. "Is there an address with that?" There was. She had the information they'd been asked to find.

To make sure, she dialed the number in Florida. On the fourth ring, a woman's voice answered. "Is this the lady of the house?"

"Yes." The tone was grumpy, as if she'd been sleeping.

"Ma'am, do you have small children?"

"Three of them." There was pride in her voice.

"May I ask their ages?"

"The oldest is ten, Mari is nine, and Isaac is six."

"We're offering a special sale today on the Children's World Encyclopedia. It suits ages six to thirteen."

"I'm not interested." There was a harsh clunk as contact was broken on the Florida end, but Carrie had what she wanted. The names matched Cabot's children. She replaced her own phone in its cradle with a smile of satisfaction.

***

Jack entered the Records Department of the Genesee County Courthouse, unsure where to start. As he leaned his crutches against the counter, a pretty brunette rose from her desk and approached. She wore a fake-cashmere sweater in soft green with short green-and-black plaid skirt that emphasized slim legs covered in black-patterned nylons. Her perfume reminded him of flowers he'd noticed overseas, exotic and pleasing on some primitive level.

"Did you fall on the ice?" Her guess showed how close most people's imaginings stay to home.

"Something like that. My business partner came here a while ago to look up some information. I need to find out what he looked at."

"Can't you ask him?" The smile that accompanied the question was flirtatious.

A month ago Jack would have avoided her gaze, mumbled a reply, and beaten as quick a retreat as possible. Today he smiled back. Maybe Carrie isn't the only one who's growing. "He's not available."

She shrugged. "Lots of people come here to look things up. I'd need more to go on."

"It might have been military," Jack suggested. "My partner had a square-ish build, dark hair, and a chin like Dudley Do-Right."

"Do you mean Todd?" Just like that.

"Yeah, Todd Sachs."

"What happened to him?" Her fingers tapped at her lips, as if pushing angry words back. "We were going to go see *2001: A Space Odyssey* together, but he never called."

Jack shouldn't have been surprised. Todd would have moved quickly to get close to this lovely little number.

"I hate to be the one to tell you, but Todd was murdered." The girl's eyes grew big. "What he found out here might connect to why."

"Oh, no!" She put a hand on her lips in the classic gesture of disbelief. "I've been calling him all sorts of vermin, and the poor guy is dead!"

It took a few minutes to explain the basics of the situation and a few minutes longer for the clerk to collect her thoughts. Finally, Jack again approached the subject of Todd's visit.

At first, she was less than helpful, still fluttery from shock. "Of course we don't stand over people while they look at the books." She couldn't keep her hands still. They moved from her face to her hair and to the countertop as if seeking assurance that the world went on, even when someone you liked died a violent death.

"Of course you don't." Jack spoke softly, using a comforting tone. "But Todd was a talker. He would have told you what he was thinking."

"We did talk a bit." She was settling down now. "I remember he looked at military service records first. Then he left for a while." She frowned, remembering, and added, "He asked if there were pay phones he could use, and I told him they were downstairs." Later he came back up and looked through several listings: marriages, I think, or maybe census records. By that time, I was busy with someone else, and he helped himself. We're pretty informal around here."

Jack was disappointed. Past the brunette were shelves and shelves of huge books full of records. Where should he begin to look? "Will you let me see the military records for the past two years, please?"

Happy to be of help, she deposited a large binder on the counter with a thud. In it were typed listings of all those who'd served, but

153

after Jack perused them, he knew no more than he had before. Todd Sachs and Packard Somers had been honorably discharged from the U.S. Army, Crate in 1967 and Todd in April of this year.

When Jack slid the book back across the counter, the brunette remembered something. "Todd did ask how he could find out about marriages that took place overseas. I asked him if he had a war bride somewhere who might object to our going to the movies together, and he said no. He was checking for a friend."

It was interesting that Todd had connected the Vietnamese wives with Stan's accusations. Thanking the brunette, who smiled and suggested hopefully he could come back any time, he set his crutches under his arms and left the records office.

CHAPTER TWENTY-THREE

When Jack returned from the courthouse, he seemed tired, but Carrie could tell from the set of his jaw he wasn't giving in to it. "You know, I don't think you're supposed to wear that all day at first," she told him, wincing as he limped to his desk and dropped into his chair like a stone. "It's like wearing contact lenses. You get used to it slowly."

"What do you know about contact lenses?" he asked with an air of innocence that didn't fool Carrie for a second.

"How did you find out?"

"Your mother called." Jack raised his hands as if denying guilt. "Don't ask me how she found out, but she thought I should talk with you about the dangers, being a man of more experience in the world."

Carrie was exasperated. "I am in no danger."

Jack smiled despite the ache in both legs. "I have a feeling I'm seldom going to agree with your mother, and I'd like to see you try them if it makes you happy." In a burst of honesty he added, "But you look great the way you are."

Carrie blushed and looked away, which was how she caught a glimpse of a tiny pair of shoes sticking out from under the couch. Li's shoes. Jack's wife.

"Thank you," she replied stiffly, "but we were talking about you. You're no good to the agency if you collapse from overdoing it with the new leg."

"Point taken. Now how did things go on the Cabot case?"

When he heard how Carrie had located Mrs. Cabot, he commended her and confirmed she'd been wise to confirm it was the right Madeline Cabot with a phone call.

"I hope she didn't run away because Mr. Cabot was mean to her or anything like that," Carrie commented.

"She might just be vindictive or selfish. The courts did give him visitation rights."

"I'll call him this afternoon." She flipped her notebook closed and slid the pen into the wire loop on top. "What did you find out at the courthouse?"

"All they list is a man's name and address, dates of service, and rank achieved. Todd was there, Packard Somers was there, but no one else I recognized."

"Dead end?"

"I guess so." Jack reached for the lighter as if touching it could somehow bring Todd's message to him. "Next I'll get hold of this insurance agent Su mentioned. Su was going to try to find a number for him."

"I can give her a call, since Mr. Cabot doesn't get home from work until three." She rose from her chair, adding, "You might want to think about what I said. That leg isn't meant to be worn all day at first."

He nodded to show he'd heard, but Jack being Jack, the prosthesis stayed in place.

***

Jack stroked the engraving on Todd's lighter, trying to recall the faces of the men they'd served with. He'd had no contact with them, didn't even know in most cases if they'd made it home alive. His injury had caused a sudden separation from even those few he'd chummed with. Everyone had to deal with friends suddenly dead or gone from the group, and each man handled it in his own way. There were no cute get-well cards, for sure. Some came briefly and sat at the bedside of the wounded, trying to be cheerful. Others ignored them completely, as if they were dead. Many refused to even speak those names again, as if the bad luck might rub off and stick to their clothing.

After his injury Jack never saw the other men who'd sat around the poker table with him or slept in the bunks nearby. Though he'd never forget the smells of the country: the damp of mildew, the odor of fish, and the sweat of guys crammed together in too-hot conditions, he'd forgotten the individual men. Todd's face was the only one he remembered clearly, and Todd was gone forever.

He didn't even remember full names. A few habitual troublemakers came to mind, the memory there from having typed their names on discipline reports so many times.

Letting his mind work on it, Jack watched Carrie go about her tasks. She'd had a good time at the restaurant in Chicago, trying unfamiliar foods—

Just like that, a name came to mind, and it even had an address with it. Corfa, the guy they'd called The Greek, had once had escort duty with Jack. For three hours, while an incompetent company commander dithered and swore and yelled into a radio, the two MPs sat miserably in the monsoon rain. They'd talked about lots of things, starting with idiot officers, but eventually they'd come to post-war plans. Corfa said his family owned a restaurant in Manitowoc, Wisconsin.

"How did a bunch of Greeks get to Wisconsin?" Jack had asked.

"I think we took a wrong turn at Sicily," Corfa responded, his white teeth flashing in his tanned face.

What they'd had couldn't be called friendship: poker and jokes about the guy's fanatical cleanliness. Still, Corfa might know names or remember Sean Green, GI turned insurance agent. A name like his shouldn't be hard to track down in northern Wisconsin.

Jack picked up the phone and contacted Information. There was a listing for Corfa's Family Restaurant and two residential listings: a Stamos Corfa and a Nicholas Corfa, Nicholas—Nick—sounded right, but Jack bet he'd be at the restaurant this time of day. He wrote all three numbers down, thanked the operator, and dialed the restaurant.

A woman's voice answered on the third ring, sounding way too Brooklyn for Wisconsin. In the background he heard a blend of activities associated with meal preparation: dishes clattering, the sizzle of meat on a grill, and the whump of café doors settling back into place after someone passed through. "Is there a Corfa there who recently returned from Vietnam?"

"Who's asking?"

"I'm—I knew him over there, and I'd like to talk with him."

There was no answer, but the phone clunked, and he heard her call, "Nicco, some vet wants to talk to you."

There was muffled conversation and Jack heard, "How the hell would I know?"

Finally, a voice he recognized said tentatively, "Hello?"

"Nick Corfa? It's Jack Porter. The Joker."

"Jack? Jack Porter, well, I'll be damned." Corfa's face appeared in Jack's mind: sharp lines, a slightly feral smile, and a cleft chin. He'd often smelled like bleach: his clothes, his boots, even his skin had been subjected to the stuff lest he catch some dread tropical disease. "How you doin', man?"

"Pretty good, Nick, pretty good. Back at the family business, huh?"

"Yeah. My father wants to retire now that I'm home, so the place will be mine." Jack thought a restaurant was a good fit for a guy with a germ phobia, but he didn't' say it aloud. Corfa continued, "I'm gettin' married, too. That was her answered the phone."

"I'll bet she's great." Good public relations. Carrie would be proud.

"Yeah, she is."

That was it for small talk, so Jack came to the point. "Nick, I'm a private detective now, and I have bad news. Todd, you remember Todd Sachs?"

"Sure, everybody knows Todd."

"Todd was my partner, but he was murdered."

"Man, that's terrible. Murdered?"

"Another guy we knew, Crate Somers, is dead too."

"Was that the goofy little guy that followed Todd around all the time?"

"Yeah." Jack could picture Corfa rubbing his chin, as he often had when deciding whether to fold or not.

"He's dead, too?"

"They said it was an accident, but another vet, Stan Bartkowski, died too. All this in a week. He had called Crate claiming someone was trying to kill him."

"Don't remember Bartkowski."

"Todd called him Stosh."

"Yeah, that might ring a bell. He's dead too?"

"Drowned. The police think it might suicide. I think differently."

"Geez, Porter, you got a mess there. Where are you, anyway?"

"I live in Michigan. Listen, I wonder if you recall a guy named Sean Green. I'd like to talk to him, but I don't remember him from 'Nam."

"Green." Jack could almost hear Corfa's brain clicking through memories. "I don't think I knew a Green, but you meet a lot of guys."

"There's something else. Both Crate and Bartkowski had Vietnamese wives."

Corfa hesitated before commenting, "I guess we all could have had one of those."

"What do you mean?"

"There was this little gook that went around trying to hook GIs up with local girls. If their fathers had enough money, he'd set it up so the girls got to go to the states."

"How'd he get the men to agree?" Jack's head began to feel heavy, as if it couldn't hold what was coming.

"Sometimes he picked real lonely guys, the kind who didn't stand much chance of getting a girl back home." After a pause he added, "I heard he even worked on poor clods with bad wounds, telling them they'd get a woman to take care of them."

Jack kept his tone casual. "How do you know about this?"

"He tried it with me once, said if I'd marry one of his girls, I could divorce her when we got to the states. I sent him packing pretty damn fast, I can tell you. Told him I didn't need no slant for a wife. Somers fell for it, huh? His wife's a gook?"

"She's a widow now. Thanks for the information." He rang off before the blithely oblivious Corfa could insult him further.

***

"Tell me something, Jack," Todd said once when they were looking at office spaces for rent in the city. Jack had known a serious topic would follow the use of his real name. "How'd you and Li meet? We saw her that night at the bar, but you didn't know her then, right?"

"No," he admitted. He didn't want to discuss his marriage with Todd. For one thing it was an obvious failure, and Todd could see that. Jack hated Todd knowing Li didn't come home many nights, that she paid no attention to him most of the time. It would be worse if Todd knew he'd married her in a moment of despair, in fear he'd be alone for the rest of his life. Even half-conscious, Jack Porter, the guy who could handle any situation, should have been able to handle that.

Todd didn't drop it. At a stoplight he turned in the pickup seat and faced Jack directly, turning the volume down on Petula Clark's warbling. "I wondered if Kelly talked you into marrying her."

"Kelly? The card shark Kelly?"

Todd was silent for a moment. "After you...left, I heard rumors. Kelly was always looking for an angle, and what I heard was he took money from rich Vietnamese to get their daughters out of the country and away from the war."

"I met Li in a store in Phu Bai one day. We got to talking and hit it off. I liked her, and I thought she liked me." Jack let his tone signal the end of the conversation.

The light changed, and the ride continued in silence. Jack sat there, feeling sick to his stomach for the lies he'd told the only person on earth who might have understood why he'd done what he did.

CHAPTER TWENTY-FOUR

Li wandered into the office about a quarter after three, giving Carrie a curt greeting before peeking in at Jack, who was on the phone. Returning to the front, she stood staring out the window. The day was mild for November, and sunshine made it almost warm. A line of cars came by, horns beeping. The lead car, decorated with tissue flowers and a "Just Married" sign on either end, stopped in the middle of everything. Four people climbed out four doors and circled the car at a run: a laughing bride, a grinning groom, a giggling maid of honor, and the driver, a nervous-looking best man. The bride and groom stopped as they passed each other for a long kiss, which brought toots from car horns both in the wedding party and around it. Each then climbed back in the same door he or she had left, and the parade continued down Dort Highway.

Li looked at Carrie, who was watching and smiling, "Why they do that?"

"It's called a Chinese fire drill."

"Why they do it?" she repeated in an irritated tone.

"They're happy. It must have seemed like the right thing to do at the moment." The phone interrupted shrilly, and Carrie turned to answer it. Li stood staring out the window. Her beautiful face wrinkled in a sneer as she muttered, "And what about the next moment?"

***

VIETNAM, 1967

The night she first saw Jack Porter, Li had gone to a horrible local bar to meet a man who said he could get her out of Vietnam. The GI had been recommended to her father, a widowed general in the Army of the Republic of Vietnam with only one child, Li. The general had little faith in South Vietnam's future, and he'd decided he wanted his daughter out of harm's way. Eventually the communists would take over, he told her, in two years or three— whenever the Americans tired of spilling their blood far from home. What would happen then to those who'd stood for the republic? The thought was not pleasant to contemplate.

General Nguyen explained that his daughter must escape

Vietnam. He would pay whatever it took for her to do that. In return she'd help him get out once she was established in America. Of course an ARVN general could not be discovered arranging such a thing. It would mean an end to his post and possibly his life. Li herself would have to meet with the man who'd approached him, Sean Green.

Green didn't show, and she sat in that squalid place for an hour, surrounded by lewd comments and the smell of cheap liquor. Eventually she gave up and started for home, but a drunken soldier attacked her when she left the hut. Two Americans, some kind of army policemen, intervened and saved her from rape and possible murder. If she'd been calmer and less afraid and angry, she might have bypassed Green altogether, but Li wasn't used to controlling her temper.

The next morning, she couldn't forget the one with blue eyes and light, light hair. A few days later, in one of those odd coincidences life offers, the same young American appeared in her life a second time. He followed her into a store and hung around, obviously as taken with her looks as she was with him. Li filed the information away for future use. She liked the crispness of his movements, the watchful posture, as if he were ready for any eventuality. If she had to marry an American, Li chose him.

Her father sent Uncle Ho to find out what he could about the man. His name was Jack Porter, they learned. Ho approached him with the marriage proposal, but Porter refused. That made Li so angry she broke several of her favorite knick-knacks. When she calmed enough to consider her next step, she decided Ho had been too blunt and scared the man off. Ho apologized a thousand times, offering to contact Sean Green, an American who worked with him on such schemes. A day later Ho reported Green would sound Porter out at the first opportune moment.

That was when a land mine changed everything. Uncle Ho reported Porter was in the hospital, his leg gone. Li was furious, and more small bits of furniture were destroyed. She'd found someone who suited her, but he'd become a cripple. Why was life so unfair?

Within a day, Sean Green visited with Uncle Ho, the latter dwarfed by his bear-like companion. Ho served as interpreter, since Li's English was poor. Green, a handsome man with a ready laugh and no patience for Asian politeness, came right to the point. He surprised Li with the claim Porter's injury was a good thing for her.

"He was a tough guy before," he contended, "but now he'll be off-balance and confused. His confidence is shattered, he's dopey with pain meds, and he's scared to death. We can talk him into anything."

"But he has no leg," Li objected. "How would we live?"

Green laughed, showing large, white teeth. "Porter's eligible for a pension from the U.S. government for the rest of his life. And you? Once you get to the States, you'll have all kinds of prospects." One hand rose as if to touch her arm, but he thought better of it and let it drop to his side. "All you have to do is remain beautiful." He looked at her in a way that would have made her father furious. "And you can't help doing that."

Another woman might have smiled to acknowledge the compliment. Though she savored it, Li gave no response. Green was undaunted, and his gaze said he understood and even approved of her haughty behavior.

Li paced the garden for an hour after Green and Ho left. Did she want to burden herself with a crippled man? Still, her father wanted her to do this, and Porter was handsome. She wondered how much money the wealthy American government paid a man who'd lost a limb. Probably enough. Possibly a lot.

Did she have a choice? The home of her childhood was fast becoming the land of bomb craters and terror. Tired of worrying about the future, Li made up her mind. If Green could talk Porter into this marriage, she'd smile and say the words. Once she made it to America she would succeed. If Porter wasn't the man she wanted him to be, surely there would be other men.

***

Carrie was on the phone when the other line rang. Li had left the office in a sulk, saying nothing to either of them about her destination. Jack answered and found it was Su Somers. "I finally found the insurance policy. It fell behind the desk. The company is Duncan Family Insurance in Gavenna, Ohio, but I can't find Sean Green's name on it anywhere. The line for the agent's signature has the name Mark Bolenz on it." Su seemed apologetic. "I had my mother-in-law look at it too, in case I am missing something, but that's what it says. Shall I call the company?"

"If you don't mind, I'll do it," Jack answered. Su gave him a phone number for the main office. "I'll call you back soon."

It took only a few minutes to reach a prim but helpful personnel manager, Mr. Benac, who checked his records and reported, "No Sean Green employed here, not in the last three years. The older records are stored in the basement."

"This policy was written six months ago. Does the name Mark Bolenz ring a bell?" Jack idly watched the clock's second hand pulse as it ticked off twelve seconds.

"Mr. Bolenz worked for us until recently," Benac reported.

"He left the company?"

"As of October 30."

"Do you have any idea where he went?"

The manager put the phone to his chest, and Jack heard muffled voices, "Anybody know where Mark Bolenz went when he left here?" There was a pause. "It's some private detective from Michigan." Benac returned to the phone. "Someone here thinks Bolenz took a job in Florida. Is there a problem with a policy?"

"We don't know of anything improper," Jack replied. "A man died, and the company paid his widow."

"That's as it should be," Benac said righteously.

"Yes, but the agent said his name was Green."

Benac thought about that. "Perhaps he was a trainee. They travel with experienced men and observe their work before taking a territory of their own."

"Then shouldn't someone have been with Green?"

"Yes." He sounded irritated to admit there might be faults in their system. "If an agent let a trainee go out on his own, we would definitely want to discuss with him his responsibilities to the company and his clients. It doesn't do to take an afternoon off because there's someone who can cover for you."

Or several months. "Shouldn't Green be on your payroll now if he was a trainee?"

"Unless he never actually hired on." Benac struggled with the company's image versus telling the truth, and Jack heard tapping that was probably a pen on the desktop. "I can't guarantee an agent wouldn't subcontract the work. They cover more territory that way, and as long as they personally check things over, we don't complain?"

"So someone might pay Green to do the legwork while he stays at a central location and does the paperwork."

The man seemed relieved that Jack made it sound reasonable. "Yes. It's against official policy, but an ambitious agent might do that, blending his expertise and another's time to maximum value."

"My client says the agent paid her in cash. Is that usual?"

Another pause, a few more taps. "Is there some reason why your client might not be able to handle the paperwork? Is she blind, or incapacitated in some way?"

Jack considered it from the company's point of view. "She's foreign-born, only been here for a short time."

"That would explain it. We stress personal service, coming into people's homes and all, so the agent would have wanted to be sure she got her money. He probably figured she needed help with the language and the procedures."

"She said Green paid the funeral expenses and then gave her the remainder."

Now the manager's manner became less defensive. "As I said, personal service. You won't get that at Sears."

"Right." Jack consulted a list of notes he'd jotted prior to making the call to be sure he'd covered everything. "One more question: what amount was paid on the policy?"

It probably wasn't something he should reveal, but Jack had established enough rapport that Benac never hesitated. "Thirty thousand dollars."

Covering his surprise, Jack thanked the manager and hung up. He stared at the phone, absently wiping away the moist handprint he'd left on the black plastic headset. In the outer office Carrie was explaining to Mr. Cabot they didn't have the time to go to Florida. Cabot apparently argued his case, but Carrie was firm and finally rang off. She turned to see Jack watching her and grimaced in mild frustration.

"Mr. Cabot was determined we should go to Florida and speak with his wife. He doesn't trust himself to face her, but he doesn't want to set the police on his children's mother." She rose and picked up a bowl of spice drops from her desk, took one for herself and brought the bowl in to offer them to Jack. "He offered to pay our expenses, but I told him we couldn't."

Jack looked thoughtful as he chose a red one. It wasn't his candy choice he was considering; he always chose red and after that white, green, and yellow last. "We need to make a couple of calls," he told her as he chewed, "but after that you might be able to call Mr. Cabot back and tell him we've changed our minds."

CHAPTER TWENTY-FIVE

As Carrie watched with a puzzled expression, Jack re-dialed Duncan Family Insurance, this time asking for the claims department. When a woman answered, he identified himself as Stanley Bartkowski. "I'm sorry to bother you, but I lost my copy of my life insurance policy. My wife has died, so I need to change some things."

"I'm so sorry to hear it, Mr. Bartkowski," she said with professional sympathy. "What's your policy number?"

"That's just it, I can't find the policy." He gave her the address they had unearthed for the Bartkowskis in Waukegan, Illinois.

"I'll have to leave my desk to find that information. Shall I call you back?"

"I'll stay on the line." The phone clicked, indicating he was on hold, and Jack whistled softly and dug for another red spice drop.

It was some time before the woman returned. "I have the policy, Mr. Bartkowski. What do you need to know?"

"I've forgotten some details. My wife handled all those things..." He let his voice trail off as if grief prevented his finishing. "Can you tell me how much I'm insured for?"

"Your death benefit is thirty thousand dollars." He circled what he'd already noted during the previous call.

Reading upside down from her chair across the desk, Carrie's eyes widened. She tapped the last zero and looked at Jack questioningly. He nodded. "I need to change the beneficiary, but my agent left the company. I don't know who's got my territory now."

There was a pause as the clerk verified Jack's statement. "Your new agent is Carleton Stiles." She gave Jack a phone number.

"Thanks a lot."

"We're glad to be of help," the woman told him, "but please put the information in a safe place this time. My records show you requested a copy of your policy in mid-September, and we sent one out right away."

"I promise not to be so careless again." As it if were a last-minute thought, he asked, "Do you have an address for my old agent, Mark Bolenz? He's in Florida now, but I'd like to let him know about my wife's death. We served together in Vietnam."

"I'm sorry, but we cannot give out that information." She sounded like his sixth-grade math teacher.

"I understand."

"Once again, our condolences on your loss."

Jack thanked the woman and hung up. "Well, it was worth a try."

"Let me take a stab at it." With a mischievous grin, Carrie took the phone from Jack's hand and dialed the number a third time. Checking his notes, she said, "Administration, please," and waited for an answer.

"What are you—?"

Carrie stopped him with a hand as the call went through. "Hi, this is Cheryl over in Mr. Benac's office. He needs to contact a guy who used to work here, name of Mark Bolenz, B-O-L-E-N-Z. Can you give me a current on him?" Seconds later she was writing it down, "Thanks, I owe you one." She handed the note to Jack triumphantly. "His final paycheck went to a post office box in Tampa, Florida."

Jack affected a scolding tone. "You've become scheming and devious, Miss Walsh."

"It's all thanks to you, Mr. Porter," she accused with a chuckle. "Once I was an honest, upright secretary. Now I've sunk to deceiving honest, upright secretaries."

Sobering, she frowned at his notes. "I guess you're thinking Mr. Cabot will bankroll your trip to Florida, and while you're down there you'll look up Mark Bolenz."

"Right. When Stan asked for a copy of his policy in September, probably after the first attempt on his life, two things happened. He and his wife became targets, and Mark Bolenz quit his job."

Carrie had been pacing, but she stopped. "Stan told me Jen saw Sean Green with a ghost."

"Green and Bolenz could be the same person. Crate knew him as Green in the army, but he's taken the name Bolenz for some reason."

They were silent for a few moments, and Jack took out the Nerf ball and squeezed it between his fingers. "Here's a theory: Green writes policies on guys who think he's their buddy since they served together. He makes them out for a lot more than they should be and gives the company and the client different sets of papers."

Carrie dropped into the chair opposite Jack and leaned her elbows on the desk. "How could he get such large policies on average guys like Crate and Bartkowski?"

"Fudge the details, I suppose." Jack dug out more red candies as he spoke. "Instead of a mechanic, Crate becomes the owner of the dealership."

Carrie finally realized what was under discussion. "You're saying this guy sets up big insurance policies on people then kills them and keeps the difference between what he gives the beneficiary and what the policy was written for?"

"It's pretty smooth, actually. The widows aren't likely to question the system, being new here. The deaths happened miles apart from each other, in different states, and they appeared to be accidents."

"How did he cash checks made out to the beneficiaries?"

"I don't know."

The exterior door opened, and they looked up to see Li returning. Squinting into the darker space of Jack's office she saw the two of them, sharing spice drops and earnest discussion. Her face registering disapproval, she swept through the place, picking up various items she'd left lying around. When she had everything, she gave them an angry glare over her shoulder and left, pushing the door open with more force than necessary.

Carrie searched Jack's face before she spoke again, "Remember Jeffrey Mancuso, the hockey fan who cheated the Callenders?"

"Yeah," Jack answered.

"He hired Elaine Harris to set Jim Callender up. What if Green hired an Asian woman to play the part of Su Somers?"

Jack nodded. "Sure. He calls the bank and says he's bringing in a client's wife to cash her insurance check. He's got agency ID, and he says she doesn't know much English."

"She'd have to have identification."

"Which isn't hard to fake. All Asians look alike to Americans, right?"

Carrie ignored the bitterness in his voice. "So he sets up an appointment, takes his ringer to the bank, they cash the check. Then he pays her off, gives Su a small part of it, and keeps the rest."

Jack sat back in his chair, resting Buddy—as he'd dubbed his prosthesis—on a wastebasket. Carrie resolved to make him a padded footstool for Christmas. "It would take a lot of nerve."

"Sean Green is an artist when it comes to scams. He arranged the marriage between Crate and Su, probably with the help of Uncle Ho."

"I thought Su said Ho wasn't in on it."

"I think they worked together, each working the system from his side." He shifted the leg again. "When Green's tour ended, he came home and started taking advantage of the same guys a second time."

"He must be a real charmer."

"He knows how to push the right buttons. Crate was wounded, worried his parents would always have to take care of him."

Carrie felt her cheeks warm as she took a bold step. "How did they get to you?"

Jack's face registered shock, anger, and finally disgust. "I was just plain stupid."

Carrie's face softened. "You were traumatized, in pain and in shock. Not a good time to make an important decision."

"No." He left it at that. Carrie thought it might have made him feel better to tell her about it, but he didn't seem ready, so she left it alone.

"Green sells insurance now."

"Maybe he was in it before the war, I don't know. Guys like Crate Somers come home wanting to make their lives normal, to put Vietnam behind them."

"Then there could be other cases and more men in danger." A frown etched a line on Carrie's forehead. "Bartkowski was an unemployed drunk. How did he buy a policy?"

"Green might have convinced Jen she needed to insure Stan in case he drank himself to death."

"But Stan discovered the policy was for a lot more than they thought."

"Right. He calls Crate and Crate calls Todd, believing he can solve any problem."

Carrie shook her head doubtfully. "This all sounds so weird. Are you sure we're on the right track?"

"Remember what Todd said to you? 'Viet wives, kali, something shur-enz.' Insurance."

"Not assurance, insurance."

"What he learned that day got him killed." Jack glanced away, his gaze lowered. "He wouldn't have told me what he suspected until he had proof, since I was so touchy about the subject of my marriage."

"Then the man in the alley I saw was Green?"

"And whoever helps with the dirty work, the guy Jen said was a ghost. They didn't have time to set up an accident for Todd."

"They made it look like a random crime, a mugging."

Easing his leg to the floor, Jack took up a pen. "Call Mr. Cabot and see if the offer is still open for Florida. You can handle Mrs. Cabot while I try to track down Bolenz."

"I'm going again?"

He shrugged. "Li did okay last week, and it's good for her to have something to do."

Li did drift along, apparently without purpose, but a disturbing idea had begun nagging at Carrie's mind. If Sean Green needed a Vietnamese woman to play Su Somers, wasn't it likely he'd go to someone he knew, someone close by? Someone like Li Porter?

CHAPTER TWENTY-SIX

While Carrie wondered if Li Porter was involved in Sean Green's crimes, Li herself entered a house where she spent most of her nights. Situated in an exclusive neighborhood off Miller Road, the place was nothing short of elegant, with marble floors and high, arched windows that overlooked a small copse of elm trees. Her footsteps echoed hollowly across the foyer and went silent as she stepped onto the deep pile carpeting of the den. There was no one else to hear. The place belonged to Sean Green until the end of December, though he'd grinned and added "sort of" to the statement of ownership.

After the holidays, Li would have to decide what she would do. Sean planned to leave Flint, and Jack didn't want her, wouldn't care if he never saw her again.

He'd been attracted by her beauty, but that wasn't enough anymore. In the early days she might have won him over, but Li had never in her life gone out of her way for another person. She didn't know how to begin, even in the moments when she wanted to.

As a result, they'd begun living inside themselves, neither knowing what the other was thinking. Though Jack was never unkind, it was obvious he wished she was out of his life. That was when Sean Green had reappeared in hers.

***

VIETNAM, 1967

The night Li left Vietnam forever was both exciting and disappointing. Green had warned her to be ready to go when he came for her, so she'd put a few things in a bag and set it beside her bed. When she got to America there'd be all new things, beautiful things. Every American woman had all the clothes she wanted.

Green warned it would be a cold, rough trip. "GI wives aren't a high priority, with the war and all. You'll be transported in whatever plane has room and is going in the right direction."

The plane was a C-130. Green, who picked up another young woman after stopping for Li, hurried them up the ladder as the engines roared to life. He left them in the care of a dour man in coveralls who pointed for them to sit and strapped them into seats of nylon webbing on the side of the plane without so much as a word of reassurance. The other seats remained unoccupied. The center area was empty except for two large crates.

As the plane took off, the noise grew to a deafening whine. Frightened, the women covered their ears and shut their eyes. The place smelled of fuel and what was probably vomit. Though Li was frightened, she was at the same time interested in the process of flight, which she'd never experienced. The other girl, whose name was Su sat with her head lowered throughout the trip, lips clamped together to keep from being sick.

When they landed at another base, the same man motioned for them to follow him down a rickety metal stairway. He pointed to a truck with canvas over the back such as Li had often seen carrying troops, and the two women climbed in. Whatever had been carried there last had left an oily spot in the center of the bed, which they tried to avoid sitting in as the vehicle lurched away. They rode for some time, a bumpy, stuttering ride, as if the driver didn't know how to handle the shifting mechanism. When the truck stopped, a man who was Asian but not Vietnamese opened the flap and politely invited them in their own language to step down.

They were outside a hotel, but Li couldn't read the sign over the door. The man informed them it was the Bangkok Blue Dragon. Bangkok meant Thailand, which gave Li some satisfaction. At least she knew where she was.

They were given a room in the hotel and told to stay quiet. The man took a picture of each of them against a white wall with an ancient box camera. Another day he took them shopping and bought them clothing very different from what they owned. Li loved the new items, telling herself that soon she would have a whole closet full of such things, all in modern style and new, synthetic fabrics.

Finally, Mr. Ghiavali gave them passports and coached them on their part in the rest of the journey. "I will take you to America," he told them. "You must do exactly as I tell you."

Once she got over her initial fears, Su didn't question anything, but Li had begun to be concerned. The lonely flight at one a.m. and the newly created documents caused her to conclude the U.S. authorities had no idea two GI brides were entering the country. That didn't matter to her, but it did make her wonder. If the government didn't know they were coming, were they aware there'd been two weddings?

They came into the States with no problem, landing at O'Hare airport with only fatigue to dampen their excitement. Crate, who'd been stateside for weeks, was there to meet Su, pale but grinning like a baboon. His parents accompanied him, as was proper, but Li found the Somers family loud and common. Su's father-in-law was obscenely fat, and his wife smelled like medicine. Li could barely be civil.

Packard and his parents insisted on taking them to lunch, but by the end of the meal even the older couple felt Li's disdain. Despite that, Su's mother-in-law invited Li to stay with them until Jack was able to come for her. Her strong "No!" caused Su to frown in irritation. There was relief on all sides when the Somers family departed for Michigan, leaving Li on her own in Chicago.

Those first weeks were frightening. Jack was in the U.S., she didn't know where, receiving therapy. Using money Jack sent, Mr. Ghiavali found an apartment and helped Li achieve a rudimentary understanding of the necessities of her new life.

Eventually, Ghiavali returned to Thailand and Li was alone. She spent several days in the apartment, terrified of venturing outside alone. When she absolutely had to, the experience wasn't as bad as she feared. A city was a city, and there were always people who would stop to help a pretty young foreigner who demanded, "Fish? Where buy fish?" After a few times Li began to enjoy deciding her own schedule and finding new experiences each day.

When Jack finally appeared, they were embarrassed and ill at ease with each other. The handsome, confident man she'd been attracted to was gone. He was pale and reticent, avoiding the eyes of those he spoke to. Though Li tried to appear willing to keep her end of the bargain, she was disgusted by his injury and irritated by his presence. Jack saw it immediately and withdrew even further.

Sick of everything military, he'd left the doctors' care halfway through fittings for his artificial limb. There followed two months of depression, when he stared all day at a small black-and-white television, hardly speaking. A pall descended over the apartment, the TV laugh track a pitiful replacement for genuine communication. Never the patient type, Li began going out at night to escape Jack's dour mood. There was a club not far from their apartment, one of the discotheques she had read about but never experienced. The music was so loud no one could talk anyway, so looks and a cool smile were all she needed to make an impression. In almost no time she met people who better fit her idea of the American lifestyle. Jack hardly seemed to notice.

Within a short time Li and Jack were two people who shared an apartment and nothing else. Li stayed only because Jack's disability pay meant they could live comfortably without working, something Li had no intention of ever stooping to.

The call from Todd Sachs changed everything. He was six months behind Jack returning to the states, physically unscathed by his tour. Todd was shocked at how low Jack's morale had gone, and Li sensed he blamed her, at least in part.

Todd came to Chicago full of plans for a detective agency. Li didn't understand most of it, since he talked even faster than most Americans, but his enthusiasm was contagious. They would move to Flint. He'd find them an apartment. Though it sounded silly to Li, she had to admit Todd's proposal made a change in Jack. For the first time, he took an interest in living. He even talked to her about it.

"Li, this is something I want to do. I know I haven't been easy to live with, but I'll try to make it up to you. Todd will help us."

Li liked Chicago. She'd learned to navigate the El. She could spend hours shopping. At the clubs her looks attracted men despite her poor English. Flint would be very different. Even Todd admitted that.

Li didn't like Todd Sachs. She sensed his negative opinion of her and feared he might encourage Jack to take more interest in her activities. Still, she agreed to the move. Something in Jack's changed mood was appealing, as if the man she'd chosen might yet re-emerge.

The tiny apartment in Flint smelled like dust. Here there was no elevated train, only a smelly bus, and her foreign looks and speech were cause for distrust. Every day, as Jack became more animated and excited about the business he and Todd were creating, Li wilted farther into sulky silence. Her unhappiness focused on Todd, who'd brought them there to rot.

"Your friend Todd brought strawberry today," she told Jack once. "Why he bring us this? I no cook strawberry."

"You don't have to cook them. You eat them like this," Jack responded, biting a juicy example in half.

"I no like this." She swatted away the carton he offered her. "Tell him no bring more. Why he give us things?"

Jack had tried to explain. "Todd has no family. I have no family—except you," he amended quickly. "Todd's brother died in the war, and I'm sort of his replacement."

"What replacement?"

"His brother. I'm like Todd's brother."

"I understand. You hurt. He take care of you."

Jack frowned. "It's not like that with Todd. He doesn't feel sorry for me, he wants to..." He stopped, unable to put into words the difference between Todd's help and what the rest of the world offered. Li turned away, uninterested.

Within a month of Todd's arrival home, the Eagle Agency was nearly ready. Todd and Jack spent their days there, so Li was alone in the apartment when Sean Green showed up.

She answered the door to find him smiling at her in the old, half-charming, half-sneering way. He had a wolfish charm, and even his hair was bristly and brindled. His green eyes glowed with an inner fire Li recognized as desire: desire for things, desire for power, desire for her.

"Good afternoon, Mrs. Porter. Do you remember your old friend Sean?" He touched her arm in a strangely intimate gesture.

Li felt a thrill of excitement. Green radiated strength, sexuality, and a kind of atavism that spoke to her own self-centeredness.

Neither would ever trust the other, but they recognized a commonality that might benefit them both.

"Please come in."

His eyes took in the smallness of the place and her discontent with one sweeping glance. "Where is Mr. Porter?"

"He and Todd Sachs work on their business." She tried to keep her voice level, but contempt colored the last word.

Green seemed to understand that she'd expected more. She'd thought, as so many did, that every American drove a Cadillac and dined out in restaurants several times a week. "Are you getting out a bit? Seeing the night life?"

"What is life in this town? Dirty factory workers drink beer until they go to sleep."

He raised a brow. "I can see you haven't met the right people. Shall we see what we can find together?"

Li's petulance evaporated. "Yes. I like this very much."

Sean removed a folded sheaf of bills from his pocket and peeled off two crisp fifties. "Get yourself something nice to wear, and this evening I'll show you some places you'll enjoy." As she took the proffered bills, his hand closed over hers briefly.

"You very kind."

Green laughed. "It will be worth it to have a woman as beautiful as you at my side, Mrs. Porter." He asked lightly, "What will you say to Jack about where you're going?"

Li lifted an eyebrow. "What I always say. I go out."

Green nodded. "I'll be out front at eight, but let's keep my visit our little secret." He ran a hand down her cheek lightly. "I'll see that you enjoy your evenings, and you can tell me what your husband is up to."

After that Li and Sean Green met often. Eventually he'd invited her to stay at the house, which was much more to her taste than the apartment. She'd been nervous the first time she spent the night with Green, wondering what Jack's reaction would be. He'd said nothing. He didn't care what she did.

Green took care to see that Li had everything she wanted, and they became lovers almost casually. Li had no delusions she was Sean's only woman, but she believed he liked her best.

Sean came and went frequently. When he was away, Li often went back to the apartment, though she didn't know why. It certainly wasn't the atmosphere. The drab furniture was depressing after Sean's stolen palace, and the pitifully inadequate, noisy air conditioner made her head ache. Once during the summer Jack had taken enough notice to talk with her about dangers a woman alone might face in the city. When Li laughed and told him she had a strong man to protect her, he retreated into his shell, his face closing like a door.

In September Sean proposed she go on a trip with him. He had some business she might be able to help with. They would spend a few days in Chicago if she liked. Once again, he gave her money with which to buy clothes for the trip and even made suggestions as to what would be appropriate. They were gone almost a month, and the experience brought the most contentment Li had known in a long time. Dining in fine restaurants, visiting night clubs, and sleeping until noon in fine hotels were things she'd always wanted. As she soaked in the hotel spa, baked in the sauna, and allowed herself to be anointed with lightly scented, full-bodied oils, Jack Porter seldom entered her mind.

In return for his generosity, Sean asked little of her. She accompanied him when asked to and did as she was told, signing as she was taught. Only once was their peace disrupted. A woman Li knew from home saw her waiting for Sean on Michigan Avenue and hurried to her, thrilled to meet an old acquaintance. Jen's flow of Vietnamese made Li feel at home, and the two women talked until Sean and his business associate came along.

The change in Jen had been abrupt. She'd gone pale, excused herself in unfinished phrases, and scurried away. Sean had seemed unhappy, but his urbane manner soon returned. Li recalled his comment to the man beside him. "We'll have to see to that, won't we, Greg?" He'd left Chicago the next morning but encouraged Li to stay at the hotel and enjoy herself.

A few weeks later Sean called from Flint. He needed her back there, at least temporarily. "I need to know what Jack is up to," he told her. "Todd was killed by muggers, and I'm worried about him." After he explained the unfamiliar term to her, he went on. "I thought Jack would give up this crazy detective agency idea, but he's going through with it." Sean paused and Li heard the threat in his voice. "I hope he doesn't get in the way of our plans."

So, Li showed up at the Eagle Agency office, which smelled of mimeograph ink and potpourri, with no explanation of where she'd been. Jack requested none, as if her absence or presence made no difference to him.

The jarring note was the woman, Carrie Walsh. Though she was careful to be polite, Li's presence made her uncomfortable. Li took fully advantage of that. The fact she had no further use for Jack didn't mean she'd step out of the way so some mouse-like creature could have him. Li was surprised that it bothered her, but the way Jack looked at the Mouse caused her pain.

Soon the Mouse began to be more confident. First her hair changed dramatically. Gradually, her clothing became more flattering. Even her posture improved. She met Li's eyes when she spoke and no longer blushed when "Jack" slipped out instead of "Mr. Porter."

Li toyed with the idea of winning back Jack's affection to spite the Mouse, but in the end, she convinced herself it didn't matter. It was enough to see him live each day knowing she was his wife. No matter how attracted he might be to his partner, he couldn't change that.

CHAPTER TWENTY-SEVEN

Jack and Carrie took a longer than usual lunch hour to replenish their office supplies. Though neither of them said it, they didn't talk about the case when Li was present. Her obvious interest made Carrie uneasy, but in the truck they could speak freely.

Jack watched the road carefully as he drove, since a sleety rain was falling. He'd turned the defroster on full to warm the windshield, and Carrie found herself blinking repeatedly to keep her contacts from drying out.

"All it takes is nerve," Jack said when Carrie expressed disbelief at the boldness of the insurance scheme. He could have mentioned guys in 'Nam who had learned to take their chances when they came. The ruthless ones learned they could get away with a lot. Officers who were incompetent sometimes didn't live long enough to face the enemy. Peasant girls who wandered alone into the jungle failed to return to their villages. Once some men were taught to kill the barriers fell, and it no longer mattered who died. Anyone who got in the way was fair game. You could see it in their eyes.

***

VIETNAM, 1967

Greg Laughton had those eyes. He'd been around much longer than Todd or Jack, was on his third tour. Part of a reconnaissance unit that slid into the jungle late at night and stayed out for days, Greg often told stories when he returned that Jack didn't want to hear. Kelly liked him, so he ended up at a couple of their poker games. Jack sat through the first one but was sickened by Laughton's enjoyment of the freedom war gave him to dispense with any humanity he might once have had. Even his milder stories, such as using a farmer's only water buffalo for target practice, left Jack furious. After the first time, if Laughton showed up Jack made an excuse and left the game.

Each time, Laughton noticed and made a derisive little clicking sound with his tongue that irritated Jack still more. Todd explained the stories away as so much bull, but Jack had known others like Greg in Chicago. Born to be cruel, they were always looking for someone to practice on.

Jack felt no sorrow when it was reported Laughton was killed in a firefight a few clicks to the north. A mortar shell had landed directly on his position, Todd reported, and Laughton had been incinerated. It was a fitting start for the hell Jack was pretty sure the guy merited.

***

Carrie arranged for the two of them to fly to Tampa, where she'd rent a car and drive up Highway 19 to see what the situation was with the Cabot children and their mother. Jack would check into the whereabouts of Sean Green, alias Mark Bolenz. They wouldn't bill Cabot for Jack's expenses, only Carrie's.

The last thing Carrie did was call her mother and tell her about the trip, knowing as she dialed that it meant trouble. Her grip on the phone was so tight it hurt her hand, and she made herself relax.

"You're going to Florida?"

"Yes, mom. On business."

"Alone?"

She sighed. Truth or lie, she was in for it. Truth then. "With Mr. Porter."

"And who else?"

"No one else."

"Sweetheart—" Endearments were the worst possible sign.

"Mom, it's business. We have to track down a man's children because they were taken away by their mother."

"He probably deserved it."

"We don't know that."

"Does Jack understand your reputation could be ruined?"

"Mom, traveling for work is something people do all the time."

"My daughter doesn't. Staying in a hotel with a man!"

Carrie couldn't help but smile. "There are lots of men in hotels, Mom. I'm not sleeping with any of them."

The conversation wound on, but agreement came no closer. Carrie finally made up a story. "I have to go. Someone's here." She hung up, shaking her head. There was no pleasing her mother: three months ago she claimed Carrie had no life and never went anywhere.

Now she argued her daughter should stay home and do nothing.

Before they left Flint, Jack had several things he wanted to accomplish. First, he called Detective Molineaux in Chicago and asked if Jen Bartkowski had indeed been Vietnamese. "No way of knowing," he replied. "She had a passport, and the picture was of her, but the number belongs to one Nan Ghiavali, born in Bangkok."

"Can you find out where the real Nan Ghiavali is?"

"Porter, I have a job. I don't need you to find me things to do."

"One favor and I'll go away. I'm leaving for Florida in an hour."

"That makes me jealous, but I'll call you back."

As they waited, Carrie read Jack's note and tapped the name Ghiavali excitedly. "Jack, there was a man here one day, talking to Li. His name was Ghiavali, and he's Thai. He was headed for Chicago."

"He's the transporter then." Using their second line, he called Su and confirmed that Ghiavali was the one who'd escorted her and Li to the U.S. He spent some time questioning her on the details of the trip then thanked her, promising to call when they knew more.

"It sounds like they were smuggled out of Vietnam on a supply plane," he told Carrie. "How would they know it wasn't the way things were done? They stayed in Bangkok while Ghiavali prepared the false documents. They came to the States with him, probably traveling as his daughters. Who'd notice it's different girls each time?"

Molineaux called back. Nan Ghiavali and her sister Rhee were students at Northwestern University. Both were present and in good academic standing. "By the way, you asked me to check for drugs in Bartkowski's body. Nothing except lots of alcohol in his blood, but a bruise on the side of his head makes the M.E. suspicious. Could be accidental, he says, but the odds are against it."

"Thanks a lot. I'll think of you when it's eighty degrees." Jack turned back to Carrie. "I'll bet the records show those girls traveling between here and Thailand several times in the last two years."

Picking out a phone book, Jack located the number for the United States Department of Immigration and Naturalization. After being cycled through several offices, he found someone with access to records and held a long conversation.

Hearing his questions, Carrie began to understand what he was thinking. She listened as Jack learned Li Kai Baht had never entered the United States, according to government records. Nor had Li Porter or Su Somers. There was no record of marriage between Jack, Stanley Bartkowski, or Packard Somers and any Vietnamese national.

As he replaced the phone in its cradle, Jack turned to Carrie with a stunned look on his face. "No record of Li, Su, or Jen entering this country."

"Maybe it takes a while for the records to get updated."

Jack looked at his watch. "We've got to go or we'll miss our plane. Lock the office. Li can use her key when she gets here." Carrie sensed he wanted to be out of there before he had to face the woman who had lied to him for months. Gathering their suitcases, they walked to the corner where the taxi Carrie had arranged met them.

The business of travel absorbed the next hour, but once on the plane, Jack took up the questions on both their minds. "Okay. Green takes money from wealthy Vietnamese families, promising them security in America, but the women are brought here illegally."

"Do you think the wives know?"

"I doubt it," Jack replied. "They were disoriented, scared, and hopeful. They wouldn't question the procedures."

A stewardess passed along the rows, checking preflight compliance. She was pretty, as they all were, and by airline rules she'd be single as well. Her gaze lingered a second longer than necessary on Jack's face. He didn't notice, but Carrie did.

As the woman closed overhead compartments with a series of decisive clicks Carrie said, "The GI's think their wives were okayed by the U.S. government, but it was all a show."

Jack rubbed a hand through his hair. "I never even questioned it."

"You had other things to think about," Carrie reminded him

gently.

"But in the months since then I never asked myself where the paperwork was. The army, immigration, all the government stuff that naturally accompanies this kind of thing." He twisted impatiently in the seat. "We have to find Green, Bolenz, or whatever he's calling himself now or he's gotten away with killing four people."

"He isn't acting alone. There are two of them, maybe more."

Jack rubbed his eyes as if trying to force an image. "I wish I could place Green. I can't picture him or even recall hearing the name."

"How did he get away with it? I thought the army was all rules and regulations and everybody obeying orders from the top."

Jack struggled to find the words to answer. "War is chaos, Carrie. Even though the military has strict procedures, it's a body that follows orders. If a person had official-looking papers, if he moved around so no one commander observed enough to get suspicious, if he had nerve and a few connections, he could get away with a lot."

She nodded. "Now that person is playing the same game here at home. Police in Wisconsin, Chicago, and Flint won't connect three apparent accidents and a fatal mugging, because they don't know about each other's cases. If not for the connection between Todd and Crate, you wouldn't have noticed it either."

As the stewardess rattled up behind them with her beverage cart, Jack summed it up. "Green and his helpers have the nerve successful confidence schemers need. Unfortunately, they also have no compunction against killing, both for money and to keep anyone from uncovering what they've been up to."

CHAPTER TWENTY-EIGHT

It wasn't eighty degrees in Florida, but the sun shone, and sixty-five by noon sounded good to Carrie. The Cabot children awaited the school bus like a downward staircase, six-year-old Isaac first, then a gangly middle girl and finally the oldest, herding her siblings like a mother hen. They appeared healthy and content, smiling at the driver and greeting friends on the bus as they climbed on. Carrie watched the bus pull away then slid out of the rental car and approached the house. The door opened to her knock, revealing a woman of medium height with brown hair and hazel eyes. She was neither beautiful nor homely; everything about her seemed average.

"Mrs. Cabot?"

Shock flashed across the sunburnt face and denial formed in her eyes. Then resignation set in. "What." It wasn't really a question.

"I represent your ex-husband. He wants to see his children."

Her face hardened and she ran a hand through sandy blond hair that had yet to be combed this morning. "It's always about what he wants. He never cared what I wanted."

Carrie thought of Mister Cabot, also a mediocre type. It was hard after he left the office to remember the man's physical characteristics or defining mannerisms. Two unremarkable people had married, created three children, and then found themselves poorly matched. Now both of them wanted to forget each other's names, but that wasn't possible. Carrie felt like an intruder in a private matter, but she did what she'd come to do. "Mrs. Cabot, may I come in?"

***

VIETNAM, 1967

"Did you ever think about it, Joker?" Todd asked one night as they sat on their bunks after chow. "Marriage, I mean?"

"Nope." Someone had adopted a monkey, which had the run of the tent. It sat beside Todd, appearing to follow the conversation and grinning widely at Jack's answer.

"Never?"

Jack flashed his infrequent grin, "In all my twenty years I never found the right girl."

Todd chuckled and the monkey chattered, probably more interested in the peanuts they were handing it than the topic of marriage. "Okay," Toddy admitted. "We aren't all that old. But you think about it sometimes, right? My parents were pretty happy, so I think about it. But lots of married couples don't make it, and I wonder how you know, how you decide, 'This is the one'?"

Jack shelled another peanut for the monkey, which accepted it gravely. His parents hadn't been anyone's example of an idyllic couple, and he'd pretty much avoided the thought of marriage entirely.

"There was this girl," Todd went on. "She was nice, and pretty, too. Her name was Diane, I thought she and I would go along for a while and then get married, you know, sometime in the future. Then one day Diane says she can't wait any longer for me to grow up. She wants a man with serious intentions. The next month she's engaged to a guy whose father owns a lumber company." Todd raised his hands, palms up. "At seventeen she had it all planned out. I wasn't on the same wavelength, I guess."

"How much did her leaving bother you?" Jack asked.

Todd frowned. "I was mad and a little hurt."

"A little? You weren't that crazy about her then."

"No, I guess not. But that's what I wonder about. Was she right we weren't ever going to work, or was I right we'd have been okay with a little more time? Do you know when the right person comes along, or do you grow into it after you're married?"

"Can't help you there, buddy. I have no experience with women long-term." Apparently bored with the conversation, the monkey jumped to the upper bunk and wandered off. Jack gave a rare elaboration on his thought. "I've known people I thought would never stay together who make it for years, and marriages that look perfect that don't last three months except on paper."

"I'll tell you what it is," came a voice behind them. "It's money. That's all that matters to women."

Todd looked up at the newcomer. "Hey, Kelly!"

"Sachs, Porter." Kelly wore his usual outfit, fatigue pants, a cotton undershirt, and boots. Either the man had a strong dislike for shirts, or he liked to show off his chest. Jack had never seen him with a shirt on. Over his wiry hair he wore a camo hat customized almost to the point of destruction. "You guys interested in some poker?"

"We have to check our social calendars," Todd replied. "How about it, Joker?"

"Sure, why not?" Jack answered. It occurred to him he was relieved Greg Laughton wouldn't be there. His eyes met Kelly's, and he knew Kelly read the thought from the ironic arch of his eyebrow. Jack flushed. He wasn't glad the man was dead, just glad he wasn't around.

Kelly kept his eye on Jack as he spoke to no one in particular. "You want to know what I heard the other day when I was up at Bong Son? Somebody claims they saw Laughton out in the paddies."

Todd shook his head. ""Laughton bought the farm. People just like prolonging the legend."

"Yeah," Kelly agreed. "Greg was quite a legend around here." His eyes met Jack's again, and Jack looked away. Though Kelly had never done anything to him, he couldn't warm up to the guy. Todd liked everybody and included almost anyone in his circle. Why couldn't he be like Todd, who believed in goodness despite the bad things that had happened to him? Jack believed in his own mind, strength, and heart. As long as he could take care of himself, he'd be okay.

***

Just before noon Jack rejoined Carrie, who had returned from New Port Richey with the rental car and sat waiting in the sun, both doors open to let the slight breeze waft through. She looked cute in a red and white dress with matching red pumps. The hair trailing down the back of her neck curled even more in the moist heat of Florida, and Jack thought it was altogether too becoming. As she handed him a fairly cold bottle of soda and took a sip of her own, he had trouble not reaching out to touch a spiral that dangled above one eyebrow.

He covered with a request for her report.

"Mrs. Cabot will call Mr. Cabot today and work out a fair visitation schedule. She was pretty angry with him when she moved, but she's had time to see the unfairness of taking his children so far away."

Marriages gone bad generate a lot of getting even, Jack thought, but Carrie went on. "Anyway, we'll check with Mr. Cabot tonight and see what he wants us to do. Now did you at locate the mysterious Mr. Bolenz/Green?"

Jack couldn't report equal success. His visit to the county courthouse had brought only negatives. Duncan Family did not operate in Florida, and there were no registered insurance agents in the state named Sean Green or Mark Bolenz. "No Bolenz in the phone book. I called several Sean Greens, but none of them was the right guy."

"We'll have to get creative," Carrie said, her tone encouraging.

"Okay." Jack finished the six-and-a-half-ounce Coke. "But let's get lunch first. I'm much more creative on a full stomach."

CHAPTER TWENTY-NINE

Li left Sean's house for Jack's office but returned a few minutes later when she realized she'd left her wallet on the bed while changing purses. She slipped her wet boots off in the foyer and padded softly down the hall in her stockings to retrieve it. Sean was in the library, talking on the phone. He was turned away, so he didn't see her.

"—I'd guess they're there by now, but I can't get a flight until morning. Can you arrange something?" At the threat in his tone Li stopped to listen. "Both of them. She's seen too much, and he's too damned smart for his own good." He listened for a moment then said, "You've missed her twice. See that it gets done right this time."

Li turned and tiptoed out of the house. Sean was planning to hurt both Jack and the Walsh girl. Why? Like scattered notes of a song finally played together to form a melody, she suddenly understood the events of recent weeks. She'd known Sean's activities weren't legal, but was she involved in murder?

Sean said the auto wreck that had killed Jen Bartkowski was an accident. Then Jack had found the husband dead, an apparent suicide. He thought Crate Somers had been murdered as well, but Sean couldn't have done that. He'd been in Chicago with her.

But now Sean had told someone in Florida to "arrange something." Li shivered. Sean's schemes were worse than she'd imagined, but what could she do about it? The answer came quickly. A smart woman was always ready to side with the winner.

***

Jack and Carrie ate lunch in a cafe on the Gulf that advertised excellent fish. The lot adjacent to the place was being developed to accommodate the growing influx of tourists, winter residents, and move-ins. Some of the restaurant's parking area was taken up with equipment, a bulldozer, a roller and a paving machine. Along the edge a large pit had been dug, and soil was piled high beside it. Backed halfway up the dirt-pile was a dump truck, filled but left waiting as the crew crossed the lot and headed for the restaurant.

"Must be a good place if it's where the working men eat," Jack commented as he parked the car parallel to the building.

Carrie was pleased that the big machines would be shut down

so they could eat in peace. Only the distressed call of seagulls disturbed the silence, and she paused to savor the warmth, so different from what she'd experienced only yesterday.

Entering the little diner, they chose a scarred wooden booth in a corner and ordered the special. As they waited for their food, Carrie entertained Jack with stories of fishing trips with her father, brought to mind by the coastline she'd traced that morning. "It was only a twenty-two-footer, but we'd haul it over to Lake Huron on summer weekends. Mom wouldn't go, said it ruined her permanent wave, so it was just the two of us."

"Sounds like fun."

She giggled as a memory arose. "One time it was almost me alone. Dad was standing at the tiller when I lost my hold on the boom line. The sail went spinning, and the boom almost knocked him into the bay. It was lucky he was quick, because if he'd gone overboard, I'd never have been able to turn that boat around to go back for him."

As the waitress set a perfectly pan-fried grouper before each of them, Jack chuckled, picturing Carrie's horror. "You almost dunked your father in the middle of a Great Lake?"

She could laugh too, years later. "I was so scared when that boom went swinging at him, but Dad didn't get upset. He said we were both lucky, him to be dry and me to have learned a lesson about paying attention without anyone getting hurt." She sampled her fish and gave a purr of approval.

"Your dad sounds like a great guy," Jack commented.

"He was the best." Carrie had deduced Jack's family wasn't the supportive kind, but he never talked about it. "Did you ever go fishing on Lake Michigan?"

Jack turned with a look of amused scorn. "Are you kidding? Chicago tough guys don't fish. Our hobbies were skippin' school, playin' pool, and lookin' cool."

They'd finished eating, and he led the way to the till and handed the waitress a ten. She returned his change with a hurried smile and a "Y'all come back."

"No sports?" A bell over the door tinkled as they exited the restaurant.

"I used to be pretty good at basketball."

His smile had turned rueful, and Carrie wished for a moment she'd kept quiet. Then she changed her mind. "I'll bet you could play again. You're doing pretty well with old Buddy."

"Maybe." He seemed cheered by the thought. Stepping ahead of Carrie, he opened her car door then moved around to the driver's side and got in.

Carrie saw the impending crisis a second earlier than Jack did. "Jack!" The dump truck they'd noticed earlier bore down on them, careening driverless across the parking lot.

Though the noonday sun reflected off the windshield, Carrie thought a human form dropped from the far side of the truck and disappeared behind it.

Their car was about to be crushed against the building wall. "Get out!" Jack shouted. Carrie was already doing that, and she thought irrelevantly that in a crisis we order each other to do the obvious. Sliding across the bench seat after her, Jack pulled the artificial leg after him, put his good leg on the concrete, and pushed off as hard as he could toward the back of the car.

The truck hit where he'd been seconds before, but the car's sturdy frame resisted the onslaught just long enough to allow them to get out of the way. It shuddered violently for a couple of seconds then collapsed as Carrie grabbed Jack's arm to help him stay balanced. The noise of the collision was deafening, and several workers hurried out the door at the front of the restaurant. They stopped, horrified at what they saw. As the truck came to rest against the crumpled car, Carrie heard astonished voices from another direction. Turning, she saw that a hole had appeared in the wall of the café. Cooks and waitresses peered out at the scene, surprised but apparently unhurt.

"Carrie?" Jack's voice penetrated her consciousness, and she realized he'd said her name several times.

"I'm fine. Just a little fluttery." She laid a hand over her heart. "What about you?"

"I guess I can still make some moves." Jack's calm voice belied the pulse she saw beating on his forehead. "Basketball might not be out of the question after all."

Two hours later, the rental company had sent out another car and arranged for disposal of the ruined one. The police had questioned everyone at the scene and termed the experience an unfortunate accident. The worker who'd parked the truck insisted he'd set the brakes and left the gearshift in reverse. "I can't understand how it could have happened," he insisted.

Jack's jaw tightened at that, but Carrie followed his lead and made no mention of their purpose in coming to Florida. No one was particularly interested in them once it was clear they were uninjured.

When they were alone Carrie described what she'd seen, and he nodded grimly. "I missed it, but I don't doubt you saw someone there. We're supposed to be dead."

"Looking back, some things that happened to me recently take on a different aspect." She told him about the car that almost ran her down and the men who tried to pull her into the alley. "I took them to be isolated incidents, but there's only so far that idea can stretch."

"They're afraid you can identify them," Jack said flatly. "You need to take the next flight home."

"What good will that do?" Carrie argued. "If they're after us, we have a better chance if we're together, watching each other's backs."

"That cop in Flint will see you're safe until this is wrapped up."

He was worried about her, but she was equally worried about him. "Listen, Jack. We didn't know before what we were getting into, but now we do. Someone is really good at committing murder and making it look like something else. We're both on his list, so I'm not going anywhere without you until this is over."

"You sound like Onalee right now," Jack observed. "I guess you have a little of her in you."

"Oh, pooh!"

In the end he agreed with her. "These people are apparently as good at figuring out where you and I are as they are at arranging accidents. I am going to call Molineaux, so there's someone who knows everything we know."

As he hoped, the detective took the threat seriously. "You two need to get yourselves to a police station."

"Why should the Florida police believe our crazy story?" Jack asked. "They don't know us from Adam and Eve, and we have no proof of anything. If we knew where Bolenz is, we might pull it all together."

"Bolenz might be a murderer many times over," Molineaux cautioned. "Let the cops handle it. I'll call down there, so you at least get a fair hearing. Get yourself and that pretty partner of yours to police headquarters—now."

"Right, Detective. We're on our way." Jack replaced the phone, his expression doubtful. "Molineaux wants us to go to the police."

"But all we've got right now is a theory."

"True. Even if they believe us, how would they check it out?"

Carrie thought a moment then picked up the phone Jack had just set in its cradle. Removing one earring, she dialed the operator. "Do you have a new number listing for Sean Green in Tampa?" As she waited, she tapped her foot in unconscious impatience. "No? What about Mark Bolenz? B-O-L-E-N-Z?" Another pause, more tapping, "Great. Give me that number, please."

She wrote down the number then dialed it. A man answered. No, he wasn't Sean Green. No, he didn't know when Sean would return or where he could be reached.

"I'm sorry I missed him," Carrie purred into the receiver. "If you talk to him, will you tell him Joan called? Joan from Chicago?"

"Sure," the man answered. "I'll tell him."

"Thank you, um, what'd you say your name was?"

"I didn't, but I'm Sean's half-brother, Mark. Mark Bolenz."

CHAPTER THIRTY

"Okay, so Sean Green has been using his brother's name."

"Hold on." Carrie dialed the operator again. "I'm wondering if Sean Green at CE2-3425 is the one who lives on Poinciana Street. No? What's the house number? Gee, I guess I got that wrong too. Thanks." She hung up the phone, looking pleased with herself. "The house is at 192 Palatia. We can give the police a location."

Jack looked thoughtful. "I'd sure like to get a look at this guy."

Carrie reattached her earring. "Why don't we drive over there? You can stay in the car, and I'll knock on the door. You'll either know the man or you won't. I say, 'Oops, wrong house,' and we proceed to the police station."

"Too dangerous," Jack said firmly. "He might be a killer."

"He probably doesn't kill everyone who knocks on his door," Carrie reasoned.

"What if he's the man you saw that day in the alley?"

Carrie grinned. "Tell me this, Mr. Porter. If you put me next to the Carrie in that alley, would you know we were the same person?"

Jack had to smile. "No, Miss Walsh, I have to admit I would not."

"Then let's go."

Consulting a Tampa city map, she acted as navigator, and they found Palatia with no difficulty. The wide street was lined with what could only be called stately homes, most long and low with screened porches and swimming pools. Carrie peered out the window at house numbers. "There." Jack pulled over on the opposite side.

The house was pale stucco. Arched porches lined the front of it, shading the windows and the doorway, which was recessed and ornate. The wide, slightly sloping lawn was perfectly managed with shrubs and trees neatly trimmed, and the brick driveway formed a semicircle that brought visitors right to the door. The perimeter of the property was enclosed with a wrought-iron fence that provided security without detracting from the property's beauty.

"Somebody's making money," Jack commented.

Carrie listened impatiently to a long list of instructions and warnings. "I'm not going to take him down and cuff him," she protested. "I'm going to let you get a good look." Sliding out of the car she crossed the street, her red heels clicking on the pavement.

The door was opened by a man in his thirties, small of frame and meek-faced, with large glasses and thinning, light-brown hair. "Yes?" Even his voice was tentative.

"I was wondering if I could speak to the lady of the house."

He looked at her for a few seconds, as if she'd spoken in a foreign language. Finally, he said, "Can you step inside?"

"Excuse me?"

"Step inside, please. I have the air conditioning on, and I don't want to cool the whole county."

"Oh." She wanted to glance back to let Jack know it was okay but didn't want to alert the man to the fact that she wasn't alone. She entered a foyer that smelled of untended garbage.

"If your wife isn't home, I'll just come back later."

He closed the door behind her with a finality that made Carrie aware she'd made a mistake.

"I can't--"

"Shut up." The man turned the deadbolt and peered out the sidelight. When she glanced at his hand, she saw that he held a small pistol, not aimed at her but definitely accessible. "Let's go in there."

The house was almost empty, as if the movers hadn't delivered the furniture yet. The entry opened onto a large living room on the right and a den on the left. Between the two a hallway led to the back of the house, where she glimpsed glass patio doors past what appeared to be a galley kitchen. Bolenz gestured toward the living room, where two kitchen chairs sat before a flickering television set. He turned the volume down but not off.

"I don't know what you think is going on, but I'm not alone," Carrie said. "My partner is probably calling the police right now."

"I'm afraid that's not true, Miss Walsh," said a voice. Carrie turned to see Jack standing behind her. Apparently, he'd come in through the patio doors. Why?

As her mind grappled with that question, she saw movement behind him. In the shadow of the hallway stood the man who'd spoken. His face was in shadow, and his frame was much larger than Jack's. He also held a pistol, and Carrie felt her hopes fade. Jack spoke to her, his voice tight. "Carrie, meet Sean Green. In Vietnam I knew him as Kelly."

CHAPTER THIRTY-ONE

The big man nudged Jack into the room with the muzzle of the gun. "Kelly, yeah. That name was your buddy Todd's invention, like you were the Joker and Somers was Crate."

He spoke again to Carrie, ignoring the two men. "To Todd, an Irishman named Green was Kelly. He was trying to say, 'Kelly, 'Nam wives, insurance.'"

He'd failed in so many ways. He shouldn't have let Carrie go to the door. He shouldn't have missed Kelly sneaking up behind him. And being less than a whole man, he shouldn't have deluded himself into thinking he could do this job.

"So you're the murdering insurance man." Carrie's voice shook with fear, but her disgust came through too.

"I told my brother you'd be coming around. He and I watch each other's backs, like Jack and Todd did in the 'Nam." He gestured with the gun. "Don't suppose you brought your M-16 with you, Joker?"

"What happens now, Sean?" Bolenz sounded tentative, and he looked like he'd never held a gun before. Jack knew that didn't improve their situation. An amateur shooter and one who was proficient were dangerous in different ways.

"You're going to take this nice couple's car back to the rental agency for them. I'm sure you'll find the paperwork in the glove box. When you've done that, pack their things and check them out of their hotel." He took Carrie's purse from her long enough to remove the room key from inside. "The address is right there."

"Jack?" Without a word Jack took out his own key and handed it over. "Separate rooms with such a delightful lady for company? You always were slow to take advantage of a situation."

"What about them?" Bolenz asked.

"You do your part while I take Jack and his pretty secretary for a ride in the car." Green indicated a door, and they went before him into a garage where a white Thunderbird convertible waited.

"Did Crate Somers' death pay for that?" Jack asked.

Green ran a hand lovingly over the spotless, highly polished fender. "My brother and I have expensive tastes. It takes a good deal of money to live according to them." He directed Jack to the driver's seat and Carrie to the back with him. "Drive where I tell you, Joker, or the lady you brought to the party is going to die."

Jack did as ordered, backing the car out and then heading west as Green indicated. When they came to Highway 19, they turned south toward St. Petersburg. As he drove, Jack struggled to stop the voices of blame in his head. He was no good to Carrie if he kept beating himself up for what was over and done. Forcing his shoulders to relax, he let his military training take over. Wait for an opportunity. Keep your mind on the goal. Believe you can do it and you will.

Green wasn't the type to keep silent, especially when he was feeling smug. "Joker, I have to say I'm thrilled you overcame your injury. Walking again, that's great." His tone shaded to dark. "Too bad you had to stick your nose into our business."

"You killed Todd, Kelly. That made it my business."

"And look where it got you." Green regarded a neat grove of orange trees. "I always kind of liked the guy. Couldn't play poker worth a damn, but otherwise, a pretty good head." He shifted his shoulders in the seat. "Blame Somers. The dork never did have a clue, and when it didn't pay to think, he finally did."

Jack tensed again at the light tone of Green's dismissal of the death of a former comrade. "Stosh told him Sean Green might not be the buddy he seemed to be."

"Luckily old Stanley's communication skills weren't the best. Crate didn't believe he had it right, so he called me."

"Big mistake."

Green shrugged. "Somers asked his questions, nothing I couldn't handle. I assured him Stosh had chemical problems, which was true. Then Somers tells me he talked to Todd, and if anything happens to Stosh or his wife, Todd will know where to look." Green's tone dropped lower, "The little runt wouldn't have talked like that if he hadn't always had Todd to back him up. We'd already done Stosh's wife by then, so Crate had to die."

"That would have happened anyway."

He gestured vaguely with his non-gun hand. "Right. We just moved the timetable up a little."

In the rear-view mirror, Jack saw Carrie shiver. "You arranged a few more accidents."

"We haven't had a finding of murder yet." He shook his head in mock regret. "Crate broke his neck—kid never did have any luck."

"He had more class than you'll ever understand, Kelly."

"Money or class, Joker? I'll take money every time."

"Like the time the poker pot disappeared during a mortar attack?"

Green chuckled gleefully. "You see, Joker? A guy can get away with a lot if he has the guts to take a chance here and there." He shifted his feet, bumping Jack's seat as he made himself more comfortable. "How's your wife these days, Jack?"

"What wife would that be?" Jack shot back.

"So you figured that out too? You're good."

"Those women will be deported when it comes out they're here illegally."

"Some might be okay," Green said airily. "If they've been good little girls, their husbands will make things right for them."

"Su Somers is a widow with two small children."

"Hey, she got what she wanted. She's in the States. I got what I wanted, a large amount of money."

"You cheated everybody involved."

"And in ten cases, only one GI got suspicious."

"Let me guess. He didn't make it home."

"Like I said, you're good." Green had been watching the road, and he ordered, "Make a right at the next road."

About a mile down, Green directed him to turn once more, this time down a road marked *Pelican's Beak Harbor*. As the shell-gravel mixture crunched under the wheels of the car Green said, "Take a right, Jack."

The road was little more than a track. A small sign at the turnoff had the words *Boat Launch* routered into wood. "I have to say that your wife has been very helpful to me."

"She's not my wife."

"Good thing, or there'd be horns growing out your forehead." Green laughed at his joke, and Carrie lowered her eyes, unable to meet Jack's in the mirror.

"I like that girl," Green went on, "but in some ways she's the reason it all fell apart. After you went back to the world, Todd started watching me. He didn't figure out my scheme, but he was suspicious." He looked at Jack questioningly. "You never told your best buddy the truth about your marriage?"

"No." Anger made his voice lower than usual. "If I'd known you had anything to do with it, I'd have walked away."

"Limped away. You couldn't walk, remember?" His grin was nasty. "It doesn't matter. You came home, I came home, and eventually Todd came home. He forgot all about me until Somers called him."

"And that brought you to Flint in a hurry."

"Yeah, Somers was one thing, but Todd was smart, and he already had ideas. After a look at the records and a few phone calls, he learned Li wasn't a legal alien." The road had become bumpy and narrow. "One more right up there."

As Jack turned in at the drive of a small marina, he smelled Tampa Bay, a blend of fish, decaying seaweed, and wet, mossy wood.

"We relieved your partner of a notebook that would have put me in a bad spot. It would have gone well, but Miss Walsh came along."

Green smoothed Carrie's hair away from her face, and she cringed at his touch. "Li says you couldn't have seen much, but my partner's motto is 'Better safe than sorry.'" He glanced at Jack. "If you'd stayed away from Porter, you'd have lived a lot longer."

"It's not his fault you're cowards and murderers," Carrie said.

"I suppose not, but it's your funeral."

Green slid forward and gestured to the right. "Pull in over there, next to the Shelby. It belongs to an old comrade of yours. Kinda like a reunion, isn't it, Joker?"

Jack parked the car. Though he planned to take any chance that arose to go after Green, he had to consider Carrie's safety, and despite his willingness to talk on the way, Green hadn't been the least bit sloppy.They walked to the end of a dock where a trim little twenty-eight-foot sailboat floated lightly on the water. Teak gleamed in the sunlight, and there was not a speck of dirt anywhere. As they approached, a man who'd been resting on the deck stood up, and Jack swore softly. He turned to Green, who was enjoying the moment. "Come on, Jack, say hello to your old friend Greg Laughton."

***

VIETNAM, 1967

Sean "Kelly" Green returned to his hooch a little after midnight, satisfied with the day's work and ready for some sack time. Ducking through the entry flap he smelled cigarette smoke, which irritated him. No one smoked in his tent.

A figure sat in the darkness, the only illumination the glowing red tip that moved up to where the face would be then down to rest on the thigh.

"Who is that?" Green asked, unhappy with uninvited company.

"Leave the light off," said a voice. "I like it better this way."

"Who are you?" he repeated.

"Think." The voice was raspy from smoking too many cigarettes. From the tone, the speaker was pleased with himself. It was a voice from the grave.

"Laughton?"

"Bin-GO."

"We heard you were dead."

"I started that rumor myself—faked my death so I can start over. Some things in Greg Laughton's past aren't right, you know?"

Green understood at once why Laughton was there. "You need transport stateside."

"Right again. And you're the guy who can arrange it."

"I am," Green agreed. He was already figuring how it could be done. "I'm about to end my tour as well."

"You got anything set up back in the world that could make use of my talents?" Though Laughton tried for a light tone, Green realized he was in a spot. A man who didn't exist anymore, a man whose "talents" tended to violence—what would Laughton do back in civilization?

"Maybe we can do business," he said casually. "I need a man who doesn't mind the means if the end is profitable enough."

CHAPTER THIRTY-TWO

"It got a little uncomfortable for me in the military," Laughton drawled as Green directed Jack and Carrie onto the boat. "Sorry if my death caused you any grief." Looking Carrie up and down he added, "I see you brought the entertainment."

She suppressed a shiver. Jack started to say something but apparently thought better of it. He sat down on the boat's portside bench, near the stern, leaving Carrie the seat farthest away from Laughton. Distance didn't help much, because she could still see the smirk on his face and the snub-nosed revolver in his hand.

Green remained on the dock. "Take our comrade-in-arms for a sea cruise, Greg. I think he'll be impressed with your boat."

Laughton looked pleased, as if the trip really were to show off his craft. Carrie thought she'd never seen a person with such cold eyes. Laughton was not much taller than she, but his frame was tightly muscled. A tattoo of a naked woman showed on one arm where his sleeve was rolled back. His movements were compact and studied, like a snake watching its prey before striking. She had no doubt he'd attack as quickly and mercilessly as a reptile.

"Unless you need me, I'll be on my way," Green said briskly.

"It's under control. You just keep making us lots of money." As Green retreated up the dock, Laughton made a clicking noise with his tongue that might have signaled disgust or amusement. He pulled the cord on the boat motor and, as it roared to life, ordered Carrie to untie the lines that held them to the dock. She obeyed, clumsily since her hands shook with fear. When she finished Laughton expertly guided the boat out of its slip with one hand, holding the gun low and confidently with the other. He kept it trained on her, no doubt figuring Jack would be reluctant to endanger her life.

The boat headed out to sea, the motor chugging as the turquoise water parted smoothly over the bow. Laughton looked back to the dock once, and Carrie mouthed to Jack, "Talk!" He frowned, but she couldn't repeat it before Laughton's flat gaze came forward again.

"Should I put up the sail?" she asked innocently. "I know how to do it."

Laughton's face split in a grin. "Is this where the little lady tries to be helpful so the big mean guy won't kill her? It ain't gonna work. You got nothing that could make me change my mind, get it? Nothing."

"Fine," she replied. "Maybe someone will see us motoring in a perfect wind and wonder what's wrong."

He considered that. "You know how?"

"My father had a boat a lot like this one."

"Okay. Set the main. But I'll be watching."

Carrie obeyed, though it wasn't easy in heels and a skirt. Taking the furling line, she wrapped it around the winch then cranked the sail up. The sail billowed as it filled with air, and Laughton adjusted the tiller accordingly. Once the sail was up, she locked both the furling line and the boom line into cleats that held the sail steady.

"Not bad," Laughton observed.

"Carrie sat down near the cleat that held the boom in place. "I didn't mind sailing when I was a kid, but it's terrible once you grow up and have to worry about what it does to a permanent wave."

Laughton gave her a look that revealed disgust for her comment.

Jack finally seemed to get what Carrie's plan was. "I thought you took a direct hit from a mortar, Laughton."

He chuckled. "Some kid from Idaho did, so I took his ID and gave what was left of him mine."

"And hung out in the jungle until Green could smuggle you back to the States."

"Yup. Things worked out okay."

"Until Jen Bartkowski saw you in Chicago. She told her husband she'd seen a ghost."

"It's tough staying off the radar, but we took care of her." Laughton squinted at the horizon and made a minor adjustment to the steering. "Most things are doable after some time in-country."

"Like killing old friends?" Jack challenged.

"Friends? Are you kidding me? Getting stuck in that hell-hole didn't make us brothers or comrades or especially not friends, Porter. It just made us unlucky."

Laughton glanced at Carrie, who sat primly silent, her hands in her lap. Jack drew Laughton's attention back to him. "Does it bother you that Green has you killing people while he lives in expensive houses?"

Carrie listened with half her mind. Only a few hours earlier they'd laughed about the time she almost dunked her father in Lake Huron. Did Jack remember, and would he react quickly enough to what she had in mind? Laughton was having fun baiting Jack. The next gust of wind would be the time to act.

"Green can have his women—actually your woman—and all the crap he likes so much," Laughton was saying. "He's smart, and he can kill if he has to. He doesn't like it but that's okay, because it means he needs me." Laughton glanced at Carrie again. "Me, I like the rush I get when somebody dies."

"You're some kind of sick monster."

"You always were holier-than-thou, Porter. Too good for the rest of us. How'd you feel when you woke up with most of your leg gone?"

"What I'm missing doesn't make me less than human. What you're missing does."

Laughton's expression hardened for an instant, but he recovered his smirk. "You're right. I'm a sick mother, but you know what, Joker? I feel alive, and you? Very soon you're going to feel dead."

***

As Laughton spoke, Jack saw Carrie signal a warning with her eyes. Reaching out in a swift, sure motion, she pulled the boom line free of the cleat. The sail, puffed full of air, came swinging aft with all the speed of the wind on the bay. The heavy metal pole struck Laughton in the head as it wheeled, knocking him sideways. The boom went on in its circle, but Jack ducked out of its way.

Though he roared in pain, Laughton didn't drop his weapon. Crouching, he shook his head, trying to clear it. Jack knew he had to take advantage of his enemy's disorientation quickly. Moving in with his shoulder lowered, he tried to knock Laughton off his feet. It didn't work because of Laughton's crouched position and Jack's inability to find purchase on the slippery deck. The boat slewed wildly as its sail swung back and forth, and Jack saw Carrie scramble to manage it, fighting the wind as he fought an angry, deadly Greg Laughton.

Jack fell on Laughton more than he attacked him, but they both went down. Grabbing the man's gun hand, Jack beat it against the deck, trying to make him let go. Laughton flailed briefly under Jack's weight but managed to bring his fist around and land a sharp blow to his head. Jack rolled away, coming to his knees and countering with an uppercut that snapped Laughton's head back. In the second of respite he gained as Laughton recovered from that, Jack stood, setting the prosthesis under him as stably as he could. As soon as Laughton got to his feet Jack swung again, this time punching him high in the stomach. The response was not what Jack hoped for. Laughton bent for a second but stepped forward and wrapped his meaty arms around Jack's chest. Lifting Jack off his feet, he squeezed his chest so tightly he couldn't breathe.

Jack beat on the back of Laughton's head with his fists, struggling desperately for oxygen. His one useful foot scrabbled on the deck, but he couldn't get purchase. The prosthesis was more encumbrance than help, and he realized he couldn't hurt his opponent enough to make him release his grip. In a few seconds, Jack would black out, and that would be the end of it.

Suddenly the pressure on Jack's chest lessened and he sucked air into his lungs with an audible gasp. Laughton staggered backward, and Carrie stepped out of his way. In her hand was one of her pretty red shoes. A red dot appeared on Laughton's temple where the heel had made contact. Snarling, he gave her an angry swat, like a bear at a blackfly. The blow sent her reeling against the cabin door.

The few seconds' respite was the break Jack needed. Moving in quickly, he landed a series of blows to chin, midsection, and chin again before Laughton could defend himself. Though he still didn't go down, he staggered backward, toward the rail. Marshalling his remaining strength, Jack rushed forward, pushing Laughton with all his strength while at the same time throwing himself sideways to avoid following the path his opponent took.

Laughton's arms waved desperately, but he couldn't keep his balance. He hit the rail just below hip level and went over the side with a resounding splash. The boat sped on as he floundered for a moment, gasping and shaking the water from his eyes. Glaring at them, he calmed somewhat and began treading water. Not surprisingly, he made no cry for help

Jack sat on the deck while Carrie finished the work of securing the boom. "Are you all right?"

Her lip was bleeding slightly from the cuff she'd received, but she pressed it with one hand. "Fine. You?"

He nodded, still panting from the exertion. After a moment she helped him stand, righting the cockeyed prosthesis as if she'd done it a hundred times. They stood side by side, watching Laughton's head become smaller. "Do we go back and get him?"

"We're not that far out. Let him prove how tough he is." Satisfied with that, Carrie took the tiller and turned the boat in a long arc that would take them back to shore.

CHAPTER THIRTY-THREE

When they were once again on dry land, Jack and Carrie made their way to a waterfront bar that offered a telephone and a place to recover from almost being murdered. The friendly bartender retrieved a sweater from lost and found and wrapped it around Carrie, who shivered from shock. Jack refused his offer of something similar but did ask the man to make a fresh pot of coffee.

Carrie called the Coast Guard and reported the man in the bay, giving landmarks and warning he was a multiple murderer. A businesslike voice assured they'd investigate and strongly suggested she remain where she was so the police could interview her.

"Now what?" she asked Jack as she hung up the telephone and sipped the fragrant brew their new friend set before her. "I can't believe those creeps would have killed us."

"What's a couple more dead to them?" Rage trembled in Jack's voice, and Carrie empathized with his losses, the deaths of men who'd been his friends at the hands of men who had served with them and should have been like brothers.

"The police are on the way."

Jack drank half his coffee in one gulp. "By the time we explain all this, Bolenz and Green will be long gone from that house."

"And we have no idea where they'll go next."

"We don't, but we know someone who does," Jack replied grimly. "Have you got our return tickets in your purse, or were they in the car?"

"In my purse." Carrie laughed nervously. "I can't believe I still have it after all that." She opened the clasp of her shoulder bag, checked to see that the tickets were still there, and snapped it shut.

Jack smiled, though his eyes revealed fatigue. "I've never known a woman to willingly let go of her purse." He finished the coffee, and the jolt of caffeine seemed beneficial, because he tapped the bar in a brisk drum rhythm. "As soon as we're done with the cops, we'll fly back to Flint. I have to find Li."

Carrie understood on one level. Whatever had happened between them, Jack felt he'd failed Li somehow. She thought it was the other way around. For Jack's sake, she hoped Li hadn't been a party to murder.

Jack seemed to be thinking the same thing. "Li isn't a criminal," he asserted. "She's spoiled—I guess self-centered is the word—but she didn't get such a hot deal when she got stuck with me. I came home angry at the world and sorry for myself. Where she'd pictured glamorous night clubs in Chicago, I gave her Hamady Grocery Stores in Flint."

"She probably didn't know what Green was up to," Carrie suggested. "He fooled a lot of people for a long time."

"Still, she did as he asked, which makes her an accessory at the very least. If I can talk her into turning state's evidence she might stay out of prison." He frowned. "She'll be deported for sure."

Carrie's head lifted in alarm. "Green knows if she were to testify, they'd be sunk. Li could be in danger."

Jack tapped the cup nervously on the wood surface. "Get us the first flight you can find. I'll tell the police the short version over the phone. We have to find Li before Green realizes there are cops after him in three states."

They arrived at the Tampa airport an hour later. Carrie sat in a plastic chair while Jack paced the length of the lounge. Though she was sure it wasn't good for his already abused leg, he couldn't sit still so she didn't suggest it. She'd managed to get an earlier flight, but to Detroit, not Flint. They would have to drive from there. Carrie called Detective Bill Stevenson and filled him in on the situation. He promised to try to locate Li and put her in protective custody, but if she wasn't at the Eagle, closed now for the day, she had no idea where to direct the police to look for her.

"There's a nasty storm here," Stevenson told her. "Hope you get in before it gets too bad."

Jack was unhappy when she passed along the warning. "Murder, fraud, snowstorms, how many other problems can crop up?"

"You can't fight Mother Nature, Jack."

He grinned ruefully. "Sorry. I'm not much good right now at being objective, so it's good that you can be."

"I'm not married to someone who might be in danger."

His face turned serious. "Neither am I, remember?" Realizing what that meant for the two of them, Carrie felt her face go red.

"I—I meant—" She dropped her gaze.

"It's okay." Jack slumped into a chair beside her. "Listen, we've got time, and I ought to tell you some things, if you want to hear them."

"Of course I do."

"When I got to Vietnam, I was tough, even cocky. I hadn't had a single girlfriend, but I'd had lots of women. I thought they were all pretty much the same." Jack seemed both aware and unaware of her as he went on. "Then one night I saw Li. She was beautiful, like a statue, and different from other woman I'd seen. Unattainable." He chuckled. "She let me know beyond any doubt I didn't impress her one bit. Reaching her, having her, was kind of like a fantasy, like winning an Asian goddess. I wasn't into marriage, so it would have stayed a fantasy except for a land mine in the road."

Carrie wanted badly to take Jack's hand, to let him know she could imagine how he'd felt. She feared he'd recoil from her sympathy and end the story, so she stayed still and listened.

"When I woke up in a hospital bed with only one leg, suddenly I wasn't so tough. All my plans were ruined, and aside from Todd, nobody cared what happened to me.

"I don't remember much, but somehow I agreed to marry Li. I took advantage of her because I was scared."

Carrie's intention to listen quietly couldn't stand him taking the blame on himself. "Sounds to me like it was the other way around."

"She just wanted out of that hell-hole. You can't know what it was like for her." He rubbed at his stubbly chin. "Back here we set up housekeeping and tried to be a couple, but it didn't work. I was hard to live with, I admit that, and Li was disappointed in America. She really thought we all were like characters in the forties movies they get over there, cocktails at six and dinner in formal clothes every night. She began going out nights, looking for the life she was sure I was denying her. We drifted farther and farther apart."

A garbled voice came over the intercom and Carrie heard "Detroit" and something about five minutes.

As Carrie dug for their tickets, Jack finished his story. "I don't love Li, Carrie. I never did. I was attracted to a beautiful face, like you told me once your dad was when he married your mom."

"It's none of my business why you did what you did."

He grinned at her. "Sure it is. You're my partner, and you have a right to know--that is, when I know myself."

The intercom squawked again, and people rose to get in line for boarding. Carrie shifted topics. "You said we're partners. Does that mean the Eagle Agency might continue to operate?"

"We're batting a thousand so far." He spread his fingers, tracing an imaginary logo in the air. "'We never fail!' Now we need to stay alive long enough to print that on a business card."

CHAPTER THIRTY-FOUR

The plane landed in Detroit after midnight, and as Stevenson had warned, a full winter storm raged across mid-Michigan. Jack was anxious to reach Flint, so they rented a car and started homeward. I-75 turned treacherous north of Pontiac. The road was a slick, slushy mess, with the left lane completely unusable and the right not much better. Cars slewed and fishtailed as drivers fought to stay in the narrow lane kept open only by constant plowing. Any deviance pulled the tires this way and that with a sickening lack of control.

Jack drove with cautious confidence, both hands on the wheel as it bucked each time the tires slipped. They crept along in a line of well-spaced, slow-moving vehicles, strain telling on both their faces. The road ahead of them appeared and disappeared as the wipers flopped noisily back and forth, making clear spaces on the windshield for only moments at a time. The heater in the rental was pitifully inadequate, and Carrie's feet were freezing in her flimsy red shoes. The windows kept fogging up, making visibility even worse.

At the Holly exit sign Jack narrowly avoided a pileup. Someone had tried to merge into traffic, but the cars on the road couldn't see it and ran into the newcomer and each other. Newly arrived state troopers had parked their cars, lights flashing, on both sides of the road as they set up flares. An officer informed them they'd have to leave the freeway. "Jack, Marsha and Roy live in Holly," Carrie said as he followed instructions. "We can stay there for the night and go on in the morning."

Reluctantly admitting that going on was reckless, Jack let Carrie direct him to the Wozniak home.

Marsha answered the door in a turquoise chenille robe and matching slippers. "You were driving in this mess? The television is telling everyone to stay home." Within minutes and while slicing squares of chocolate cake, she arranged for one son to sleep in the other's room to allow Carrie a bed, had Roy convert the sofa to make a place for Jack, and put her daughter to work making Sanka to still the shivering Carrie tried unsuccessfully to hide.

Jack asked to use their phone and called the police station.

Stevenson was out but had left word that he was unable to locate Li. Tampa officers reported the coast guard had found no one stranded in the bay, nor had there been anyone at the house on Palmetto when they arrived.

"They're on the way here," Jack muttered, tossing some bills on the phone stand to cover the long-distance charges.

"They'll have to deal with the same storm we did," Carrie said.

"Not if they chartered a plane direct to Bishop."

Marsha's husband Roy spoke up, his Tennessee background discernible in his twang. "Airport's closed, I heard it on the tee-vee. They're routing everybody to Detroit." Carrie shivered once more despite the liquid that warmed her hands and her insides. They might have traveled the same road as the men who wanted them dead.

"You can't do a thing right now," Marsha soothed. "Get some sleep and tackle your problems tomorrow."

Typically for Michigan weather, the sun shone brightly the next morning, and by eight o'clock the roads had been cleared. After eating a hearty breakfast of waffles, bacon, eggs, and orange juice and thanking the Wozniaks for their hospitality, Jack and Carrie started for the office. It was their hope Li would be there, but when they arrived, the only sign of her presence was a list of four phone numbers. Because she knew few English letters, Li had written down only numerals with no explanation of who or why.

Two numbers she recognized: the Callenders and her mother. She put off calling Onalee, and the Callenders' office hours began at nine, which left fifteen minutes. The third number was a man selling cemetery plots. He was insistent but Carrie was more so. Finally, she got rid of him and dialed the fourth number. "University of Michigan Flint, how may I direct your call?"

Carrie handed the phone to Jack, knowing he'd asked for information. Taking the receiver he said, "I called several days ago about military personnel marrying foreign nationals."

Jack listened, thanked the woman, and hung up. "Anyone who comes to the U.S. from the Republic of Vietnam under false papers will be returned forthwith. They told that to the woman who

213

answered the phone here yesterday."

"Li knows she'll be deported if they find her."

"Yes."

"Do you have any idea where she'd go?"

Jack sighed. "I know a lot less about that than Green does."

Carrie's brow furrowed as she tried to think. "Might she go to the Thai man, Mr. Ghiavali?"

"I'll call Sergeant Molineaux and ask him to check."

Chicago police had already located Lin Ghiavali's apartment, but he was no longer there. They found an array of forged passports, student visas, and the paraphernalia for making them. While Jack heard all about it from Molineaux, Carrie busied herself setting the office to rights, cleaning up half-full cups of tea and watering the plants Li had left to languish in the front window. When Jack snapped his fingers to get her attention, she hurried over in time to hear the detective's warning.

"—a new piece of information you should know about. Checking with Duncan Family Insurance, we found four policies that involve vets and payouts large enough to look suspicious. Somers and Bartkowski we know about. A third ex-GI in Ohio is heavily insured, married to an Asian, and enrolled by Mark Bolenz, so we're checking into that one. The fourth policy is made out on you."

Jack glanced at Carrie, his eyes troubled. "I never bought insurance from anyone."

"Your policy is paid up and valid, fifty thousand dollars' worth. Try not to let anybody collect on it, eh?"

Jack's expression turned grim. "I'll do my best."

The phone jangled as he broke the connection with more than usual force. "No wonder my imaginary wife has been hanging around." He ran a hand through his hair, leaving it a mess. "And to think I busted my ass to get back and save her from the evil Sean Green."

"Jack—"

He laughed bitterly. "They wouldn't even have had much

trouble arranging an accident for a one-legged cripple."

"Stop it!" she ordered, but his face had turned stony.

"Go home, Carrie, take some time off. I'll call when I feel like working again."

"Listen—" she began, but a glance stopped her. He had to deal with this last act of betrayal, and he was determined to do it alone. "All right, but I'm not far away. If you hear anything or...if you need...I mean..." He was silent, and she couldn't continue. "Okay, but call me."

Taking her coat from the hook on the wall, Carrie returned to the front and tidied her desk slowly, hoping Jack would say something more. She slid her chair into place, locked the file cabinets, and unplugged the coffee pot, reluctant to leave him to his black mood. When she'd delayed as long as she could, she ripped a sheet of yellow legal paper from a pad and scribbled a note. Sticking it under the dial of the telephone, she went from one kind of cold into another.

***

It was late when Jack finally stirred from his chair. He'd needed to be miserable for a while, to let waves of despair wash over him. He'd surrendered to the past: his unhappy childhood—the deaths of Crate, new father, and Todd, his best friend. The terrors of war and the destruction of his leg. And the betrayal of a woman he had treated as his wife. Questions that arose generally started with *Why?* His mind whirled with a crushing sense of the evil in the world, and for a while it wasn't possible to bear the weight of it.

But for Jack such moods were temporary, and after some time his spirit of determination re-asserted itself. Looking around, he realized darkness had deepened the shadows in the room. Life went on, and there were things that needed doing.

Ignoring a heavier-than-usual ache in his leg, Jack rose to close the place up. It was unnecessary, of course, because Carrie had already done it. After checking the lock on the front door, Jack noticed the slip of paper propped on the phone and leaned down to read it. *I'm making chocolate chip cookies. Bring 2 Cokes.*

Jack smiled. Carrie Walsh was doing her best to see he remained a member of the human race. For some reason, she believed in Jack Porter, and her faith gave him hope. He grabbed his jacket and locked the door behind him, once more able to look forward.

her jeans and pointed it at the roiling flock as a whole. If only she wasn't such a terrible shot, hadn't relied on Dakota so much. She whistled a keep-away call, as she would have done at home. Rather than scattering them, it only seemed to rile the mantas more. They swerved away, gathered themselves, then bore down on her and Dakota.

Verity tried to steady her breathing, failed, and aimed as best she could. One, two, three shots in close succession and none of them hit. She didn't have enough time to aim, she didn't have enough paintballs to not aim. She could do this. She'd practiced with Dakota before, for the hell of it. Another shot—there, a wing. And then the mantas were on top of her and she had no more time.